AN AMISH TABLE

OTHER NOVELS BY THE AUTHORS

BETH WISEMAN

THE AMISH SECRETS NOVELS
Her Brother's Keeper
Love Bears All Things
Home All Along

THE DAUGHTERS OF THE PROMISE NOVELS
Plain Perfect
Plain Pursuit
Plain Promise
Plain Paradise
Plain Proposal
Plain Peace

THE LAND OF CANAAN NOVELS
Seek Me with All Your Heart
The Wonder of Your Love
His Love Endures Forever

OTHER NOVELS
Need You Now
The House that Love Built
The Promise
An Amish Year
Amish Celebrations (Available July 2018)

STORIES
A Choice to Forgive included in *An Amish Christmas*
A Change of Heart included in *An Amish Gathering*

Healing Hearts included in *An Amish Love*

A Perfect Plan included in *An Amish Wedding*

A Recipe for Hope included in *An Amish Kitchen*

Always Beautiful included in *An Amish Miracle*

Rooted in Love included in *An Amish Garden*

When Christmas Comes included in
An Amish Second Christmas

In His Father's Arms included in *An Amish Cradle*

A Love for Irma Rose included in *An Amish Year*

Patchwork Perfect included in *An Amish Year*

A Cup Half Full included in *An Amish Home*

Winter Kisses included in *An Amish Christmas Love*

The Cedar Chest included in *An Amish Heirloom*

Vannetta Chapman

The Amish Village Mystery Series
Murder Simply Brewed
Murder Tightly Knit
Murder Freshly Baked

The Shipshewana Amish Mystery Series
Falling to Pieces
A Perfect Square
Material Witness

Stories
Where Healing Blooms included in *An Amish Garden*
An Unexpected Blessing included in *An Amish Cradle*
Love in Store included in *An Amish Market*
Mischief in the Autumn Air included in *An Amish Harvest*

KATHLEEN FULLER

THE AMISH LETTERS NOVELS
Written in Love
The Promise of a Letter
Words from the Heart

THE AMISH OF BIRCH CREEK NOVELS
A Reluctant Bride
An Unbroken Heart
A Love Made New

THE MIDDLEFIELD AMISH NOVELS
A Faith of Her Own

THE MIDDLEFIELD FAMILY NOVELS
Treasuring Emma
Faithful to Laura
Letters to Katie

THE HEARTS OF MIDDLEFIELD NOVELS
A Man of His Word
An Honest Love
A Hand to Hold

STORIES
A Miracle for Miriam included in *An Amish Christmas*
A Place of His Own included in *An Amish Gathering*
What the Heart Sees included in *An Amish Love*
A Perfect Match included in *An Amish Wedding*
Flowers for Rachael included in *An Amish Garden*

A Gift for Anne Marie included in
An Amish Second Christmas

A Heart Full of Love included in *An Amish Cradle*

A Bid for Love included in *An Amish Market*

A Quiet Love included in *An Amish Harvest*

Building Faith included in *An Amish Home*

Lakeside Love included in *An Amish Summer*

The Treasured Book included in *An Amish Heirloom*

An Amish Family (Available June 2018)

AN AMISH TABLE

THREE STORIES

Beth Wiseman

Vannetta Chapman

Kathleen Fuller

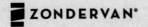

ZONDERVAN

An Amish Table

Copyright © 2018 by Beth Wiseman, Vannetta Chapman, Kathleen Fuller.

This title is also available as a Zondervan e-book.

Requests for information should be addressed to:
Zondervan, 3900 Sparks Dr. SE, Grand Rapids, Michigan 49546

Mass Market ISBN: 978-0-7852-1757-2

Library of Congress Cataloging-in-Publication Data

Printed in the United States of America

18 19 20 21 22 / QG / 20 19 18 17 16 15 14 13 12 11 10 9 8 7 6 5 4 3 2 1

Contents

A Recipe of Hope by Beth Wiseman............................1

Love in Store by Vannetta Chapman.....................123

Building Faith by Kathleen Fuller..........................215

A Recipe for Hope

Beth Wiseman

Glossary

ab im kopp—off in the head, crazy
ach—oh
bruder—brother
daadi—grandfather
daed—dad
danki—thank you
dat—dad
dochder—daughter
dumm—dumb
dummkopp—dunce
Englisch—non-Amish person
fraa—wife
fremm—strange
guder mariye—good morning
gut—good
gut nacht—good night
hatt—hard
haus—house
kaffi—coffee
kapp—prayer covering or cap
kinner—children or grandchildren
kumme—come
lieb—love
maed—young women, girls
maedel—girl
mamm—mom

mammi—grandmother

mei—my

mudder—mother

nee—no

Ordnung—the written and unwritten rules of the Amish; the understood behavior by which the Amish are expected to live, passed down from generation to generation. Most Amish know the rules by heart.

rumschpringe—running-around period when a teenager turns sixteen years old

sohn—son

wedder—weather

Wie bischt?—How are you?

ya—yes

CHAPTER 1

It's going to be a long two months.

Eve Bender finished packing the necessities to take to her parents' home, trying to follow the same instructions she was giving to the children: "Pack light, take only what you must have."

Moving back in with her parents at age thirty-eight was bad enough, but she also had a husband and three teenage boys in their *rumschpringe* in tow.

Eve shook her head as she struggled to zip a large brown duffel bag. *Of all the things to happen.* Yesterday a storm had knocked a tree down onto their two-story farmhouse, and the damage was extensive. It was going to take members of the community two months to completely repair the structure, but Eve knew it was a miracle that none of them had gotten hurt. She'd been thanking God since it happened.

She placed the duffel bag next to an old red suitcase she'd bought at a mud sale in Penryn a few years before. She'd paid two dollars for the piece of luggage and only used it once when she and Benny traveled to Harrisburg to attend a cousin's wedding. She folded her arms across her chest and stared at the bags, hoping she'd remembered everything they'd need at her parents'.

Benny, along with several men in the district, had cleared the tree earlier this morning, using a chainsaw to break the large limbs into logs that could be carried to the woodpile. Her husband had also checked to make sure the boys could get safely to their rooms upstairs. The tree had fallen through Eve's sewing room upstairs and crushed the kitchen below it. They might have lived around the mess if it weren't the middle of January. Benny and the boys had done the best they could to hang thick tarps over areas exposed to the elements, but Eve wondered if the clear sheeting would hold against a strong wind. She pulled her long black coat snug around her and went down the hall to check on the boys.

She walked into Leroy's room. At eighteen, her oldest son was sitting on his bed with earbuds plugged into whatever his latest gadget was. He pulled one from his ear when she walked in.

"Are you packed?"

Leroy pointed to a dark-green duffel bag on the far side of the room. "*Ya*." He put the plug back in his ear.

"Very *gut*."

Shivering, Eve headed toward the twins' room. She knocked on the door, then entered slowly, not surprised to find Elias sleeping on his twin bed and Amos sitting on the other bed with his pet lizard lying on his stomach.

"I'm trying to keep him warm," Amos said when Eve put her hands on her hips and scowled. She wasn't fond of the foot-long Chinese water dragon that Amos usually kept in a cage.

"*Mammi* is going to have a fit when you bring that lizard into her *haus*."

Amos's hazel eyes grew round as he sat up, cradling the reptile in his hands. "I—I can't l-leave him here. He-he'll freeze."

The younger of her sixteen-year-old twins—by nine minutes—Amos, stuttered when he was upset or nervous. "I know. I'm just saying *Mammi* isn't going to like it." She walked over to where Elias was sleeping and gently slapped him on the leg. "Elias, get up."

Elias rolled onto his back and rubbed his eyes. "It's Sunday. A day of rest."

"Not today. I told both you boys to pack whatever you need to go to *Mammi* and *Daadi's haus*."

Elias slowly sat up, his sandy brown hair tousled. "I don't know why we have to go over there. This half of the *haus* is fine." He rubbed his eyes again as he yawned.

"Don't be silly. It's going to be in the teens tonight and snowing. Even with the tarps and the fireplace, I can't even cook us a meal."

Eve's gas range was only a year old, and her propane refrigerator wasn't much older than that. Both would have to be replaced, along with the oak dining room set Benny had built when they were first married, with seating for eight. Losing the dining room furniture upset her more than the other losses. But she reminded herself that they were all safe and silently thanked God again.

"Now get moving," she said with a clap of her hands. "We need to be there before dark."

Back downstairs, she carefully stepped over debris and made her way to what was left of the kitchen. Benny was holding his black felt hat in one hand, stroking his gray-speckled brown beard with the other, and eyeing the mess.

"Is it really going to take two months before we can move back?" Eve shuddered. She and her mother didn't see eye-to-eye on most things, and *Mamm* wasn't used to having three teenage boys around either.

"Depends on the weather." Benny finished looking around before he walked to Eve and pulled her close. "It won't be so bad."

Eve's head rested against her husband's chest as he towered over her by a foot. "You don't know my mother the way I do." She sighed.

. . .

After making up the sleeper sofa in her sewing room, Rosemary put fresh sheets on the two beds upstairs where the twins would sleep, then made her way to Eve's old bedroom. Her daughter's room hadn't changed all that much since Eve had moved out to marry Benjamin over twenty years ago. She ran her hand along the finely stitched quilt on the bed with its mottled cream background, golden yellows, and soft blues bursting from a star in the center. Rosemary had given Eve the quilt on her sixteenth birthday, but Eve left it when she'd married, opting to take a brand-new double-ringed wedding quilt that Benjamin's mother and sisters had made for her.

As it should be.

Rosemary sighed.

She eased a finger across the top of the oak dresser and pulled back a layer of dust, then reached for a rag in her apron pocket. After wiping the piece of furniture from top to bottom, she inspected the rest of the small room, dabbing at a cobweb in the corner above where the rocking chair was. She could remember sitting in the rocker, Eve swaddled in her arms, rocking until late in the night. Her only child had suffered a bad case of colic. She turned toward the bedroom door when her husband walked in.

"Everything is *gut*, Rosie. You're fretting too much." Joseph pushed his thick, black glasses up on his nose. "You'd think the bishop was coming to stay. It's just Eve, Big Ben, and the *kinner*." Like most folks in the community, Joseph referred to Benjamin as Big Ben because he was a bear of a man, stout and tall, towering over almost everyone. Rosemary still called him Benjamin because that's what she'd called him since he was born.

"I'm not fretting." Rosemary raised her chin as she folded her trembling hands together in front of her. "I just want things to be nice for Eve and her family."

Joseph shook his head and stared at her. "You worry too much."

"I do not. I'm not worried about their stay. Why do you say that?" Rosemary looked away from her husband's soft brown eyes as she positioned the Bible and box of tissues on the nightstand.

"You know just what I'm sayin'." Joseph tipped back the rim of his black hat just enough so that Rosemary could see how much his gray bangs needed a trim. He tapped a finger against his thick beard of the same color and raised a bushy eyebrow. "You know that when Eve is here in our *haus* for two months, she will see . . ." He paused as Rosemary clenched her fingers tightly together. "She will see how things are."

"Joseph Chupp, you don't know what you're talking about." Rosemary moved toward the bedroom door and tried to ease past him, but Joseph blocked her, gently grasping her shoulders.

"Talk to Eve, Rosie. Tell her everything. Let her help you."

"There is nothing to tell." Rosemary shook loose of his hold. "And I don't need any help. I am quite capable of running *mei* own home, preparing meals for you, and tending to everything else around here. I'm not a feeble old woman." She scowled. "So stop acting like I've got one foot in the grave."

"I didn't say that, *lieb*. But I think—"

She maneuvered her way around him and shook her head. "Let me be. I have much to do."

Once she'd reached the bottom of the stairs, she crossed the den and went into the kitchen, going straight to a large pot of stew she had simmering on the stove. She fought the tears forming in the corners of her eyes as she picked up the spoon on the counter. With concentrated effort, she gripped the ladle full-fisted and shakily swirled it around the thick, meaty soup, praying that the Lord would keep her hand steady.

Eve's family lived almost nine miles outside of Paradise, just far enough to make it quite the haul by buggy, so most of Rosemary and Joseph's visiting with their daughter and her family was done after worship service every other Sunday. The thought of all of them under the same roof for two months was exciting. And terrifying.

Rosemary jumped when she heard a knock at the front door.

CHAPTER 2

Eve forced a smile when her mother opened the large wooden door, then pushed the screen wide. *"Wie bischt, Mamm?"*

"Gut, gut. Come in." Her mother smoothed the wrinkles from her black apron as she stepped aside so Eve could enter the living room, then waited while Benny and the three boys toted in the suitcases and duffel bags.

Eve breathed in the aroma of her childhood home. There was always a piney clean fragrance mingled with a hint of whatever *Mamm* might be cooking. Eve hung her black cape and bonnet on the rack by the door and glanced around the room. Her mother's oatmeal-and-honey hand lotion was on the end table next to her side of the couch. She'd been making and using the lotion for as long as Eve could remember. After devotion time in the evenings, her mother would smooth the silky balm on rough hands, worn from a hard day's work.

Eve hadn't been in her parents' home in a couple of months. She blamed it on the distance between their houses and the fact that she saw them every other Sunday at someone else's homestead for worship, but she knew it was more than that. Her mother didn't approve of the way Eve and Benny raised the children. "Too many freedoms," she'd always say. Eve had grown weary of her mother's lectures years ago.

It also upset Eve to see the way her parents lived. She'd tried for years to get her mother to upgrade to appliances and other household fixtures that would make their lives easier, things that Bishop Smucker approved of, like propane lighting. But *Mamm* insisted on using lanterns to light the entire house, which became more and more of a fire hazard the older her parents got. The same lantern was on the mantel from many years ago, and when Eve turned to her left, she saw another one on the coffee table—just the way it had always been. Both her parents had poor eyesight, especially her father, who was almost blind without his thick, black-rimmed glasses. Eve had told them repeatedly that propane lighting would brighten up the room and help them to see better, but *Mamm* said such technology wasn't necessary. She also used the same gas stove that she'd had since before Eve was born, one so ancient she had to light the pilot in the oven as well as the top burners.

Eve walked to the fireplace, pulled off her black gloves, and warmed her hands by the fire as Benny and the boys continued to haul in their necessities.

"I have you and Benjamin in your old room." *Mamm* joined Eve by the fire. "We'll put the twins in the extra bedroom and Leroy in my sewing room on the pullout couch."

"That sounds *gut*." Eve managed another brief smile,

although she couldn't help but wonder if God was punishing her for something. Two months here with her mother would be a nightmare. That wouldn't be the case with her father. He mostly stayed in the background and let *Mamm* run things, which was exactly the opposite of how it should be. Everyone knew that the man should be the head of the household.

Her father came from his bedroom around the corner from the living room, waving to everyone as they entered. "Come in, come in . . . out of this *wedder*." He kissed Eve on the cheek the way he always did when he saw her, then shook hands with Benny and all three boys. Eve glanced at her mother, who had never been affectionate. Eve didn't have the energy to change things. Instead, she was overly affectionate with her own children and made sure they'd never feel unloved.

"Follow me, and we'll get you all set up while the womenfolk work on some supper." *Daed* motioned for Eve's clan to follow him upstairs, and Eve followed her mother into the kitchen. She could see snow starting to fall outside the window as night was almost completely upon them. They'd made it there just in time, and Eve was hoping her house wouldn't be damaged any further from bad weather.

"It smells *gut* in here." Eve walked to the old white gas range and fought the urge to say anything. She'd asked her mother only once why they didn't buy a newer model, one with an electronic ignition that would be easier—and safer—for them to use. *Mamm* had scowled and said it was too *Englischy*, a term that Eve had never heard anyone except her mother use. "What can I do to help?"

"You can set the table." *Mamm* pointed to a hutch on the far wall in the large kitchen. "And use the *gut* dishes."

Eve hesitated. Her mother only used the good dishes at Thanksgiving, Christmas, or other special occasions. But Eve didn't want to give her any reason to argue so soon after they'd arrived, so she went to the hutch and pulled out seven of the large white china plates. She was setting the last one in place around the large table in the middle of the room when her father, Benny, and the boys walked into the room. Eve had already instructed her sons about not using cell phones, earbuds, or other electronics around her parents—especially their *mammi*. After a small rebellion, they'd all agreed. And Eve had told Amos, "If possible, try not to let *Mammi* see that lizard."

Eve remembered when she'd turned sixteen, excited to participate in all the things that the *rumschpringe* offered. It should have been a time to explore the outside world, go to movies, ride in cars, wear *Englisch* clothes, listen to the radio, and own a cell phone—if portable phones had been common and affordable back then. But Eve's parents had been much too old-fashioned and overprotective for any of that. Eve had hidden the few things that she did do from her parents—the same way she was making her own *kinner* do now.

She wasn't thrilled that all of her boys were actively taking advantage of this time period, but that's the way things were done. Children should be allowed to experience the outside world, then make a decision whether or not to be baptized into the community. It was every parent's fear that one of their children would choose not to stay, but Eve knew that she and Benny had educated the boys well about the *Ordnung*. All she could do was pray that they'd all seek baptism. Leroy was scheduled to be baptized in the spring, which made Eve think that there would be a proposal in the works too. Her oldest son had been courting Lena Byler for almost a year, and Lena was going to be christened into the community at that time as well.

Eve's father sat in his spot at the head of the table, Leroy and Elias took the two seats to his left, and Amos and Benny sat across from them. When Eve's mother sat down across from her father, Eve slipped into a chair beside Benny. They all bowed their heads in silent prayer, and Elias was the first one to speak.

"It's so dark in here." He glanced at the lantern hanging above the middle of the table, then at two others on the counter. All the *kinner* were used to the large propane lamps they had in their house.

"This is the way it has always been done, Amos." Eve's mother raised her chin as she passed a bowl of chow-chow to her right.

Eve cleared her throat. "*Mamm*, that's Elias."

Her mother shook her head. "*Ach*, I still can't tell those boys apart."

Eve smiled. "Most people can't." She ladled herself some stew from the large pot in the center of the table. Despite her anxiety about staying with her parents, she still thought her mother's cooking was the best in the world.

Of course, if *Mamm* would wear her glasses more

often and invest in some propane lighting, she'd have a better shot at identify-ing her own grandchildren. But to be fair, everyone in the community confused Amos and Elias. They were as identical as any twins could be, and the only thing most people used to distinguish them was that Amos stuttered sometimes. As a parent, Eve could tell them apart instantly before they even came within ten feet of her. Elias's eyebrows were a tad bushier than Amos's, and Elias had a freckle to the left of his right eye. One of Amos's teeth on the bottom row was crooked a bit to the left, and his thumbnails were different from his brother's, rounder. And to Eve, the boys just had a different scent. Maybe that was some-thing only a mother noticed.

"I'm the handsome one," Elias said with a mouthful of food.

Eve quickly corrected him. "Don't talk with your mouth full."

From there, the conversation turned to the work to be done on the house. The plan was that Eve's father, Benny, and the three boys would tackle outdoor chores here first thing in the morning—get the chickens and pigs fed, stalls cleaned, horses tended, and cows milked—then they would go to the house to work. Various members of the community would show up as they could to lend a hand. Eve knew they could raise a barn in a day, and at first she'd questioned Benny as to why they couldn't get her house put back together in a day too. Benny had started to explain the structural damage, but then he just shook his head and said, "We'll get it livable as soon as we can."

Eve glanced out the window, and the only propane light her parents allowed illuminated the yard, large flakes of snow falling in blankets. If bad weather continued, it was going to make repairs that much more difficult.

She thought about spending her days inside with no one else but her mother, and she wondered how this part of God's plan for her life could be a good thing. It was only a matter of time before they began to disagree about everything from how Eve raised her children to updating this old house. As she finished the last of her stew, she determined that she was just going to keep quiet and let her mother run her own household and try not to cause any upset.

. . .

Elias put the lantern on the nightstand between him and Amos before he climbed under the covers fully dressed, leaving his shoes next to him on the floor. He flipped open his cell phone.

"You better not try to sneak out here. It ain't gonna be as easy as at home." Amos sat up on his bed, frowning in the dimly lit room.

"Mind your own business." Elias propped himself against his pillow and tapped Elizabeth's number. While it was ringing, he said to his brother, "Besides, I'm closer to Elizabeth's *haus* here. Just barely a run through the Lapps' pasture, and I can meet her at the barn behind her *haus.*"

"I—I reckon if you'd got caught sneaking out at

home, you would've been in a b-big enough heap of trouble. But if you get caught sneaking out of *Mammi* and *Daadi's haus*, you're r-really gonna get it."

Elias closed the phone when Elizabeth didn't answer, then glanced at the battery bars. Only one left. Tomorrow he'd need to find some power to recharge, which might be a challenge since he'd be with his father and other members of the community working on their house. His father had insisted both Elias and Amos take a leave from their part-time jobs at the market in Bird-in-Hand to work full-time on the reconstruction. Leroy had also been told to put his job on hold at the construction company where he worked. Leroy's supervisor hadn't taken the news as well as the twins' boss at the market, but the older man had eventually agreed.

This new work schedule put a glitch in Elias's plans. First, it would be hard to charge his phone. Second, he wouldn't get to see Elizabeth. She'd been visiting him every day for two months during her lunch break from the bakery. Elias was sure their first kiss was coming soon.

"She's not answering anyway." Elias put the phone on the nightstand. He glanced out the window at the steady snowfall. It would have been a cold trek across the pasture, but seeing Elizabeth would have been worth it. "And ya know, Amos . . . you ain't ever gonna get a girlfriend if you don't give it more effort."

Amos grunted. "Give it more effort? N-Now you're talking like the *Englisch*. You probably want to—to be one of them."

"Don't be *dumm*. I'll never leave here. I'll marry Elizabeth, and we'll have lots of *kinner*." In the darkness he pointed a finger at his brother. "You're the one always reading them *Englisch* magazines. You probably want to go live out there." He waved his hand toward the window.

"Ain't true. I mostly like the pictures anyway." Amos lay down.

"You're gonna be living with *Mamm* and *Daed* until you're old, like twenty or something." Elias folded his hands behind his head. His brother was so shy that he'd barely even talk to a girl; all he did was bury himself in books and magazines. Elias knew that it was partly because of his stuttering, but Amos was a good-looking guy. Elias grinned at the thought.

"Sh-shut up, Elias."

"You shut up, Amos." Elias shook his head, not in the mood to fight. He stood up and was just about to slip out of his trousers when the phone rang. He grabbed it and answered quickly as he sat back down on the bed.

Elizabeth's sweet voice was a whisper as she spoke. "Can you *kumme*?"

"*Ya*. Same plan. If I'm not there in thirty minutes, then I got caught leaving the *haus*." He paused. "But since I'm at *mei mammi* and *daadi's haus*, I'm closer, so maybe less than thirty minutes."

"*Gut*. I'll be in the barn. Be careful, Elias. It's snowing *hatt*. Sure you want to *kumme*?" Before he had time to answer, she said, "I really want to see you."

Elias smiled as his heart thumped in his chest. A blizzard wasn't going to keep him from Elizabeth. He swallowed hard. "I want to see you too. Putting on my shoes and leaving."

As soon as they hung up, Elias slung his feet over

the side of the bed and reached for his flashlight on the nightstand. He looked at the clock. Nine forty-five. His parents were always in bed by eight thirty, since they started their day around four thirty, so he was pretty sure his grandparents would be asleep too. But their bedroom was downstairs, so he'd have to be extra quiet going out the front door. He reached for his shoes.

"I—I wouldn't wanta—wanta be you if you get caught." Amos sat up in bed, and Elias pointed the flashlight in his face.

"Don't worry about it. It's late. Everyone's asleep."

Amos chuckled. "I hope she's worth it."

"*Ach*, she is, *mei bruder*. And I'm going to kiss her tonight."

"I'm going to sleep." Amos lay back down. "When four thirty comes, you'll be sorry."

Elias didn't answer, but instead shoved his pillow beneath the quilt on the twin bed. His mother rarely checked on them, but just in case she poked her head in the room, he'd be covered. He bundled up in his coat, stuffed his hands in his gloves, and pulled a thick stocking cap over his head.

He cringed when the bedroom door squeaked, then two stairs creaked on his way down. Crossing the living room, he decided not to go out the front door, but instead use the door in the kitchen since it was farthest away from his grandparents' bedroom. He tiptoed into the kitchen, and a bright light hit him in the face.

"Going somewhere?"

CHAPTER 3

Elias's feet felt rooted to the wooden floor in the kitchen as he stared at his grandfather. "Uh . . ."

"Just going out for a late-night stroll?" *Daadi* pulled the flashlight from Elias's face and put it on the table so the light was shining at the ceiling. Elias didn't move. "Mighty cold for a walk, *ya*?"

"Uh, *ya*."

Daadi picked up a glass and took a swallow. "Nothing like warm milk to help a man sleep." He pointed to a plate on the table. "And a slice of your *mammi's* apple crumb pie. Have yourself one." His grandfather pushed his glasses up on his nose, then scooped up a bite with his fork.

Elias was sure his chance of seeing Elizabeth was gone. He pulled off his knit stocking hat—the black one his mother had made him two years ago—and rubbed his forehead. "I was just . . ." His heart ached at the thought of lying to his grand-father, and he wasn't sure what to say.

Daadi nodded as he swallowed. "*Ya, ya.* I know." He stood up from the table, pushed in his chair, and pointed a finger at Elias. "I reckon we don't need to speak of this."

Elias felt his face turning three shades of red, and he opened his mouth to respond, but his grandfather spoke first.

"Your *mammi* doesn't like when I get up to eat cookies or pie this late at night. Gives me heartburn, and she says it's not *gut* for me." He smiled, his coke-bottle glasses hanging off his nose again. He was dressed in a long white shirt atop black trousers and black socks. *Daadi* picked up the flashlight from the table, and Elias brought a hand to his face when his grandfather shined it in his direction. *Daadi* stroked his long gray beard. "Which one are you anyway?"

Elias considered his options for a moment, then told the truth. "Elias." He held his breath as he waited to see what *Daadi* would do next.

His grandfather lowered the light, shuffled past him, and patted him on the shoulder. "Well, Elias . . . have a nice stroll. *Gut nacht.*"

Elias stood still as his grandfather scooted in his socks across the living room. Elias heard the bedroom door gently close. Was this a trick?

He waited a full five minutes as he tried to decide what to do. Then he imagined how Elizabeth's lips would feel on his, and he tiptoed out of the kitchen and closed the door behind him.

. . .

Elizabeth's teeth chattered as she pulled the back door open, forcing it against packed snow. She pulled her flashlight from the pocket of her heavy black coat and turned it on, scanning for critters as she strode down the path to the barn. When she didn't see anything, she walked to a haystack in the corner of the barn and sat down. Luckily, their three horses, four pigs, and three goats didn't seem disturbed by her visit. She wrapped her arms around herself, knowing she shouldn't have tempted Elias to travel on foot in this weather, but her heart fluttered every time she thought about him. Seeing him only once a day at lunchtime had been hard enough, but now that he would be working on the family's home, she wasn't sure when they could get together. This seemed like the only way, and she was sure that he was going to kiss her soon.

She stood up and paced, thinking it had been longer than thirty minutes. She poked her head out the barn door to see that all the lights at her house were still off. It was a miracle she'd managed to get out of the house with three younger sisters in the same bedroom, two older brothers down the hall, and her parents around the corner. It would be worth it when Elias walked through the door.

Elizabeth had known both the Bender twins for as long as she could remember, and from the time she was six or seven she was sure that she would grow up to marry Elias. While the boys looked the same to most people, Elias was more outgoing and confident. He never got riled or upset, and he was always happy. Elizabeth loved that about him. Amos seemed like a fine fellow, but he was incredibly shy, kept his head down, and stuttered when he got nervous. Elizabeth had tried to talk to him lots of times after the worship service, but she doubted Amos would ever venture out into the night to visit her. The barn door eased open, causing her heart to skip a few beats. *Elias, or Mamm or Daed?*

Her heartbeat returned to normal as Elias crossed the threshold into the barn. She brought her hands to her chest and bounced up on her toes once. "You made it." She walked quickly toward him, stopping a couple of feet away. His face was drained of color, his breathing ragged. His black jacket and stocking cap were covered in white flakes, his teeth were chattering. She walked closer and began rubbing his arms. "You're freezing. I should never have asked you to do this."

But I'm so glad you're here.

Elias wrapped his arms around her and pulled her close. She wasn't sure if it was just to warm himself up; but whatever the reason, it felt good to be in his arms.

"*Ach*, Elias. You're trembling."

"I'm fine." He shook as he held her. "I just wanted to see you."

"I feel the same way." She nuzzled her head into his chest. "I can feel your heart beating."

He chuckled. Not what she was expecting. He eased away, grinning. "I almost got caught."

"*Nee*. What happened?" She'd thought it had taken longer than thirty minutes.

He peeled back the rim of his black stocking hat, which had almost fallen over his eyes. "*Mei daadi* was sitting at the kitchen table when I tried to sneak through the kitchen."

Elizabeth gasped. "What did you do?"

Elias shrugged, still grinning. "He was eating a piece of pie and drinking milk. He asked if I was going for a stroll. I never really answered, and he went on to bed."

Elizabeth wrapped her arms around herself again. "That's *fremm*."

"I know." He pulled her back into his arms. "But I had to see you."

They stayed in the embrace for a few moments, both shivering, until Elias slowly pulled away. He gazed into her eyes, and Elizabeth was sure he could hear her heart beating.

"Elizabeth . . ." He leaned down until his lips were inches from hers. "I love you."

Before she could answer, his mouth was firmly on hers, and she went weak in the knees. The kiss went on forever. Twice he eased away, but kissed her again. When they finally parted, she said, "I love you too, Elias."

He pulled her into his arms. "I can't stay long. But I'll try to come tomorrow night."

Elizabeth pulled from his arms and gazed into his eyes. "*Nee.* Don't come." She cupped his cheeks with her gloved hands. "It's much too cold for you to travel by foot like this. And tomorrow is supposed to be even colder. It's enough knowing that you love me."

Elias smiled. "I'd walk through a blizzard to be with you, Elizabeth, even if it was only for a few minutes like tonight." He kissed the top of her gloved hand. "I'll be here."

"But—"

"Don't you want me to come?" Elias tipped his head to one side.

Elizabeth fell into his arms. "*Ach*, Elias. I always want to be with you, but it's just so cold."

"I'll be here."

And as Elias kissed her for the last time that night, Elizabeth was sure that she would one day be Mrs. Elias Bender.

· · ·

On Monday morning the men and boys left to go work on the house, leaving Eve and her mother alone. Eve wasn't sure how much work the menfolk would be able to get done on the house with the weather predictions, but of more concern to her was how she and her mother were going to fare all day together. Eve noticed her mother's right hand trembling as she washed the breakfast dishes. They'd all known for over a year that *Mamm* had Parkinson's disease. Eve had tried several times to get her mother to see a doctor in Lancaster, but *Mamm* always said that Fern Zook's herbal recipes were working just fine.

Eve loved Fern and appreciated the work that she did, but she suspected that modern medications could help her mother's condition far better than an herbal remedy.

Mamm's right hand shook with might as her four fingers met with her thumb, then the familiar circular patterns began as her mother tried to steady the plate so she could run the dishrag across it.

"*Mamm*, I'll finish the dishes." She reached for the plate her mother was holding, only to have her mother shakily jerk it away.

"I'm not an invalid, Eve. I can wash the dishes. I take care of your father every day." She scrubbed at the white plate.

Eve's mouth hung open for a moment. "I didn't say you were an invalid. I just offered to help." She set her dish towel on the counter, walked to the table, and picked up the butter and jams, stowing them in the refrigerator. "What can I do to help around here today? I'll clean the bedrooms and bathroom upstairs, but what else?" She was hoping there was plenty to do to keep them both busy and out of each other's hair.

Her mother didn't look up. Her hands were still in the soapy water, and strands of gray hair had come loose from beneath her black *kapp*. "I was hoping you'd do a couple of things for me while you're here."

Eve stood still, dreading what might be coming. "What's that?"

Mamm slowly turned toward her. "I haven't updated the family Bible since you were born. I was wondering if you'd add the boys, their birthdates and such." She turned away and resumed washing another plate. "And there is a large section in the back for notes. Maybe you could write down certain dates that are special. Things like that."

That was an easy enough task. Eve pointed to the living room. "The Bible you keep on the end table?"

Mamm shook her head. "*Nee*, I have the big family Bible in *mei* bedroom. It goes back five generations." She turned around to face Eve again, wiped her hands on a dish towel, and smiled. "I always meant to update it after the boys were born, but I needed to verify the times and how much they weighed." She paused. "And especially note the differences in the twins, since most of us can barely tell them apart."

Eve smiled. "That's an easy task. I'll be glad to." *And that will take about five minutes.* "What else?"

Mamm picked up her recipe box from the kitchen counter and motioned for Eve to join her at the kitchen table. She pulled out a stack of blank index cards from the back of the box.

"Most of the meals you and I make we know in our minds, *ya*?" *Mamm* raised an eyebrow, and Eve nodded. "But someday the boys will marry, and we'll want to share the recipes. I thought you could spend some time while you're here writing them all down." Her mother flipped a finger along the top of the categorized cards. "Most of these are from friends, although a few of them are mine." She leaned over and touched Eve's hand. "But I've never taken the time to write down the ones I know by heart."

Eve glanced at her mother's hand on hers, a rare and welcome gesture, but then *Mamm* quickly pulled her hand away. Again Eve wondered why there'd always been such distance between them. Eve's grandparents had passed before she was born, and her aunts and uncles lived in Ohio, along with a few cousins Eve had never met. She'd often wondered what kind of relationship her mother and grandmother had.

Mamm handed her a pen. "Do you want to start now?"

Eve slowly took the pen. "There are probably hundreds. You've been showing me how to cook since I was a little girl."

"*Ya.* Exactly." Her mother tapped her hand to the

table, then hastily got up. "You get started, and I'll bring you the Bible for updating. Don't worry about the upstairs, I'll get it."

Eve stared at the recipe box. She thumbed through the cookie section and randomly pulled out a card. It was a recipe for boiled cookies from Rachel King. Eve remembered when Rachel gave *Mamm* the recipe. Rachel's daughter, Hannah, couldn't have been more than a year old the first time Eve babysat her. She could still recall the scrumptious cookies that Rachel had left for her to snack on. Eve had made sure not to leave that day without Rachel's recipe. Her mouth watered as she thought about the chunky peanut butter cookies.

Eve placed the card back in its spot as she thought about Hannah, who was now a grown woman running the family's bed-and-breakfast. She pulled out another card from the box, a recipe for sour cream pancakes that had come from Esther Stoltzfus. Esther had died years ago, but her famous sour cream pancakes lived on. Eve recalled the first time her mother prepared them, when Eve was about ten. "But *Daed* doesn't like sour cream," she had protested.

"Then we just won't mention that there's sour cream in them," her mother had said, then giggled.

Eve stared at the recipe box, figuring that there was probably a story behind every card. The best times she'd ever shared with her mother were when they were cooking.

As memories filled Eve's mind, she positioned one of the blank recipe cards in front of her. Smiling, she started to work.

CHAPTER 4

Think, you old woman. Think. Rosemary thumped her palm to her forehead repeatedly.

"*Mamm*, are you okay?"

Rosemary spun around and grabbed her chest as she leaned against the kitchen counter. "What?" She scowled. "You scared me near to death, sneaking up on me like that."

Eve had taken up working on the recipes in Rosemary's recliner near the fireplace for almost a week. She wrote all day and kept the fire going while Rosemary cleaned, did the mending, and kept up with the rest of the normal household chores. Every day her daughter offered to help with the routine tasks, but Rosemary just needed her to write down those recipes. All of them.

She hadn't heard Eve get up and walk into the kitchen.

Eve pulled her black sweater snug around her. "I didn't mean to sneak up on you. I was just wondering if it feels cold in here to you. I'm freezing."

"Add some logs to the fire." Rosemary waved a hand in the air as she tried to remember where she'd put her glasses. She'd looked everywhere: on the nightstand by the bed, on the coffee table and end table in the living room, in the bathroom, even in the refrigerator. Although she'd never admit it to a soul, she'd found her spectacles next to the butter on two separate occasions.

Eve took a couple of steps into the kitchen. "Those propane heaters in the bedrooms upstairs work great. Why don't we get a couple for down here?"

"What?"

"Heaters, *Mamm*." Eve walked closer to Rosemary. "*Heaters*." She edged even closer and spoke louder. "Our Daily Bread has some nice propane heaters on sale. I can pick up a couple when I'm there tomorrow afternoon."

"That's fine." Rosemary grimaced as she scanned the counter-top, continuing to look for her glasses. "And I'm not deaf."

"What are you looking for?" Eve moved closer, and Rosemary sidestepped to her left as she reached behind her and clutched the tiled countertop. She locked eyes with her daughter. For the life of her, Rosemary didn't know what Eve was talking about.

"What?" Rosemary's heart thudded in her chest. *This is what it's like to lose your mind.* It took a lot of effort to pretend it wasn't happening. "What?" she asked again in a calmer voice.

"You're looking around like you've lost something." *Yes, that's it. I've lost something. Now, what was it?*

Eve moved closer, and it felt like every nerve in Rosemary's body was twitching, then centered in her hand. She reached for her right hand with her left and squeezed, but the shaking was worse than usual. She could feel Eve's eyes on her, the same way people at church stared at her when the shaking started.

"*Mamm*, why don't you let me take you to Dr. Knepp? I'm sure he'll prescribe some medicine for your Parkinson's. Fern's herbal recipes are fine, but the *Englisch* doctor can give you some better medication, and—"

"My glasses!" Rosemary let out a huge sigh of relief. "I'm looking for my *glasses*." She smiled. "I've lost my glasses." She shook her head a couple of times. "Now, what were you saying?"

"Dr. Knepp, *Mamm*. Let's get you some better medication to help with the shaking. It's nothing to be embarrassed about."

"I'm not embarrassed. Fern's herbs are doing me fine. I just need to find my glasses."

"They're on the mantel. I saw them there earlier."

Rosemary lifted her chin and pressed her lips together. "Now why in the world would they be on the mantel?" *Maybe you put them there to confuse me.*

Eve shrugged. "I don't know. You were dusting the lanterns earlier. Maybe you set them down. I'll get them for you."

Rosemary sighed, then quietly whispered, "*Danki.*"

. . .

Eve was working on the recipes in bed when Benny crawled underneath the covers beside her. "What are you writing on the back of the card, or is that just a very long recipe?" Her husband eased up against her, his beard tickling her face. She turned and gave him a quick kiss.

"I'm writing down things that I remember about me and *mei mamm.*"

"Like what?" Benny nuzzled her with his beard again.

She gave him another kiss. "Now scoot over and let me work on this." She playfully pushed him away. "My fondest memories of me and *Mamm* are when we were cooking, so on the back of every card I'm writing what I remember related to the recipe." She shrugged. "I mean, I don't have something to write on every card, but if we had a *gut* time making this recipe, or if something *gut* happened . . . I'm writing it down."

"I think that's very nice." Benny smiled. "You're a *gut dochder.*"

Guilt flooded over Eve. "*Nee,* I don't think so." She paused as she took a deep breath. "I haven't been seeing *mei mudder* enough, and she's gotten worse. She hides it well during worship, but being with her all the time, I really notice how much her hands shake. She still refuses to go see Dr. Knepp."

"I know it frustrates you to see her suffer, but you can't make her go."

Eve set the cards and pen on her nightstand, then rubbed her eyes. "She didn't even argue today when I asked her about buying some extra propane heaters for downstairs. She was too busy worrying about her glasses she'd lost." She rolled over on her side and faced Benny.

He eased onto his side and propped his head on his hand. Her sweet Benny. He always knew when to just listen.

"She's so cranky. Worse than ever."

"We're working on the *haus* as best we can, but the

storm is supposed to blow in tonight. If we get all the snow they say we're going to get, that will slow us down."

"I'm not worried about that." Eve blinked her eyes a few times as a knot formed in her throat. "I'm worried about her. About *Mamm*." She paused again, trying to find the words to explain her feelings. "It's not just the shaking. She's different. And I don't mean just crankier. Sometimes she looks at me in a *fremm* way." She took a deep breath, then heard a movement downstairs.

"Your *daed* eating a late-night snack again?" Benny grinned.

Eve looked at the clock. Nine thirty. She and Benny were up later than usual. "*Ya.*" Eve pushed back the covers on her side and swung her feet over the side of the bed. "I'm going to go talk to him. About *Mamm*." She wrapped her hair in a tight bun, pinned it, then found her robe. After she picked up the lantern, she leaned down and kissed her husband. "Sleep, *mei lieb.* I'll be quiet when I come back in."

Benny nodded as he yawned, then his face faded from view as Eve moved with the lantern toward the bedroom door.

A minute later she entered the kitchen. Her father was sitting at the table with a flashlight illuminating a round circle on the ceiling. His eyes grew wide when Eve entered the room.

"*Ach*, you scared me," he said through a mouthful of cake. "I thought you were your *mudder.*"

Eve smiled. *Mamm* had told her years ago that *Daed* got out of bed every night for a late-night snack. "He needs to feel he's getting away with something," her mother had said. "But it does give him an awful case of indigestion the next morning."

She pulled out a chair and sat down across from her father. He pushed a pan of sliced *kaffi* cake toward her. "Taste this." He frowned. "Something don't taste right about it."

Eve picked up a slice of the cake her mother had made yesterday. She took a bite. "It's not bad. It's just not really . . . good."

Her father frowned. "Your *mamm* is the best cook in the district." He put down his half-eaten piece of cake and shook his head.

"I wanted to talk to you about her. She's getting worse, isn't she? I mean, the shaking has increased, but she also seems so ill-tempered—"

"She's not ill-tempered."

Her father spoke with an authority that Eve wasn't used to hearing. Even when she was growing up, she'd rarely heard him raise his voice, and any disciplining had been left up to her mother. Although neither of her parents had ever laid a hand on her. *Mamm* would make her sit in her room when she'd mis-behaved, but that was the extent of it.

Daed rubbed his forehead and sighed, then went on. "She's sick, Eve. I've been telling you that."

More guilt. Eve bit her bottom lip for a moment, blinked her eyes a few times. "I know that."

"*Nee.* I don't think you do. Until this past week, you've only seen her every other week for a brief time. You're just now getting an idea of how sick she is because you are with her every day."

"*Daed*, I have a family to take care of. It's not that I avoid you." *Especially not you.* "I've tried to get her to go see Dr. Knepp. *Englisch* medications could help with the shaking."

Her father sighed. "I know you to be right." He gazed at her across the table in the dimly lit room. "But she needs *you*. Modern medicine can only go so far."

A tear found its way down Eve's cheek, and she quickly swiped it away. She'd just lied to her father. She did avoid her mother as much as she could, and she'd been dreading this extended visit.

"*Mei* sweet *maedel* . . ." Her father reached over and put his hand on top of hers. "Use this time to get to know your *mudder*." He stood up, then leaned down and kissed her on the forehead. "You might be surprised by what you learn."

Eve heard her father's bedroom door close. She picked up the slice of cake and took another bite.

Sugar. That was it. There was no brown sugar, which Eve knew the recipe called for. She ate the rest of the cake anyway, not ready for sleep just yet. She folded her hands in front of her and bowed her head.

. . .

Elias chuckled. "It's been so easy, sneaking out this week." He pulled Elizabeth close and kissed her again. Afterward he pushed back a strand of loose hair that had fallen from beneath her *kapp*. "*Daadi* just sits at the table eating his snack and waves to me as I go out the door. He usually tells me to have a nice walk and to stay warm."

Elizabeth frowned. "He's on to you, Elias. He knows you're not just going for a walk every night at this hour."

Elias shrugged, grinning. "Maybe so, but I never lie to him, and he has never mentioned it in front of *mei mamm* or *daed*."

"I guess that's *gut*," Elizabeth said, shivering.

"I'm going to go. You're freezing." He pulled her into his arms, kissed her again, then sent her indoors. "Be careful," he said as she made her way to the barn exit. "We don't want you getting caught either."

Elizabeth nodded, and once she was safely inside, Elias fought the bitter cold across the Lapp pasture to his grandparents' house. He knew a storm was due to blow in, and he probably shouldn't have traveled to see Elizabeth tonight. He could see a faint light shining from the kitchen, and he was surprised that his grandfather was still up. Every other night, *Daadi* was in bed when Elias returned from seeing Elizabeth.

He trekked softly up the porch steps, pulled back the screen, and twisted the handle on the wood door. A light hit him in the face.

And this time it wasn't his grandfather.

CHAPTER 5

Elias cringed as his mother stood, yelling at him in a whisper from the other side of the kitchen table. "You are grounded, do you hear me?"

"*Ya.* Yes, *Mamm.*" Elias was glad that the table was between them. He hadn't seen *Mamm* this mad since he dropped a frog down the back of Anna Mae Stoltzfus's dress after worship when he was nine. Usually she left the discipline to their father, but she'd been so furious about the frog incident she didn't even wait for *Daed*, opting to pull a switch from a nearby tree before they walked into the house. Elias wished he were young enough to take a spanking instead of being grounded.

"It is nearing zero degrees outside with a storm coming in. Do you have any idea how dangerous it is for you to be outside in this?" *Mamm* put her hands on her hips.

He could barely see her in the dim light of the lantern, but he was pretty sure her face was red as a beet, the way it usually got when she was really mad.

"How could you do this while we are staying at your grandparents' *haus*?"

Elias opened his mouth and almost said that *Daadi* knew about it, but there was no reason to get his grandfather in trouble too. "I'm sorry."

Mamm pointed toward the living room. "Go. We will talk of this in the morning. And you can be sure that I will tell Elizabeth's *mudder* about this."

Elias stopped breathing. "*Mamm*, you can't. Please. Don't tell her *mudder*. I'll never be able to see Elizabeth again. Her father will forbid it. *Mamm* . . ." He squared his shoulders, standing taller. "I'll die if I can't see her."

His mother rolled her eyes. "You will not *die*. And over time, I'm sure that you and Elizabeth will be able to see each other again."

Just the thought of not seeing Elizabeth every day caused Elias's stomach to ache. "What about the singing on Sunday?"

"That's in two days. I promise you'll still be punished."

Elias put a hand on his hip and looked at the floor. "Some *rumschpringe* this is."

His mother came around the table and held the lantern up. As he'd suspected, her face was beet red.

"You watch yourself, mister. We've allowed all of you boys plenty of privileges, but sneaking out when a storm is coming is dangerous, and you should know better." *Mamm* frowned, her eyes locked with his. "I don't want your grandparents to know about this. Now up to bed you go."

Elias stomped across the living room to the stairs. He wasn't a child and shouldn't be treated like one. He would find a way to see Elizabeth. No matter what his mother said.

. . .

Four o'clock came early on Saturday morning. Eve had trouble going to sleep after catching Elias sneaking back into the house. She knew she'd reacted out of fear more than anything. As predicted, the storm had come during the night and dropped almost twelve inches of snow. Despite the weather, her father, Benny, and her three sons left to go work on the house. She'd told Benny about catching Elias, and they agreed that two weeks' punishment would be sufficient. Benny had talked her out of telling Elizabeth's parents.

Her father's words weighed heavily on her heart. *"Use this time to get to know your* mudder," he'd said.

What is there to get to know? Eve and her mother were nothing alike. Her mother had shown little to no affection toward Eve when she was growing up. Eve had made it a point to shower her children with affection. Rosemary Chupp was also stubborn, refusing to change with the times or make use of modern medicine to help herself. Eve took advantage of certain luxuries that the bishop allowed—things that still kept them separated from the outside world, but that also improved quality of life or saved time—propane lights, certain canned goods, battery-operated mixers for baking, a modern gas range for cooking, and a sewing machine that was run by a small generator . . . just to name a few.

Eve gathered up the recipe box, blank cards, and her pen. After she stoked the fire, she curled up in the recliner and tried to focus on the happy times she and her mother had shared. Even now, as they prepared meals together in her childhood home, there was a peacefulness between them that was absent the rest of the time. Just like when she was young.

"How are the recipes coming?" *Mamm* walked into the room toting a yellow feather duster. Eve didn't think the house could get any cleaner, but she didn't comment.

"Fine. I can't believe how many recipes I have in my head. It was a *gut* idea to get them all written down."

"*Danki* for doing that." *Mamm* smiled, and again Eve's father's words flowed through her mind.

"You're welcome. I'm enjoying it." Eve paused. "We cooked a lot of things together over the years."

"*Ya.* We did." *Mamm* exhaled, sounding content, and Eve wondered if her mother wished they were closer too.

They were quiet for a few moments, then Eve decided to share her project. "I—I hope you don't mind, but on the back of each card I've written memories I have of us preparing the recipe." She bit her bottom lip for a moment, keeping her head down. "Or maybe where we took the food, or what we were doing when we first made it." She shrugged. "Just little things like that." She looked up after a moment and was shocked to see tears gathering in the corners of her mother's eyes. "*Mamm?*" Eve waited, not sure what to do. She wasn't sure she'd ever seen her mother cry.

"I think that is *gut*. Very, very *gut*." *Mamm* raised her chin, blinked her eyes several times, then began dusting around the lanterns on the mantel.

They were quiet while Eve wrote and her mother

cleaned the living room. Eve had already gone upstairs to make sure that Amos's lizard and cage were still safely hidden in the closet behind a bunch of boxes. So far they'd been lucky that Eve's mother hadn't stumbled upon the reptile while tidying up the boys' room.

Eve finished her card for Chicken in a Cloud. It was a favorite of both hers and her mother's, although Eve had long ago given up making the sauce from scratch, opting for cream of chicken soup instead. It wasn't as tasty, but it was much easier. However, it was her mother's recipe, so Eve wrote it out the way her mother had originally taught her—to save some chicken broth, then mix it with flour and butter to make the creamy sauce. But the best part of Chicken in a Cloud was the story that went with it. She turned the card over and wrote.

> I remember the day we had chicken and potatoes, and you suggested we do something other than just bake the chicken and make mashed potatoes as a side dish. I was standing on the little red stool as usual, so I was tall enough to help. You always stood to my left.

Eve paused, looking up. She could see the red stool through the doorway into the kitchen, tucked into a nook on the other side of the refrigerator; same place it had always been. She smiled.

> You added milk and cream cheese, the way you always did when making mashed potatoes, but I asked you why you didn't add any butter. You told me to

wash my hands, and we both did. Then you thrust your bare hands into the mashed potatoes and pulled out two handfuls and laughed. I wasn't sure what to do, but you nodded for me to do the same. Then we tossed the mashed potatoes into a casserole dish you had laid out, both of us laughing the whole time.

I was eight or nine, I think, and I couldn't believe we were playing in the food! We formed a crust with the potatoes, then talked about the chicken filling. I felt so much a part of the process, and when we were done, you told me to name our creation. And Chicken in a Cloud was born.

Eve leaned her head back against the recliner, noticing that her mother had left the room. *Mamm's* bedroom door was closed. She'd been known to sneak in a nap this time of day, so Eve closed her eyes and let the Chicken in a Cloud memory linger in her mind. There'd been so many good days for them; she wondered why she allowed herself to focus on the negative in their relationship. Maybe they were just two different women with varying ways of doing things.

She opened her eyes and looked into the recipe box. She'd written close to a hundred, she figured, and probably had at least a hundred more to go. There wasn't a story to go with every card, but each time she recalled a fond memory, she felt one step closer to her mother, even if it was only one-sided. Glancing at the clock, she knew she was going to miss the two o'clock prayer gathering at Our Daily Bread, but Benny had asked her not to travel in this weather. She knew he was right, but she would miss the fellowship of the local women in the community. Her mother hadn't been to the prayer gathering since the tremors in her hands had started. Sometimes Eve was surprised *Mamm* still went to church.

. . .

Rosemary sat on her bed staring at the plain white wall as shadows of her past danced in front of her. She'd gone for years without the haunting images surfacing. *Why now, Lord? Why are these demons in my head?*

She thanked the Lord every day that her relationship with Eve wasn't like the one she'd had with her own mother. Rosemary had never laid a hand on Eve. She'd made it a point to stay distant from her only daughter, just in case that type of thing ran in the family genes—like mother, like daughter. Now she wanted to be closer to Eve, but they'd been this way for so long that Rosemary wasn't sure how to change. She saw the outpouring of affection that Eve gave to her own children, even if she wasn't raising them the way Rosemary would have liked. The boys had brought all their electric gadgets along, and she reckoned everyone thought they were hiding them. But there were small boxes with wires in the twins' room, a radio in Leroy's, and Eve had lotions from Walmart. Rosemary cringed.

If there was one thing she'd learned from her mother, it was that change wasn't good. That belief had been beaten into her and her siblings. She'd tried to make sure Eve didn't evolve with the times, but she and

Joseph had rarely disciplined their daughter. Maybe it was their fault that Eve didn't feel the same way about change. As another generation was nearing adulthood, Rosemary could see that things were only getting worse. Soon there'd be generations of Amish folk who wouldn't rely on the Lord's will, but instead on all those gadgets and what-nots.

Rosemary heard a ringing in her ears—so loud she brought her hands to her head. But she could still hear Minerva screaming. *Mamm* must have the horse whip after her again. Rosemary didn't understand why Minnie couldn't just mind her manners with their mother. Most of Rosemary's beatings had come from defending her sister. She hauled herself up off the bed and burst out the door.

Minerva was curled up in a ball in the recliner. Rosemary ran to her and dropped to her knees. "Minnie, hush your cries. Stop it now." She pulled the girl into a hug to try and muffle her sobs before *Mamm* came back again. Minnie pulled away and said something, but Rosemary could barely hear her for all the buzzing in her ears.

She blinked a few times, then her heart started pounding in her chest when she realized the mistake she'd made. "Eve, is that you?"

CHAPTER 6

I t was terrible, Benny." Eve leaned her head back against her pillow Saturday evening. "She thought I was her sister, Minnie, and then when I tried to talk to her about it, she walked away. Did you see how quiet she was during supper?"

Benny didn't say anything as he got underneath the covers.

"I think she must be going crazy." Eve thought again about what her father said. This must be what he wanted her to know, that her mother was losing her mind. "Because she is surely *ab im kopp*."

"Remember, Dr. Knepp said that Parkinson's disease can cause some mind problems. Didn't he say that?" Benny propped himself up against his pillow, then stroked his beard. "It wonders me how often this happens."

"I don't know. I wish *Daed* would have told me about this, but I guess he wanted me to find out on my own." Eve shook her head, frowning. "He said she wasn't ill-tempered, and that's true. It's even worse; she's losing her mind."

"Maybe that's why she wanted you to write all the family recipes down."

"You're right. I didn't even think of that." Eve thought about the *kaffi* cake with no sugar in it. She rolled onto her side, her long brown hair cascading past her shoulders. "Do you think *Daed* is punishing me somehow—that he's mad at me for not coming around enough, so he wants me to see how bad things are with *Mamm*?"

"That doesn't sound like your father. Plus, only our heavenly Father judges us." Benny leaned over and kissed her on the cheek. "Pray about it. And I will too."

Eve closed her eyes and said her prayers.

But sleep didn't come for a while.

. . .

Rosemary was glad that worship and the meal afterward had occupied a large part of the day, but she knew that come tomorrow she'd be left alone with Eve again, and her daughter was bound to say something about Rosemary's bout of insanity.

It had seemed so clear in Rosemary's mind . . . Minnie screaming and Rosemary comforting her.

She pulled her heavy coat tighter around her, thankful for the windshield on the buggy, but freezing nonetheless. Joseph's teeth were chattering when she glanced his way, and he kept pushing his glasses back up on his nose. Twisting her neck, she turned to see Eve, Benjamin, and the twins behind them in their own buggy. The Bylers had hosted worship on this frigid Sunday, so Leroy had stayed to be with Lena.

"I want to talk to you about something, Rosie." She recognized the slow steadiness of Joseph's voice. He was about to say something important.

She looked his way.

"I want you to let Eve carry you to see Dr. Knepp."

Rosemary hadn't mentioned the Minnie episode to Joseph, so Eve must have told him. "What did Eve say?" She faced forward, raising her chin as her own teeth clicked together.

"About what?"

Rosemary turned toward him again. "About me. Did you and Eve have a conversation about me? I don't want you talking behind *mei* back like—" She sighed, unable to pick the right word for her rant . . . *like I'm a crazy person.*

"No one's talking behind your back, *mei lieb*, but I want you to get some better medication for your sickness."

Rosemary thought about the day before and briefly considered it. "*Nee.*"

"Don't you want to feel better?" Her husband pushed his glasses up on his nose again.

"I don't feel bad." Rosemary gripped her hands together in her lap, hoping Joseph wouldn't notice the shaking. She'd been praying that she wouldn't lose her senses anymore, and she'd keep praying about it. As awful as life had been with her own mother, Rosemary still remembered the day her father took her mother to see the *Englisch* doctors in Lancaster. *Mamm* never came home.

Joseph slowed the horse to a slow trot. "Rosie . . ."

He turned toward her and sighed, then looked back through the plastic shield in front of them. "I know that you think we need to avoid the modern things of the world. And we mostly do. But I want you to think about seeing the *Englisch* doctor."

Tears gathered in the corners of her eyes for the second time this week. She couldn't remember the last time she'd cried, and yet it had almost happened in front of Eve, and now Joseph. She looked down at her hands. The shaking had been getting worse, but more fearful was a trip to see Dr. Knepp.

· · ·

Elias tossed and turned beneath his covers. He'd spent as much time as he could with Elizabeth after worship service, but now as the moon shone brightly through his window, his mind filled with visions of her. They'd sneaked behind the Bylers' house twice to kiss, and Elias was sure he wanted to spend the rest of his life with her.

He glanced at Amos on the other side of the room and wished his brother would quit snoring. Usually it didn't bother him, but tonight he was just jittery in general. *This must be part of being in love.* He was glad no one could see the thoughts floating through his mind. Turning on his side, he thumped his pillow with his fist until it flattened. He was a frustrated man; he couldn't sleep, he missed Elizabeth, and work would come early in the morning. He'd be glad when he was back at his job at the market, able to see her every day for lunch.

He folded his hands behind his head and scowled. Every day this past week *Daed* had sent Amos to the hardware store for something they'd needed for the house. Once it was for more nails, and then yesterday they'd run out of wood putty. It didn't seem fair that Amos always got to make the run to the store. Elias could have used the opportunity to see Elizabeth, which was probably why his father didn't assign him the task. Amos was sure taking advantage of his break away from the job site, taking an extra long time every day. He was probably stopping in some bookstore or library to bury his head in a book.

Elias rolled over again. Elizabeth had insisted that Elias not sneak out during the two weeks while he was grounded. She was worried about his health out in the cold, and that he would get caught again and be in even more trouble. He was thankful his parents had not told Elizabeth's parents that they'd been meeting.

I love her so much. I hope she loves me half as much as I love her.

He flipped onto his other side. And wished Amos would quit snoring.

. . .

Rosemary couldn't sleep. She had been awake when Joseph slipped out of bed to go have a snack, and she was still sleepless as he tried to sneak back under the covers without her knowing. She smiled for a brief moment, but worry filled her heart. She was afraid to go to sleep. What if her mind wasn't intact when she woke up? She'd been praying about it all night, but maybe this was God's plan for her.

She watched the clock for almost an hour, and it was nearly eleven when she climbed out of bed to go to the bathroom. As she felt her way through the darkness, a glow outside the window caught her eye. She walked toward the window and leaned her face toward the pane to peer outside, then she walked to the bed and nudged her husband.

"Joseph, wake up."

He grunted.

Rosemary gave him another gentle push on the shoulder. "Wake up. One of the boys is outside in this weather."

"Is he coming or going?"

Rosemary went back to the window and peered out. "He's coming up the walk toward the porch."

"*Gut*. Then all is well."

She turned around and faced her husband. His voice didn't express one bit of concern. "How can you say that? No *kinner* should be out this time of night in this *wedder*."

"It's Elias. He goes to see the Lapp girl."

Rosemary watched out the window as Elias came up the porch steps. "Elizabeth?"

"*Ya*. That's her name. Now come back to bed."

Rosemary waited until she saw Elias safely up the porch steps and heard the gentle *click* of the door in the living room closing behind him before she went to the bathroom. A few minutes later she shuffled back to bed in her socks, pulled the covers back, and got into bed. She nudged Joseph. "That's disrespectful, sneaking out." She shook her head before she slid down onto her pillow. "What next?"

"He's in *lieb*. I used to sneak out to meet you too. Now go to sleep."

Rosemary remembered meeting Joseph at the nearby shanty when she was seventeen. She cringed, recalling the risks she'd taken. But she knew Eve wouldn't react the way her own mother would have if Rosemary had been caught. "Eve will hear of this in the morning."

"Let it go, Rosemary. I'll talk to Elias tomorrow."

Her eyes rounded in the darkness. "Let it go? I can't keep this from Eve."

"I will talk to the boy in the morning."

"You make him understand that this type of behavior is unacceptable. And in our *haus*." She rolled onto her side. "Eve would have never done anything like that."

"Really?" Joseph chuckled. "I doubt we know half of what Eve did during her *rumschpringe*. We didn't give her many freedoms, but *kinner* that age are going to break the rules, explore."

"Eve would have never sneaked out of the *haus*."

"Ask her, then."

"I will."

"Go to sleep."

Rosemary let out a heavy sigh and closed her eyes.

. . .

Elias grunted as he pulled the covers up over his head. "What do you want, Amos? It can't be time to get up yet." His brother poked him in the arm for the second time, and Elias eased his head out of the covers. Amos was holding a lantern, and Elias glanced at the clock. "I could have slept thirty more minutes."

"George is missing."

Elias bolted up. "What?"

"I must not have closed the latch on his cage good." Amos held up the lantern and shined it toward the closet, the door wide open. "He ain't there."

Elias rubbed his eyes as he stretched the length of the bed.

"Help me look for him."

"He's your stupid lizard. And I can smell breakfast cooking." Elias rolled out of the bed.

"*Danki*, Elias. I'll—I'll remember when you need *mei* help for something." Amos dropped to his knees, shined the lantern under each bed, then actually called George by name as if he were calling for a dog.

Elias shook his head but then lit the other lantern. He pulled out the dresser and held the light close, shone the light behind the rocking chair, then held it at arm's length around the room while Amos did the same thing using the other lantern. "I don't see him."

"That's not *gut*." His brother scratched his head as he continued to move the lantern around the room.

Elias pulled on his black work pants and a dark-blue long-sleeved shirt. "Let's eat breakfast. I'll help you find him when we get home from work tonight."

Amos leaned down and stuck his hand inside each of his shoes that were by the bed, then went to his empty duffel bag in the corner and pulled it wide at the zipper.

"*Nee*. Not in here." He dressed quickly. "Shut the door *gut* behind us," Amos said as he left the bedroom in front of Elias. "That way he won't get out of this room while we're at work."

Elias did as Amos asked, but sighed as he glanced behind him at the space between the bottom of the door and the wood floor.

Plenty of room for George to squeeze his way out.

CHAPTER 7

The next morning Rosemary wanted to tell Eve about Elias. It seemed the right thing to do despite Joseph's insistence that he would speak to the boy. Eve should know that her son had been sneaking out. But she looked so peaceful curled up in the recliner writing on the recipe cards. Rosemary stared at her for a few moments, still unable to believe that she'd actually mistaken her own daughter for Minnie. She shook her head, struggling to clear the images.

As she ran a broom across the wooden floor in the living room, she fought the tremble in her right hand and the ache in her back. She paused, straightening for a moment as she put a hand across the small of her back.

"*Mamm* . . ."

Rosemary turned to Eve. "*Ya?*"

"Why don't you take advantage of my being here and let me help with the housework?" Eve laid her pen across the card in her lap.

Rosemary shook her head. She was already taking advantage of Eve being here by having her write down the recipes. Eve didn't know that Rosemary had referred to them several times already, sneaking a peek when no one was around.

"No . . ." She smiled as she waved a hand in Eve's direction. "It's important for you to write the recipes down, and . . ." She paused. "And *mei* hand trembles too much to do that." It was easier to admit that than tell her daughter that she couldn't remember how to make things she'd been cooking for over forty years. She wondered if Eve was going to mention yesterday's episode. Surely she already suspected that her mother was losing her mind.

Eve twisted her mouth back and forth. "Well, you should at least let me get you something better than that old broom. They make nonelectric sweepers, *Mamm*, that are very light and easy to use."

"No need." Rosemary began pushing the broom across the floor again. "This is the way I've always done it."

"*Ya*, I know." Eve's tongue was thick with sarcasm, and Rosemary's eyes darted to the right just in time to see Eve rolling hers.

Rosemary held the broom out to her side like a pitchfork and put her other hand on her hip. "Did *mei* own *dochder* just roll her eyes at me?"

Eve put the recipe box, cards, and her pen on the end table next to her and leaned forward. "*Mamm*, I'm sorry. I don't mean to be disrespectful, but I can't understand your unwillingness to change. Bishop Smucker allows us certain items that make our lives easier, like better appliances and a new sweeper. It just doesn't make sense to me." Eve lifted her hands and shrugged. "So maybe explain it to me."

Rosemary's blood was about to boil, but she reminded herself that Eve was of a new generation. Rosemary would have never spoken to her mother in such a way. And for good reason.

"Why is it that you feel the need to change everything about our ways?" Rosemary lifted the broom a few inches off the ground. "I've had this broom for years, and it's cleaned every room in this house just fine without buying an *Englisch* sweeper. Besides, hard work is *gut* for the soul."

"*Mamm*, God doesn't distinguish your place in His kingdom based on whether or not you use a broom or a sweeper—which, by the way, isn't an *Englisch* sweeper."

"Well, the good Lord doesn't want us veering from our simple ways either." Rosemary put the broom down, turned, and ran it across the floor again. "And I reckon He doesn't want us giving our *kinner* all the freedoms that they seem to have nowadays."

Eve's eyebrows drew into a frown. "All three of *mei* boys are in their *rumschpringe*, *Mamm*. You know there are certain freedoms that go along with that." Then Eve mumbled under her breath, "Even though I didn't have any."

Rosemary thought about what Joseph had said, and she faced Eve, brushing back a piece of gray hair that had fallen forward. "Did you ever sneak out of our *haus* in the middle of the night?"

The color drained from Eve's face. "Why do you ask?"

Well, there; Rosemary had her answer. But if Eve sneaked out because Rosemary and Joseph had not allowed her enough freedom, then why was Elias sneaking out? Those *kinner* surely had more than enough privileges. Her thoughts were quickly resolved—it was just never enough these days. There was never going to be a return to the times when a hard day's work and simple pleasures were enough to keep a person satisfied. With each generation the birds wandered farther from the nest, which only set them up to be swallowed by the world around them.

She finally answered Eve. "I was just wondering. Your *daed* suggested that maybe we didn't give you enough freedom during your *rumschpringe*, but if we didn't, it was only to keep you close, to make sure that you chose correctly—to be baptized into the community."

Eve smiled, not showing any teeth. "I chose correctly."

"I hope that your boys will all make the right choices." Rosemary slowly stooped to push the little bit of dirt she'd gathered into a dustpan.

"They are all *gut* boys, but they deserve to explore the world so that they know this is what they want. You're lucky I didn't . . ."

Rosemary looked up. "What? We're lucky you didn't what? End up in the *Englisch* world? It was surely our biggest fear when you were growing up."

"I worry about that too, but you can't criticize the way we raise our *sohns*." Eve stood up. "At least they know they are loved." She turned to go up the stairs. "I'm going to straighten their rooms."

Know they are loved? Her daughter didn't know she was loved? Rosemary's head started buzzing again, and she started to call out, but instead she squeezed her eyes closed.

She put her face in her hands. *Dear Lord, please don't let me have another episode.*

Deciding that maybe a nap would help the dizziness she was feeling, she opened her bedroom door, then grabbed her heart. *It's happening again.* Another hallucination.

She didn't move as she eyed the small alligator perched atop her bed. Slowly she backed up two steps and opened her mouth to call for Eve, but stopped herself.

This isn't real.

She eyed the imaginary reptile for several moments. Then she shrugged and crawled into bed beside it.

. . .

Eve knew she shouldn't have spoken to her mother that way, but it was getting harder and harder to take the constant criticism about the way she and Benny raised their children and how she continued to move away from the simpler ways she'd been brought up with.

She walked into her mother's sewing room, which was exactly as Eve remembered. The treadle sewing machine was against the left wall, and the shelves next to it were filled with quilting scraps, bolts of material, and other sewing supplies. On the opposite wall was the yellow-and-blue plaid couch that *Mamm* had picked up at a mud sale in Bird-in-Hand. She'd said the couch was much too fancy for the living room, but she'd bought it anyway since it folded out into a bed and had only cost her ten dollars.

Eve pulled up the green and white quilt that Leroy

had tossed back this morning, then fluffed his pillows and positioned them against the back of the couch. She glanced around the room. Leroy's dirty clothes were in a hamper Eve's mother had put in the room, and his other clothes and personal items were neatly folded and displayed atop *Mamm's* sewing table in the corner. Eve smiled. If Levi did choose to marry Lena Byler, the girl would be glad that Eve had trained up her son to be neat and tidy.

She closed the door behind her and went down the hall to the extra bedroom where the twins were staying. As she eyed the mess before her—mostly on Elias's side of the room—Eve knew that the twins' future *fraas* would have their work cut out for them. She picked up two dirty shirts off the floor. As she made Elias's bed, she thought about the way he'd slipped out to meet Elizabeth. It wasn't the worst thing in the world, but it had certainly been worthy of punishment. She'd avoided letting her parents know about the incident, but maybe she should have told them. Maybe she should have made a point for her mother to see that she was quite capable of disciplining her children when they needed it.

She smoothed the wrinkles from the quilt on his bed before she went to the other bed, which was covered in a matching quilt. Once both the beds were made, she sniffed a few times, recognizing the smell of dirty socks. She bent to her knees, and sure enough . . . two dark black socks were underneath Elias's bed. Picking them up with thumb and first finger, she held them at arm's length as she looked around for any other dirty

62   BETH WISEMAN

clothes. When she didn't find any, she walked to the small hamper and tossed in the socks.

Unlike some of the rooms in the old farmhouse, this room had a closet. Eve had inspected the contents when she and the twins were deciding if it would be a good place to keep George. There were boxes stacked along the left side, and Eve knew that her old faceless dolls were in one of the crates, cards and letters that her mother had saved in another, and various keepsakes. Eve didn't open the closet, hoping Amos was remembering to feed the reptile.

The boys had managed to sneak the lizard in with a blanket draped over the cage while Eve distracted her parents. She felt a little guilty for deceiving her folks about a Chinese water dragon, but it would have been just one more thing for her mother to fret about.

Eve hadn't been happy when Amos came home with this unusual pet. Her son had saved his money and begged his parents for what he called a lizard, but the frightful-looking beast had grown much larger than any lizard Eve had ever seen. If it gave Eve the shivers, what would her mother think . . .

. . .

Elias bit down on his ham sandwich, his teeth chattering from the frigid temperatures. As he sat on the couch in his family's living room, wind blew around the plastic sheeting and swirled throughout the damaged structure. *Daadi* was sitting next to Elias, eating his own lunch. His father and Leroy had eaten earlier and were outside toting lumber from the wagon to a designated pile on the north side of the house. Amos—as usual—had been sent to town for supplies, and was probably thumbing through magazines or books somewhere.

"Elias . . ." His grandfather sighed as he locked eyes with Elias, shaking his head. "I reckon when a fellow is grounded, he should respect his parents enough to follow the rules." *Daadi* pushed his glasses up on his nose, frowning.

"Uh, *ya*. You're right." Elias wondered what his grandfather was getting at.

Daadi ran a shaky hand through his beard. "Your *mammi* caught you coming into the *haus* last night. She wanted to go straight to your *mudder* and tell your business, but I told her that I'd give you a friendly talkin'-to, and that I was sure you wouldn't disobey your parents again." He stuffed his lunch trash in his black lunch box and stood up from the couch.

Elias's jaw dropped. "But I didn't . . ." He scratched his head for a moment before he went on. "Are you sure it was last night?"

"*Ya*. It was last night." *Daadi* pulled on his heavy gloves, then pushed his black felt hat firmly onto his head. "I won't be able to help you next time."

"But I . . ." Elias wondered if his grandfather was confused. Or more likely, his grandmother was. He stood up and watched the older man walk out the door to help his father and Leroy. Moments later Amos walked in.

"I'm starving!" His brother's whole face spread into a goofy smile, and Elias walked closer to Amos, squinting.

"Where've you been?"

Amos's teeth were chattering, but the grin wasn't going away. "You know where I was. Running errands."

Elias moved even closer to Amos and thumped him lightly on the arm. "That the only place? And what about last night, *mei bruder*?"

Amos's mouth pulled into a sour grin. "Wha-wha-whatcha talkin' about?"

"I just took the blame for you sneaking out of the *haus* last night. So you best start talking."

CHAPTER 8

Elias turned up the propane heater in the bedroom, set the lantern on the end table between his and Amos's beds, then crawled under the covers and waited for his brother to come in after taking a bath.

Amos's hair was wet and sticking straight up when he walked in towel-drying it, barefoot, wearing blue pajama bottoms and a white T-shirt. "*Ach*, it's cold in here."

Elias rolled his eyes. "Put some shoes on, you *dummkopp*." He looked at his cell phone. One bar left, but no word from Elizabeth yet. He scratched his chin. He'd been trying to reach her for an hour and no answer.

Amos got into bed shivering and tucked himself beneath the covers.

Elias turned on his side to face his brother. "So where'd you go last night?" It seemed unlikely that Amos would have a girlfriend, but Elias couldn't think of any other reason for a man to trek into this weather.

"N-None of your business." Amos reached over the side of the bed and between the mattresses, pulling out a magazine with bent edges and a shiny red car on the front.

Elias glared at his brother. "It ain't, huh?" He sat

taller. "I'm the one who took the blame for you. *Mammi* saw you last night, and she and *Daadi* think it was me who snuck out."

"Sorry a-about that." Amos flipped through the pages of the magazine.

"You don't seem too sorry." Elias glared at his brother, then grinned. "Find that lizard of yours?"

Amos's jaw dropped and he sat taller, tossing the magazine to the side. "*Ach!* I forgot!" He jumped out of the bed, grabbed the lantern, and began searching the room. "Help me look for George."

Elias yawned as he snuggled into his covers. "I think one *gut* deed for the day is enough for me."

Amos grumbled under his breath, and he was still shuffling around the room when Elias drifted off to sleep.

. . .

Eve carried the lantern down the stairs, tiptoeing, knowing she was early for breakfast. She could smell sausage and biscuits already going, but she didn't realize her father was up also until she heard her name.

"Eve and Benjamin give those *kinner* too much freedom. I could hardly sleep last night, worrying one of them young'uns would be wandering around out in this *wedder*." Eve's mother paused. "And all over a *maedel*."

Eve slowed her step, gently turning the lantern down as she listened to her mother go on. "I hope you told Elias that we don't allow such doings in our home."

"*Ya, ya.*"

Eve came to a complete stop, still listening.

"Eve and Benjamin will be lucky if those twins don't end up in trouble or living out in the *Englisch* world." Another pause. "I don't think they had those types of troubles with Leroy. Or maybe they did, and we just didn't know about it."

Eve heard her father's chair scoot from the table, and Eve picked up the pace, not wanting to get caught eavesdropping. She came face-to-face with her father in the middle of the den.

"*Guder mariye, Daed.*" She scooted around him as he smiled and nodded.

"I'm gonna go milk the cows. Send those boys when they get up."

"It's still early. I'm sure they'll be down shortly." Eve edged into the kitchen, kept her head high, and poured herself a cup of coffee.

"*Guder mariye*, Eve."

Eve returned the sentiment but couldn't look at her mother. Her thoughts assailed her, but she bit her tongue. For a moment. Then she swirled around, leaned up against the kitchen counter, and glared at her mother as *Mamm* pulled biscuits from the oven.

"We live in different times, *Mamm*. We don't allow our *kinner* to do anything that other parents in the district don't let theirs do." She bit her bottom lip, wondering why she had never been good enough in her mother's eyes.

"Were you eavesdropping?" *Mamm* set down the oven mitt and raised an eyebrow in Eve's direction.

Eve folded her arms across her chest. "*Nee.* I just happened to hear the end of your conversation with *Daed.*"

Her mother sighed as she walked to the refrigerator and pulled out two jars of jam. "I just don't think you know what's going on with your own *kinner,* that's all." She shrugged, putting the jars on the table.

Eve took a deep breath, remembering to respect her parents no matter what. "At least I *love* my children. And they know that." She glared at her mother and trudged across the kitchen. "I'm going to go help *Daed* in the barn."

. . .

"Eve, wait." Rosemary watched her daughter stomp out to the barn, pouting as if she were a small child. Rosemary knew she shouldn't have said anything about Eve's child rearing, even if it had been the truth. Eve and Benjamin were going to lose control of those twins if they didn't do something. If Rosemary had those boys under her roof for a while, she could teach them a thing or two about the old ways. They'd get rid of all that modern technology—and no one would be sneaking out of the house. And twice now, Eve had mentioned how her boys knew she loved them.

But did Eve just insinuate that Rosemary didn't love her?

Rosemary shuffled across the kitchen, grasping her right hand as it began to shake. She'd hoped that she and Eve would get closer while Eve was here, but instead, she was just pushing Eve further away.

With a heavy heart Rosemary finished cooking

breakfast, hoping Eve would come in before everyone else so that maybe she could make amends with her daughter. When that didn't happen, she turned to the Lord. She'd been praying that God would show her the way to get closer to Eve, but she also wondered if God was talking and she just wasn't hearing Him.

Ten minutes later everyone was seated at the kitchen table. After they'd prayed, Benjamin spoke up.

"Eve and I have something to ask you both." He reached for a biscuit, glancing back and forth between Rosemary and Joseph.

Rosemary briefly looked at Eve, but her daughter was picking at her scrambled eggs and didn't look up as Benjamin went on.

"Cousin Mary Mae has fallen seriously ill, and Eve and I feel it would be *gut* to pay her a visit." Benjamin sighed. "The timing is bad with the *haus* and all, but it would be a *gut* chance to also pick up some supplies. I'm having trouble finding some of the hardware we need for the old door in our kitchen and a few other small things we could cart back in the van with us."

Joseph pushed up his glasses. "How long would you be away?"

"We'd like to stay for a week." Benjamin took a bite of his biscuit and swallowed. "The boys could still help you on the *haus* while we are away." He glanced at Eve. "Mary Mae and Eve write letters and are close. Eve feels we should make the trip, and I do too."

"She's got the cancer, huh?" Leroy scooped up the last of his eggs and quickly reached for the bowl in the middle of the table.

"*Ya.*" Eve kept her head hung low, and Rosemary wondered how much of her sadness was due to Mary Mae . . . or how much of if it was from this morning's scuffle.

"It's no problem." Joseph sat taller as he spoke directly to Benjamin. "You go, take the time you need to be with Mary Mae. We will keep working on your *haus*, and all will be well."

As the others chatted, Rosemary grew quiet, thinking. She and Joseph would have these three teenagers to tend to on their own. Could she maybe show them some of the old ways? Tell the boys stories about how things used to be, before all this modern technology invaded their world? And would they listen, maybe even get rid of some of their gadgets?

Rosemary glanced around the table. Leroy was a good boy. He kept busy and seemed to stay on task. He seemed mostly interested in spending his free time with Lena.

She looked at the twins. Elias was making a move for the last piece of bacon when Amos reached for it too, beating his brother to it. Rosemary was pretty sure that the slight bump under the table was one of the boys kicking the other. She'd seen the twins picking at each other continuously, more so than normal. She'd never raised any boys, and these two seemed a bit of a handful.

Well, she had hoped for this. A chance to have some say in her grandchildren's lives.

She took a deep breath as Benjamin sat up taller and firmly told the twins to mind their manners.

Careful what you wish for.

CHAPTER 9

The next day Eve shivered all the way out to the van that was waiting in the driveway, large flakes of snow dotting her heavy black coat and bonnet. Benny had already loaded their luggage, and Eve had talked to the twins about behaving themselves while she and Benny were gone.

She felt bad about spouting off to her mother yesterday, although neither had said anything about their unkind exchange.

Maybe a week away from each other would be good for both of them. Her heart hurt for Mary Mae, and Eve was anxious to spend time with her cousin, but she was also apprehensive about leaving the twins with her parents. She'd instructed Leroy to keep a close eye on things. She was almost to the car when Amos called out to her.

"What is it, *sohn*?" She turned around, putting a hand to her forehead as she tried to block the snow.

Amos lifted his feet high in the snow as he crossed through part of the yard that hadn't been shoveled. He was breathless when he reached Eve.

"We—we—we . . ." Amos blinked a few times, and

Eve knew he must really be upset about something to be having such a hard time saying the words.

"What is it? What's wrong?" She brushed snow from her cheeks with the back of her glove.

"We can't find George." Amos's teeth chattered as he spoke.

"What?" Eve swallowed hard. "Did he get out of his cage? He is a big lizard, Amos. Where is he?"

Amos raised his shoulders and held them up before slowly dropping them. "I—I guess I left the cage open a few days ago."

Eve thought she might fall over. "A few *days*? How can George be missing for that long? Have you looked everywhere?"

"*Ya, Mamm*. I've looked all over the *haus*, everywhere except *Daadi* and *Mammi's* bedroom." He tipped his felt hat down with his hand, shielding himself from the snow. "Their bedroom door is always closed."

"I'm sure George isn't in their bedroom." Eve shivered, shaking her head. "We would have already heard about it." She tried to picture the expression on her mother's face if she stumbled upon a large lizard running around in her bedroom. Eve suspected that George had either died or gotten outside if he'd been missing this long. Maybe he'd gotten into some poison her father kept in the basement for mice, or slipped outdoors somehow.

Amos hung his head, sighing heavily. He was sixteen in years, but in some ways he seemed much younger, especially now as she watched him fighting tears. She touched him on the arm.

"Keep looking. Maybe he's hiding somewhere."

She gazed up at him and grinned. "Just find him before your *mammi* does." Eve gave him a hug before she made her way to the car, then turned around and pointed a gloved finger at him. "You boys behave yourselves while we're gone."

Amos nodded as he trekked back to the house up the cleared walkway. Everyone had delayed going to work this morning until they saw Eve and Benny off.

As the van pulled away with Eve and Benny in the backseat, Eve said a quick prayer—another one—that all would be well while they were gone.

And she prayed that Amos would find George.

. . .

The house was quiet, the way it had been before Eve and her family had come to stay. Once Eve and Benjamin had gotten on their way, Joseph, Leroy, and the twins had hitched up the buggies and gone to work on the house.

Rosemary stared out the window at the snow and knew that this weather was slowing down progress. After a few moments she shuffled about the house, wondering if she'd stumble upon her glasses. She'd already checked the refrigerator but had quickly closed it. The jars and jellies had looked like they were dancing on the shelf, which Rosemary knew was not the case. But she'd had the vision just the same, and her anxiety level was rising. What else would happen? Would she lose more things? Would all objects start looking like they were dancing? Would she remember how to cook Joseph his supper tonight?

She picked up the recipe box on the counter and

brought it to her chest, thankful that Eve was writing everything down. *Now if I could only find my glasses, I could read the cards.*

Sighing, she put the container back down and made her way to the cookie jar. She'd been keeping the jar filled for the boys—and to facilitate Joseph's late-night sweet tooth. She took a peek inside but decided some dried cranberries would better suit her. Grabbing the plastic bag of fruit from the cabinet, she headed to her bedroom to read the family Bible. She'd enjoyed looking at Eve's latest entries about the boys, but today she wanted to just sit quietly and read from the Good Book.

She sat down on her bed, crossed her legs, and eased the Bible from her nightstand before she remembered that she hadn't found her glasses. She set the bag of fruit down beside her on the bed. In some ways she was no better than Joseph, eating late at night. Her secret indulgence was to eat a snack in the middle of the day while sitting on her bed reading. Joseph said the bed was no place for eating, so in her own way Rosemary felt like she was getting away with something too. She kept the Bible in her lap as she enjoyed a handful of the cranberries, trying to remember where she'd put her glasses.

It was about ten minutes later when she heard movement from underneath her dresser. She'd learned not to get alarmed anymore. Her hallucination had shown up twice before. She'd almost told Joseph about it night before last, but he surely would have dragged her to see Dr. Knepp at that very moment. She watched the lizard crawl out from underneath her dresser.

Her imaginary friend was looking a little parched today.

Rosemary left the room, went to the kitchen, and dribbled some water on a small plate. When she returned, the creature was up on her bed where she'd first spotted him. She wasn't sure how he slithered his way up there, but for all she knew, her hallucination was capable of flying or a number of other things she didn't care to think about. She set the plate carefully on the floor, a few droplets splashing onto the wood surface. Then she watched the reptile eyeing her cranberries. She eased past where he was on the bed, reached into the bag, and placed a few in front of his long snout. Or was it a *her*?

And, dear Lord in heaven . . . does it matter?

Rosemary shook her head, watching as the lizard nibbled at the dried fruit. When he was done, he slid down her bedspread, stopped at the water for a quick drink, then went back under her dresser.

She eased herself back on the bed, picked up the bag of cranberries, and leaned back against the headboard. She grasped her hand as it began to shake so fiercely that the motion of it slapping against her leg was painful.

Rosemary knew she could handle the pain.

It was all these hallucinations that she feared the most. Losing her mind.

She wondered if maybe Eve and Joseph were right. Maybe *Englisch* medications could do more for her than Fern's herbal remedies. She closed her eyes, and after a minute or so the trembling began to subside. She opened her eyes and crossed one foot over the other.

If she began to turn to modern ways for medication, where would it stop? First it would be *Englisch* pills, and next thing she knew they'd be installing propane lamps and using mobile telephones. *Too much.*

God was in control. Not Rosemary. What good could come from giving up their simple ways? If the Lord wanted to ease her ailments, He could do so, without her having to engage in worldly ways.

. . .

Elias tried not to fidget during devotions, but something was gnawing at his gut. He kept his head buried in the Bible as his grandfather recited from the book of Matthew, but he wasn't hearing much. He'd have to pray on his own later to make up for being so unfocused.

He hadn't heard from Elizabeth in several days, and he hadn't been able to reach her by phone. Earlier today he'd begged Leroy to let him use the buggy to go see her after work, but his older brother refused his plea, citing his punishment. Didn't Leroy understand that without Elizabeth's love he could hardly function? And with no phone conversations, Elias had no way to schedule a late-night meeting with the woman he planned to marry someday. Even grounded, he was ready to take the risk to see Elizabeth.

"Let us pray . . ." *Daadi* said the words loudly, as if he knew that Elias wasn't following along.

Once devotions were over, his grandmother began to tell stories about the old times, how there were no electronic gadgets or many of the modern things that their people used today. She'd never made a secret of her thoughts on the matter, and Elias had heard his mother complain about *Mammi* not accepting the new ways that the bishop allowed.

Elias tried to show as much respect for his grandmother as he could—despite the knot in his stomach—by responding to her questions, nodding when he should, and so on. But something was wrong. He could feel it.

He glanced at Amos. His brother carried on with their grandmother as if he were really enjoying her lectures and reflections on the old ways. Elias scowled, wishing he'd never taken the fall for Amos. His twin wasn't perfect—he'd sneaked out the same way Elias had—yet Elias was the one still grounded, and the one who was going to miss a party at Elizabeth's house on Saturday. Her sister Rebecca was turning fifteen, and the family was having a get-together. Elias had been to parties at Elizabeth's house before, and he knew there would be lots of food, the Ping-Pong table set up in the basement, and mostly there would be enough people there for him and Elizabeth to go lose themselves somewhere. Elias couldn't wait to kiss her again, but every time he thought about the feel of her soft lips, he thought about how she hadn't called him and how he couldn't reach her.

There had to be a way for him to attend the party on Saturday.

"Elias, are you hearing me?" His grandmother's sharp tone caused him to sit up straighter on the couch.

"*Ya, Mammi.* I'm listening."

It was a small lie, and Elias regretted it, but an idea had danced into his mind.

He knew exactly how he was going to be at Elizabeth's house on Saturday.

CHAPTER 10

"Y-You're *ab im kopp*." Amos shook his head. "You kn-know what *gut* parties the Lapps throw, and I—I ain't missing one, no matter what you try to promise me."

Elias stood over his brother, who once again had his head buried in one of his dumb magazines. He snatched the magazine away from his brother.

"Hey!" Amos jumped up and grabbed the book back from Elias. "I—I said I ain't d-doin' it, so just leave me alone." He cut his eyes at Elias before he settled back down on his bed.

Elias eased onto his own bed and sighed. "All right, then. I'll give you fifty dollars instead of twenty-five if you'll let me go in your place. You know *Mammi* and *Daadi* can't tell us apart."

Amos chuckled. "You don't even have fifty dollars."

"*Ya*, I do. I've been saving. Unlike you, *mei bruder*, I don't spend my money on expensive *Englisch* magazines." He paused, shaking his head. "You're not ever gonna own a car, so why do you like looking at them so much, anyway?" Before Amos could answer, Elias said, "Come on. Just think of all the books and magazines you can buy with fifty dollars."

There was silence for a few moments before Amos said anything. Then his brother lifted his eyes over the top of the magazine. "Maybe—maybe Elizabeth doesn't want to see you or talk to you."

Elias had thought of that plenty of times, and he was sure the notion was what kept his stomach tied in knots. "What makes you say that?"

"You ain't talked to her. There's been no sneaking out to see her, and you can't even reach her by phone." Amos shrugged. "Sounds to me like she's trying to end it."

Elias clenched his hands into fists and took a deep breath. "You don't know what you're talking about. I'm going to ask Elizabeth to marry me. I wouldn't do that if I wasn't sure about the two of us."

Amos chuckled. "Well, you won't be asking her at the Lapps' party, will ya?"

Elias glared at his brother and decided to ask him something that had been rooting around in his mind. "Who'd you sneak out to go see?"

"I told you. N-None of your b-business." Amos didn't look up as he flipped another page.

Elias shook his head, then got his nightclothes out of the dresser. He was moving out of the room when he turned around, feeling the need to jab at his brother. "Ever find that stupid lizard of yours?"

"No." Amos sighed, not looking up again.

Elias regretted poking fun about the lizard. He knew how much his brother cared for George.

He wished Amos knew how much he cared for Elizabeth. If he did, he would swap places with Elias so that Elias could see her.

Shuffling down the hall to the bathroom, Elias's mind was still whirling. There had to be a way to get to that party.

. . .

Rosemary sat on the side of the bed brushing out her thinning gray hair while Joseph was all tucked in on his side reading a book.

"Did you see how a little bit of influence from us made a difference tonight?" She smiled, recalling all the stories she'd told the boys about the old days, before modern ways invaded their lives. "I bet it won't be long before those boys give up some of those unnecessary gadgets."

Joseph grunted. "*Ach*, I'm sure they'll be tossing those cell phones and radio plugs right into the trash first thing in the morning."

Rosemary twisted to face him. "Why do you speak to me like that, Joseph? You're poking fun about a serious situation. If we don't do our part to straighten those boys out, they are going to end up fleeing to the outside world, and that will break everyone's heart, especially Eve's and Benjamin's."

Joseph closed his book and pushed his glasses up on his nose. "*Mei lieb*, those boys are fine. Eve and Big Ben have done a *gut* enough job raising them up. They'll make the right choices."

"I hope you're right, but I have a couple more days to try to talk some sense into them through the Scriptures." Rosemary stowed her brush in the top drawer of the nightstand, then crawled in beside Joseph. "Tomorrow, during devotions, I want us to spend some time on respecting your parents and elders." She poked him on the arm. "And you speak up and say something about not betraying our parents. Maybe they'll take heed and not keep up that sneaking out."

"Yes, dear."

Rosemary huffed. "You are patronizing me, Joseph. When instead you should be thinking about how we can make a difference in those boys' lives." She grasped her hand when it started to shake and quickly stuffed it beneath the quilt as she leaned back against the headboard. Her head started to spin a bit, so she closed her eyes.

"Yes, dear." Joseph eased himself down into the covers, popping his pillow with his fist a few times. He snuffed out the lantern on his side of the bed. "Go to sleep."

"I'll go to sleep after I finish tending to Minnie. Momma gave her another lashing. I'll be right back." Rosemary sat straight up, ready to go tend to her sister. She picked up the lantern on her nightstand, but Joseph quickly caught her by the arm.

"Rosie, Minnie ain't here. You know that. She's playing with the good Lord in heaven. You're thinking in the past again." Joseph held tight to her arm, and Rosemary struggled to organize the thoughts in her head. She stared at the gray streaks running through her husband's beard. *If Joseph is old, Minnie can't still be here.*

"But . . . but I heard her cries." Rosemary grasped her shaking hand and eased the lantern back down. She turned to Joseph, tears in her eyes. "I'm losing my mind."

He pulled her into his arms, running a hand through her damp hair. "You need to go see Dr. Knepp, *lieb*."

She melted into the comfort of his arms and buried her face in his chest. "I'm too afraid. He'll tell me that I'm goin' crazy, and they'll lock me up somewhere."

"That's not what they do, Rosie. They'll give you some medicine to help you, that's all."

Rosemary squeezed her eyes closed and fought the visions of Minnie crying, along with the moaning she could hear in her head.

This isn't real.

But sleep didn't come for a while.

. . .

Elias was glad that they stopped work on the house early Saturday afternoon. The party at the Lapps' started at four o'clock, and he had to figure out a way to be there. He'd been trying to call Elizabeth, but still no answer. And no calls from her.

He'd caught Amos sneaking back into the house last night, and once again his brother refused to tell Elias what he was up to. It must be a girl after all. He resented the fact that Amos hadn't gotten caught, that Elias himself had taken the blame for him once, and mostly he resented Amos's smug attitude.

I'm going to that party.

Elias was having a cup of hot cocoa with his grandfather when Amos came marching into the kitchen wearing his Sunday clothes and a smile as wide as it was irritating.

"Off to the birthday party?" *Daadi* took a sip of his cocoa, and Amos nodded. Elias resisted the urge to tackle Amos to the ground. His nostrils flared as Amos grinned on his way out the door.

"I know you're fretting about not being able to go," *Daadi* said to Elias after Amos was gone. "But the Lord always has a plan, and . . ." His grandfather shrugged. "It's just not in the plan for you to go today."

Elias nodded and fought the urge to tell his grand-father that Amos had been sneaking out. It wouldn't make a difference right now, though, and Elias wasn't a tattler.

As he sipped on his cocoa, he thought about Elizabeth. Her parents must have taken her phone away for some reason. That had to be it.

Daadi stood up, gulped the rest of his cocoa, then put his glass on the table. He pulled his hat and jacket from the rack near the kitchen door. "Tell your *mammi* that I'm going to town for a few supplies for the *haus*. I'll be back in a couple of hours."

"Yes, sir."

Elias tapped his fingers on the table, thinking. It wasn't long before an idea came to mind. He jumped from the table and ran upstairs.

CHAPTER 11

Elizabeth opened the door and smiled at her hand-some man. "I'm so glad to see you."

"Me too. I've missed you."

As she stepped to the side so he could come in, she knew they needed to talk, but her father was standing only a few feet away stoking the fire.

"Everyone is in the basement. There's lots of food, and there's already a Ping-Pong game going on. Go get something to eat, and I'll be down shortly." She resisted the urge to whisper in his ear that she couldn't wait to sneak off with him somewhere.

As he walked past her, he nudged her hand. She glanced down and saw a piece of paper, which she quickly took and stuffed into the pocket of her apron.

The front door was still open, and she saw Abram Fisher pulling up to drop off his younger brother Matthew. Two more buggies were coming up the drive-way. She'd been given the job of greeting all of Rebecca's guests, and she was anxious to be done with the task so she could head downstairs.

She fumbled at the piece of paper in her pocket, anxious to read it.

It was twenty minutes later when the buggies finally stopped pulling up, and Elizabeth hurried to the bathroom. After locking the door, she pulled the note from her pocket and read.

Dear Elizabeth,

A new love is so tender, the heart fluttering and wanting to render.

It is with you that I feel renewed and alive, like a swim in the pond after taking a dive; crisp and refreshing, but much more than that—it's the sound of my heart as it goes pitter-pat.

My feelings for you are as pure as a new baby's soul, and once lost, I now have a goal—to be the best person I can be, to spend my life loving you eternally.

She brushed a tear from her cheek as she pressed the poem to her chest. It was the third one she'd received, and with each one she knew she loved him that much more. She couldn't wait for him to kiss her later today. Somehow they'd find a place where they could go to be alone. Stuffing the note back in her pocket, she slipped out of the bathroom and made her way back to the living room.

Her father was standing at the window, and she could hear her mother puttering about in the kitchen, but otherwise all their guests had moved downstairs. Elizabeth headed toward the basement stairs, but her father spoke up.

"Hold yourself, *maedel*. Someone is walking up to the porch."

Elizabeth sighed as she turned and walked back across the living room. "*Danki, Daed.*"

She walked onto the front porch, closed the door behind her, and pulled her sweater snug as her teeth chattered. Straining to see who the last guest was, she gasped when he came into view.

Her jaw dropped, and her heart began to pound in her chest. "What are you doing here? I thought you were grounded."

Elias looked around, grinned, then kissed her on the mouth. "Where have you been? I've been trying to call. I've missed you so much."

Elizabeth eased away and swallowed hard.

Oh, this is a mess.

. . .

Rosemary found an old magnifying glass so she could read one of Eve's recipe cards. Tomato pie sounded good, and one would be enough to feed her, Joseph, and Elias. Amos wouldn't be home from the Lapps' house until later in the evening, and Leroy had gone to supper at Lena's.

As she sliced the tomatoes, she thought about Elias having to miss the party, but rules were rules. Before Eve and Benjamin left, Eve had told her that Elias was grounded, but she didn't tell her what for. It had to be for sneaking out; she'd seen him with her own eyes as he sneaked back in. She supposed she should be glad that Eve had punished him in such a manner, but as a grandmother, she assumed it was all right to feel a little sorry for him.

"Smells mighty *gut* in here." Joseph walked in from feeding the animals.

"That's just freshly baked bread you smell. I haven't even cooked the tomato pie yet." She leaned down with the magnifying glass to see how much milk the recipe called for.

"Still haven't found your reading glasses?" Joseph pulled out a chair at the table, sat down, and began thumbing through the most recent copy of *The Budget*.

Rosemary shook her head. "No. And I've looked everywhere."

"They'll show up."

"I hope."

She was quiet as she finished putting the pie together, seeing that Joseph had his head buried in the paper.

After a few moments he looked up. "Is that one pie going to be enough for you, me, and Elias?"

Rosemary nodded. "I made a fruit salad to go with it, and I have a shoofly pie for dessert." She pulled the oven door open and put the pie in. "When Amos left around four, I told him there would be some cake for him when he got home, although I'm sure there is a mountain of food at the Lapps' house."

"Four? I saw him leave a little before three."

Rosemary turned around, wiping flour from her black apron. "Well, I chatted with him for a minute or two before he left, and I know it was around four o'clock."

Joseph twisted his mouth from one side to the other. "Okay, dear."

She walked closer, hands on her hips. "I dislike when you do that. You patronize me like a child. That boy left around four o'clock. I haven't completely lost my mind, and I can still read a clock."

"Well, that's good and fine, Rosie. But one of the boys left a little before three. That's all I'm saying."

Rosemary shifted her weight, pressing her lips together for a moment. "It was Amos that left, right?"

Joseph shrugged. "I reckon. He's the one who isn't grounded."

"Well, then who left at four o'clock while you were still in town?"

Joseph closed the newspaper. "Sure you don't mean Leroy?"

"Joseph Chupp, I know the difference between Leroy and the twins. It wasn't Leroy who came through here at four. He left much earlier. It was Amos."

"Well, then I guess we both saw Amos leave, or those boys have pulled a fast one on us."

Rosemary chuckled. "I don't think so. Not on my watch."

Joseph stroked his beard, grinning. "Then you better hope that there is a twin upstairs. 'Cause I suspect there ain't."

"Well, why in the world would Elias sneak out, pretending to be Amos, when he knows he'd get caught at supper time?"

"Probably didn't care, if it's all about a girl." Joseph stood up, kissed Rosemary on the cheek, then smiled. "I think one got away on your watch."

Rosemary marched directly to the stairs and up she went. When she returned a few minutes later, Joseph was casually sitting in his rocker sipping a cup of coffee.

"Well, we are missing one," she said as she folded her arms across her chest and tapped her foot on the floor.

"*Ya*. I figured as much."

"Well, when young Elias gets home, you will extend his punishment. He's under our roof, and I reckon it's our job to—"

"Someone's coming." Joseph stood up and walked to the window. "I hear a buggy turning."

Rosemary joined him at the window, and they both waited. A few moments later Rosemary gasped, then covered her mouth with her hands.

"*Ach*, Joseph. Oh no."

She hurried to the door and out onto the porch, her heart pounding.

CHAPTER 12

Rosemary almost stumbled down the snowy porch steps, Joseph on her heels. She met Samuel Lapp in the yard; Amos and Elias were on either side of him. Although she wasn't sure who was who.

She went to the boy on Samuel's left, since blood was running down his chin from a split lip and he had a bulging black eye. After a quick inspection she moved to the other one, who'd taken quite a beating himself based on his swollen cheek and shiner.

"Who did this to you?" Rosemary's eyes watered as she glanced back and forth between the twins. They both lowered their heads as Samuel spoke.

"They did this to each other." Samuel shook his head, frowning. "I heard a commotion down in the basement, and the *maeds* starting screaming." He pointed to Amos, then to Elias. "These two were down on the floor pounding on each other."

Rosemary was speechless. Joseph stepped forward.

"*Danki* for bringing them home, Samuel. And we're sorry for the trouble."

"Well, it wonders me what would cause two *bruders* to do this to each other when it surely isn't our way."

Samuel shook his head again. "Not *gut*. And Rebecca's pretty cake her *mamm* made her ended up in a pile on the basement floor."

Rosemary opened her mouth to apologize, but nothing came out. She couldn't believe the boys could do something like this.

"Please send our apologies to your *fraa*, to Rebecca, and to the others there." Joseph waved a hand toward Amos and Elias. "You boys head into the *haus* and start cleaning yourselves up. We'll be in shortly."

"I'll tend to them," Rosemary finally said, tucking her head as she pulled her sweater around her and hurried into the house and away from Samuel's accusing eyes. She wasn't out of earshot, though, when Samuel spoke.

"I'm sure you'll be hearing from the bishop about this matter."

Rosemary moved faster, shivering. From the cold. And the thought of the bishop coming out to see them. She couldn't recall a time that Bishop Smucker had come calling about a "matter."

When she walked into the living room, Amos and Elias were glaring at each other as if they weren't done with whatever was ailing them.

"We need to get some ice on your eyes, both of you." She glanced back and forth between the two of them. "Who's who?"

"That's Amos!" Elias yelled. "Someone who is supposed to be *mei bruder*, but who tried to trick Elizabeth into loving him by pretending he was me."

Rosemary put a hand on her chest, hoping to calm

her rapid heartbeat and wishing Eve and Benjamin were here. This was way too much for her and Joseph to handle.

"And—and she d-does love me!" Amos stepped toward Elias, his bottom lip trembling, his eyes beginning to tear.

Elias stood taller. "How'd you stop your stupid stuttering while you were with her?" He leaned forward as his hands curled into fists at his side.

Oh, dear Lord. No more. Rosemary took in a deep breath and held it, not sure what to say. Or do.

"Fern t-taught me some breathing exercises t-to help." Amos's voice cracked as he spoke.

"You're a bad person, Amos." Elias ran up the stairs.

Amos swiped at his eyes.

Rosemary swallowed back a knot in her throat, hurting for all involved. She stepped closer to Amos, putting a hand on his shoulder. "We need to get some ice on that eye before it swells shut."

"*Mammi*, I have to go." He pulled away from her and dashed out the door.

Rosemary stood in the middle of the room, hoping Joseph would intercept him. But a few moments later Leroy walked in.

"I just saw Amos running down the road. Where's he going?"

"I don't know." Rosemary looked out the window. "It's dark outside. Did you see your *daadi* out there?"

Leroy pulled off his boots and left them by the front door where the twins usually left theirs. "He must be in the barn. I saw a light flickering out there."

"Leroy, there's been a problem with your *bruders.*

You might want to go talk to Elias. I'm going out to the barn and talk to your *daadi*, see what we need to do." She pulled her black bonnet and heavy coat from the rack by the door. "I don't want Amos running around at night like this, especially when he's so upset."

"I already know what happened." Leroy pulled off his heavy coat. "Lena's younger sister was at Rebecca's party, and she told us when she got home." He pulled his hat off and hung it and his coat on the rack. "Can't believe Amos done what he done."

"Well, he's hurting now, and we need him at home so we can all work this out." Rosemary opened the front door but turned to face Leroy first. "Go talk to Elias. He has to forgive Amos. He's his *bruder*." Then she hurried to the barn.

· · ·

Elias was shaking, he was so mad. Mad at Amos, and angry at himself for losing control. He sat down on his bed, propped his elbows on his knees, and held his head in his hands. His lantern was almost out of fuel, but he didn't care if the room went dark, just as his world had.

"*Mamm* and *Daed* are going to ground you both for the rest of your lives." Leroy walked across the threshold and sat down on Amos's bed. "How'd this happen?"

Elias didn't look up at his older brother. "Amos betrayed me. He's been giving Elizabeth love letters and pretending he was me. All this time I've been wondering why she hasn't been calling to meet somewhere. She's been meeting with Amos." He looked up, blinked a few times, and shook his head. "What kind of person does this?"

Leroy shook his head. "But Amos is your *bruder*. You will have to forgive him."

Drops of blood dribbled from Elias's lip as he reached for a tissue on the nightstand. "I ain't forgiving him for nothing."

They were quiet for a few moments, then Leroy spoke again.

"He must have secretly loved Elizabeth for a long time to go and do something like this. And I reckon he's hurting too."

Elias flinched as he dabbed at his lip. "Don't defend him. What he did is unforgivable."

"Nothing is unforgivable."

"Fine. Then you don't mind if I secretly start courting Lena behind your back?"

Leroy shifted his weight on the bed, then crossed one ankle over his knee. "Look . . . she wasn't the right girl, Elias. If she could so easily be swayed by Amos, then you don't want her anyway."

"She thought he was me."

"But it wasn't you, and she still must have felt something."

"She felt confused. That's what she felt. And now she's mad."

Leroy leaned forward. "That's what I'm saying. If it was the kind of love that is meant to be, all this wouldn't have happened. This is God's plan. You have to accept that. And you have to forgive Amos."

"Get out, Leroy. Please. Just go." Elias thought he might

cry, and he didn't want his older brother seeing that, nor did he want to keep listening to Leroy's lecture.

Leroy stood up. "I'm going to go check on things. *Mammi* is worried 'cause Amos took off."

"*Gut.* I hope he never comes back."

Leroy walked toward the door but turned around to face Elias. "You don't mean that. And you need to go get some ice on that eye."

Elias didn't say anything. His head was throbbing, his lip burning, and his heart hurting. "Close the door on your way out."

A few moments later he heard Leroy's footsteps down the hallway. Elias leaned back on his pillow, and a tear trickled down his cheek.

. . .

Joseph tinkered about in the barn, organizing tools on his workbench and acting as if the world hadn't just come crashing down around them. Rosemary knew better, and by the light of the lantern she searched Joseph's face for some hint of concern.

"Joseph, are you listening to me? What do we do? Should we go after Amos? Do we need to call the emergency number that Eve left for us at Mary Mae's shanty?" Rosemary edged closer to where her husband was standing.

"*Nee,* don't call Eve and Big Ben." Joseph picked up four loose nails and put them in a tin box on his bench. "Amos will be back, and Elias needs some time to cool off."

Rosemary bit her bottom lip, swallowing back an urge

to say that these things happen when *kinner* are given too much freedom. However, her thoughts ran amok as she struggled to understand how something like this could happen while the children were in her and Joseph's care.

"There's nothing we could have done to prevent this from happening," she said after a minute, hoping to convince herself.

"*Nee*. I don't think so." Joseph picked up the lantern and held it up, nodding for Rosemary to walk with him.

"*Ach*, the bishop will probably come calling, like Samuel said." Rosemary pulled the rim of her black bonnet down in an effort to block the wind as she and Joseph left the barn. She wondered if Amos had grabbed his coat. She couldn't remember.

Shivering, she walked faster, and so did Joseph. "We can't be held accountable for what the boys did," she said.

Joseph stopped abruptly and turned to face her. "Why not? You hold Eve accountable for every single thing that happens with the boys."

"Joseph . . ." She put a hand to her chest. "They are her children, and . . ." Rosemary stopped talking as Joseph held the lantern high, showing the scowl on his face.

"Rosie, everything happens according to the Lord's plan. You know this. But I don't think I've ever seen two women who judge each other more than you and Eve." He started walking again, shaking his head. "And it's a shame too."

Rosemary didn't say anything as they trudged to the house, the cold wind stinging her face.

Lord, is that what I do . . . judge?

It only took a few seconds to know the answer.

. . .

Three hours later Rosemary paced her bedroom as Joseph silently read the Bible.

"Where can Amos be? We need to go find him."

Joseph pushed his glasses up and scratched his nose. "If the boy is not home in another hour, I will go search for him."

Rosemary folded her arms atop her white nightgown. "I'm not sure I like that idea, you being out in this cold."

Joseph put a hand to one ear. "Listen. Is that the front door?"

Rosemary walked to their bedroom door and eased it open, relieved to see Amos walking in. "It's him."

She pulled on her robe, walked back to her nightstand, and grabbed the lantern, then hurried to the living room. "Amos?"

He was almost to the stairs when he turned around, but he didn't say anything.

"Are you all right?"

The boy's left eye was swollen shut. "*Ya*. I'm sorry, *Mammi*. I just had to go b-be by my-myself for a while."

Rosemary wondered if there was going to be more trouble when Amos went upstairs and confronted his brother. "Do you want to sleep down here on the couch? I can fetch you some blankets, and you'll be warm with the fire still going."

Amos turned around. "Would that be okay?"

"*Ya*." She held the lantern up. "Wait here."

A few minutes later Rosemary returned with two sheets and a large quilt from the closet under the stairs.

Once she'd fixed the couch, Amos lay down right away. "You call for me if you need anything."

He nodded, but Rosemary sensed that he wasn't in the mood to talk, so she slipped back into her room and closed the door behind her. After she set the lantern on the nightstand, she climbed into bed.

"I'm so glad he's home." She turned to Joseph. Her husband was slowly closing the Bible, and his eyes were round as saucers behind his thick lenses. Rosemary brought a hand to her chest. "What is it, Joseph? Why do you have that look on your face?"

Joseph didn't say a word; he just pointed to the floor near the dresser.

Rosemary gasped. Her hallucination's beady little eyes glowed in the dim light. She quickly waved a hand in front of Joseph's face.

He pushed it aside, frowning. "What are you doing?"

"Seeing if your eyes move back and forth. Do you know who I am?"

He narrowed his eyebrows. "Good grief. Of course I know who you are. I'm just wondering who that is down on the floor . . . that long green lizard."

Rosemary put her hands to her chest. "Oh, Joseph! You see him *too*. I've been seeing him for days."

Joseph gave his head a quick shake as he blinked his eyes a few times. "What?"

Rosemary patted his arm. "It's all right, dear. He's not real." She smiled, feeling a bit smug that she wasn't the only one losing her mind.

Joseph held up the lantern as he stepped out of the bed and moved toward the creature, who quickly vanished under the dresser. Her husband struggled down to his hands and knees, groaning as he did so. After taking a peek under the dresser, he looked up at Rosemary. "He's as *real* as the dust balls underneath that dresser."

Rosemary frowned, then joined him on the floor with her own lantern. They both peered underneath the dresser. "I thought I was just imagining things, like the jars in the refrigerator dancing, or thinking Eve is Minnie."

Joseph held the light up in her face. "The jars in the refrigerator dance?"

"Never you mind." Rosemary lifted herself up until she was sitting on the bed. "Where do you think this thing came from?"

"I suspect I know." Joseph lifted himself up and carted the lantern out into the living room.

"Don't wake the boy," Rosemary whispered when she heard Amos snoring, glad he was sleeping soundly.

"*Ach*, that thing has to belong to the boys. They must have it as a pet." Joseph headed back to the bedroom and held the lantern up as he stared down at the dresser. "I'm not sleeping in my bedroom with that critter in here."

Rosemary thought about all the times she'd shared bed space with the reptile, even given him water and dried fruit. She chuckled softly. "Oh, Joseph. Get into bed. I've slept next to him plenty of times."

Joseph was still standing, a blank look on his face, when Rosemary climbed beneath the covers.

"Good night, dear." She winked at him, but then had to bury her head in the pillow to keep from laughing at his silly expression.

CHAPTER 13

Eve had the strangest feeling as they neared home. Her stomach was churning, her head splitting, and she could feel her heart beating in her chest. As she and Benny sat in the backseat of the van, the radio was playing Christian music. Eve usually enjoyed such a treat since their people didn't listen to music, but her thoughts were elsewhere.

She leaned closer to Benny and whispered, "Do you think everything is all right at home?"

"*Ya*, of course it is." He reached for her hand and gave it a quick squeeze, but kept his eyes straight ahead, looking past the driver's shoulder at the flurry of snow that had started a few minutes ago. "I don't remember the last time I've seen this much snow in Lancaster County."

Eve took a deep breath and tried to relax. Mother's intuition was a peculiar thing, often sneaking up on a woman and taking hold. She recalled the time Elias tried to convince Amos that he could fly off the roof. Eve had dropped her broom and run outside before Amos ever hit the ground. And when Leroy was five, she'd taken him to a neighbor's house while she went to a doctor's appointment. Throughout the appointment, she'd had the same feelings she was having now, and when she returned to pick up Leroy, he'd fallen and bumped his head so hard he had to have stitches.

Something is wrong at the house.

. . .

Elias knew that he and Amos were going to be in big trouble when their parents got home. He had stayed away from his brother as best he could, but they'd been forced to work together on the house the past couple of days, which they'd done without speaking. It seemed to Elias that their grandfather had intentionally assigned them projects that forced them into the same work space.

Amos had spent the past few nights sleeping on the couch downstairs, which was fine by Elias. Then his brother would go upstairs to get dressed in the morning after Elias came downstairs. Elias knew it couldn't go on like this forever, and he'd prayed a lot about what happened. In his mind he'd forgiven Amos, but his heart was having trouble catching up. He wanted to ask Amos how he could do such a thing. But even more, he wondered how Elizabeth could have mistaken Amos for him, unless she was longing for more than Elias had given her. He wasn't one to write mushy poems like his brother. Didn't she know that about him? And he wasn't as soft-spoken or shy as Amos. Didn't Elizabeth recognize that difference?

He sighed. *The kisses.* Couldn't Elizabeth tell that she was kissing someone else? He leaned down to tie his shoelace. *Daadi* had said that there would be no work on the house today because of the weather.

Amos walked into the room as Elias walked out. Once again they avoided eye contact or speaking.

. . .

Elizabeth had searched her heart and tried to sort out her feelings for Elias and Amos, trying to forgive herself for her role in all of this. But after a few days alone with her thoughts, she was sure that Amos was the one for her. Not Elias.

It was terrible, what Amos had done, but Elizabeth knew she wasn't innocent either. Amos did what he did out of love for her, and she'd responded in kind. Amos had wanted her so badly that he'd taken risks, penned her beautiful poems, and even betrayed his own brother. She didn't feel good about that last part, but deep within she was flattered that he would go to such extremes.

Now she just had to tell Elias that she wanted to be with Amos. It was a horrible situation, but both of them needed to know how she felt. If she'd been meant to be with Elias, she could have never fallen into another man's arms. In a dark place in the back of her mind, she felt smug that she had her choice of the two men.

She leaned up against the headboard, glad to have some quiet time to think. She pictured herself and Amos lying next to each other in bed after they were married. Amos would read her a poem he'd written just for her, then he'd ease over next to her, holding her gently in his arms.

Opening her eyes, she couldn't help but think about Elias. His ways were more abrasive, even his kisses weren't as soft and gentle as Amos's, yet his outgoing nature, strength, and confidence were qualities that had drawn her to him in the first place.

She tapped a finger to her chin. Too bad she couldn't roll them both into one and make the perfect man; a nice mix of gentleness and manliness, making her laugh when she needed to, or writing her sweet poems that spoke to her heart.

But that wasn't the way it worked, so she'd chosen Amos.

It obviously wasn't a matter of looks. Most folks couldn't tell Elias and Amos apart. Elizabeth grinned, knowing she wasn't one of those people. No, it was Amos's poems that sealed the deal and showed her what she really wanted and needed in a partner.

Tomorrow she would go talk to them both. Hopefully both Elias and Amos would have calmed down by then.

. . .

Eve didn't wait while Benny paid the driver, nor did she stick around to help him unload the supplies they'd brought home or their luggage. She hurried up the sidewalk, knowing her stomach wouldn't calm down until she saw that everyone was okay.

It was almost the supper hour, and the scent of something simmering on the stove hit her as she opened the door. Breathing in the aroma of her mother's good meat loaf, she almost choked when she saw Elias walk across the room in front of her.

"What happened?" She rushed to him and reached up to cup his cheek as the churning in her stomach intensified. His eye was black and blue, and a scab was forming on his lip.

"Amos looks worse." Elias's voice sounded almost proud as he spoke, and Eve was still confused when her mother walked into the room.

"*Ach*, I didn't hear you come in." *Mamm* locked her hands in front of her, bit her bottom lip, and narrowed her eyebrows. Then she looked at Elias and spoke in a firm tone. "Best to go help your *daed* with the luggage."

Elias pulled his coat from the rack and went outside. Eve waited until the door closed behind him before she said anything.

"What's going on? And what did Elias mean about Amos looking worse?" Eve just stood there, a hand to her chest, her coat still buttoned. "What happened?"

Her mother waved a hand. "Come to the kitchen before I burn supper." She shook her head. "It's been a mighty mess around here since you've been gone."

For the next few minutes Eve listened to her mother describing what happened between the twins. All the while *Mamm's* right hand shook viciously as she struggled to stir a pot of beans on the stove. Eve was surprised her mother hadn't yet dropped the spoon.

After *Mamm* was finished, Eve rubbed her eyes as she tried to sort it all out. She had always thought that Amos was the more sensitive of the two boys, and she felt guilty for being surprised that it happened this way when she could have more easily seen Elias doing something like this. She looked up when she heard the front door open and close. Peeking around the corner, she saw Elias and Benny carrying luggage toward the stairs.

"And . . ." *Mamm* spun around to face Eve. "If all that isn't enough, there was a big giant lizard living under my dresser, which I have since learned is named George and lives in a cage upstairs in the closet."

Eve clamped her mouth tight and avoided her mother's eyes. "Oops. Guess we should have told you about George."

"Well, someone should have. Especially when he escaped." *Mamm* sighed. "I thought I was hallucinating . . ." Her mother didn't finish, but instead lifted her chin and turned back to the beans.

Eve knew that her mother was thinking of the time when *Mamm* had called her Minnie, something they still hadn't talked about. "I'm sorry that happened." Eve was sorry about both instances, but she didn't specify which she meant. "I guess we shouldn't have left you with the boys."

Eve's father walked into the kitchen then, shaking his head and grumbling.

"*Daed*, what is it?"

"Elizabeth is pulling up the driveway. One of the boys is out there—Amos, I think." *Daed* pulled out his chair at the kitchen table. "I'm too old and hungry to monitor that situation right now, but someone probably needs to make sure both boys aren't together around that girl, since they go all *ab im kopp*."

Eve walked to the window in the kitchen. A full moon lit the yard. Their people had their superstitions about the power of the full moon, as well as lots of other things, but Eve had never believed in such things. Although, today . . . she couldn't help but wonder if the moon didn't have something to do with the troubles her boys were having.

"Sit. We will pray and eat." Her father spoke with authority, but Eve didn't move. She wasn't hungry. Holding her spot at the window, she watched Elizabeth walk across the yard toward Amos.

She knew she'd never hear the end of this from *Mamm*. She would have to listen to what a bad mother she was, how the boys had too many freedoms, and on and on. She waited until her father raised his head from prayer, then asked, "How much longer on the *haus*?" It had only been three weeks, and one of those weeks she and Benny had been away.

"Big Ben will be surprised when he sees how much we got done while you were traveling." Her father reached for a slice of butter bread. "I think probably in a couple of weeks you can go back. Everything might not be perfect, but it will be livable."

Eve nodded as she forced a smile, then joined her father and mother at the table.

. . .

Elizabeth stepped out of her buggy, and Amos was quickly by her side.

"It's t-too cold for you t-to be out, Elizabeth."

"I had to see you." She glanced around him to make sure no one was on the porch, especially Elias, then she touched his arm. "Does it still hurt?"

He reached up and touched his face, flinching. "A—A little. It's okay, though."

She glanced around him toward the porch. "Where is Elias?"

"He was helping *mei daed* carry luggage upstairs. D-Do you w-want me to get him?"

"*Nee.*" She reached up and touched Amos on the cheek and smiled. He must have thought she was here to make amends with Elias. "I'm so sorry that this happened, but . . ." She took a deep breath. "I know that it's you I want, Amos. Your sweet words have won my heart." She smiled. "And your gentle ways."

Amos hung his head for a moment, then looked back at her as his eyes darkened with emotion. "I don't think I showed my gentle ways by fighting with *mei bruder.*"

"You were fighting for the girl you love," she said softly, gazing into his one opened eye. *And you won.*

"You're shivering, Elizabeth. You shouldn't have come this late." Amos's teeth chattered as he spoke. "But since you're here, I have something very important to tell you."

Elizabeth brought a hand to her chest as she felt herself blush, knowing he was surely going to tell her that he loved her. "Oh, Amos . . ."

CHAPTER 14

Somehow they'd all gotten through the rest of the week and worship on Sunday, even though Elias had said he was sick and asked to skip church. Eve had agreed, knowing it might be a bad situation with both boys and Elizabeth at church. Eve still didn't know much about what was going on, only that her younger sons were not speaking to each other. If Elizabeth had made a choice between her boys, no one had mentioned it to Eve. But she did notice that Amos and Elizabeth seemed to be keeping their distance from each other during worship service and afterward. *Maybe Elizabeth chose Elias?*

With no snow in the forecast, Benny, her father, and the boys had all left early this Monday morning. Eve was ready for a lecture from her mother about her *sohns'* behavior, but she would avoid it as long as she could. She curled up in the chair with the recipe box, but she could hear her mother upstairs. And she was talking. To herself.

Eve sighed, put the box on the table by the chair, and walked up the stairs. Her mother's voice grew louder the closer Eve got.

"You're not such a bad fellow," Eve heard her *mamm* say.

"You and George are friends now?" Eve grinned from the threshold as she folded her hands in front of her. *Mamm* was leaning down in the closet talking to George through the cage.

But when her mother stood up and faced her, Eve gasped. Both of her mother's arms were jerking and shaking. "*Mamm*, we need to go see Dr. Knepp."

"No." Her mother stood taller, but the shaking only grew worse.

"Why not? Don't you want to feel better? Don't you want medicines that will help with the shaking?" Eve didn't give her a chance to reply. "Things are changing, *Mamm*. And change can be *gut*. Going to see an *Englisch* doctor isn't forbidden by the bishop. Neither is having more modern kitchen appliances or using a sweeper in the kitchen." She could hear her voice rising, but seeing her mother like this frightened her. "It just doesn't make any sense. These things do not take away from our relationship with God."

Her mother gripped her hands together in front of her, but her shoulders still bounced forward as she edged closer to the bed and sat down.

Eve couldn't stand to see her suffering like this. "*Mamm*, please. Let's go get you something that can help you."

"I'm fine, Minnie. Just let me be, and I'll be better soon."

Eve's eyes filled with tears. "It's me, *Mamm*. Eve." She eased closer, squatted down in front of her mother, and put one hand on her leg. "It's me."

"I know that."

Eve could feel her mother's leg tense from her touch, so she pulled back her hand, but she wanted nothing more than to wrap her arms around her and comfort her. "You called me Minnie."

"I must have been thinking about Minnie." *Mamm* shrugged her shoulders as spasms still shook her.

Eve stayed where she was. *Please, Lord, help me to say the right things. Help me to help her.* She blinked back tears, longing for a different kind of relationship with her mother, yet fearful to open herself up to more hurt. But the words sprang from her mouth. "I love you, *Mamm*."

Her mother locked eyes with Eve. "I've been a bad mother, haven't I?"

"No. You haven't." *Just tell me you love me.*

"I know you think all of this change among our people is *gut*. But I don't agree, Eve. And I don't think I ever will. The more we stray from our ways, the more it scares me."

Eve bit her bottom lip, struggling not to cry. *Just wrap your arms around me and say you love me.*

"They'll lock me up. The *Englisch* doctor will." Her mother's gaze drifted over Eve's shoulder, her expression blank.

Eve's jaw dropped. "What? They won't lock you up, *Mamm*. They might ask you to have some tests, but they won't lock you up. You just need some medicine to help you with the symptoms you're having."

"They locked up *mei mudder*." *Mamm* paused, still staring over Eve's shoulder. "Because she was crazy. And not so *gut* of a mother, I might add."

Eve didn't know much about her grandparents; they had both died before Eve was born, and her *mamm* never really talked about them. "What do you mean, they locked her up?"

"She had the crazies. I guess like I do." Her mother's gaze didn't leave the faraway place over Eve's shoulder, but her eyes filled with tears. "Your father wouldn't do *gut* without me, though."

"You're not crazy, *Mamm*. These hallucinations are from the Parkinson's disease. I read about it, and problems with your mind can be a symptom." Again the urge to pull her mother close was overwhelming, but she didn't move.

Finally *Mamm* shifted her gaze and locked eyes with Eve. "I was so careful with you growing up. I never wanted to hurt you."

Eve narrowed her eyebrows. "What are you talking about?"

Mamm was quiet for a few moments.

Eve's knees were cracking, so she eased herself up and onto the bed next to her mother and waited for her to continue.

"If I've been critical of the way you raised your *kinner*, it's only because I feared that the freedoms they have will pull them from our district."

"I don't want them to leave, but they deserve a chance to experience *Englisch* freedoms during their *rumschpringe*. And it's always been done that way." Eve paused, sighing. "Except in our *haus* when I was growing up."

Her mother hung her head. "I know you don't think I'm a *gut mudder*, Eve, but I did the best I could."

"I have never said you were a bad mother. I just want to feel . . ." Eve shook her head. "Never mind." She shouldn't even have to say it. It should be obvious.

Her mother stood up from the bed and turned to face Eve. "*Danki* for doing the recipes. It will be a big help to me."

Eve jumped up off the bed. "Don't you do that!" She couldn't recall ever yelling at her mother before, but as tears threatened to choke her words, she went on. "Every time we start to have a meaningful conversation—about anything—you change the subject. Why can't you tell me you love me, *Mamm*? You've never said it! I don't even remember you hugging me. Was I so awful a child that you couldn't even hug me?" She pointed a finger at her mother. "*Mei kinner* will never feel that way. I tell them I love them all the time." She sniffled. "And I hug them."

"Is that what you think, Eve, that I don't love you?" *Mamm* was shaking so bad that her voice trembled as she spoke. She clasped her hands in front of her, but it did little to help. Her eyes filled with tears. "I've loved you since the day God graced me with the gift of you. Every breath I've taken has been for you."

Eve knew her parents had wanted more children but were never able to have any. So many times Eve had longed for a brother or sister.

"Really?" Eve rolled her eyes, then brushed tears from her cheeks. "Because except when we were cooking together, I never felt it."

Mamm briefly smiled. "The times we cooked together were my favorites too." Then she frowned, pulling her eyes from Eve's. "I never wanted to be like my mother. She was so . . . strict . . . with Minnie and me. Sometimes she'd just beat Minnie like you beat the dust out of a rug. I thought if I stayed distant from you, then I'd never be tempted to be like mother, like daughter."

"You never touched me." Eve swiped at her eyes.

"I know. I guess in my mind it was safer that way. I'm sorry, Eve. And I'm sorry for judging you for the way you've raised your *kinner*. It's not my place to judge. Only the Lord can do that." She locked eyes with Eve. "And I know we've disagreed about so many things, but all this change going on among our people frightens me."

"It doesn't have to, *Mamm*. Change can be a *gut* thing."

Her mother hung her head. "*Nee*, I don't think so." She tried to steady the shaking in her hands, arms, and shoulders. She looked at Eve as a tear rolled down her cheek. "Look how much *I'm* changing."

"We can get help with that." Eve closed her eyes for a moment, then reached for her mother's hand, grabbing it so firmly that there was no chance her mother could pull away. "I'll make a bargain with you."

Her mother's eyebrows shot up.

"If you'll let me take you to the doctor, then I won't say another word about upgrading the kitchen with more modern appliances, a sweeper for the kitchen, or anything else."

"You're sure they won't lock me up the way they did *mei mudder*? She was an awful woman most of the time, but I loved her and missed her just the same when she didn't come home."

"I will never let anyone lock you up. I will always take care of you."

Her mother pulled her hand away, then buried her face in her trembling hands and sobbed. "I'm afraid, Eve."

Eve wrapped her arms around her and pulled her close, until her mother finally relaxed in her arms and cried. "I know you are."

. . .

Elias climbed into bed following another day of not speaking to Amos. *Daed* had told Amos that he couldn't sleep on the couch downstairs anymore, so Elias waited for Amos to come in from the bathroom down the hall. His brother hadn't said a word about his conversation with Elizabeth, and prior to tonight Elias hadn't cared to hear about it. He had gotten his answer the night she'd come over. When Elias walked outside and saw her talking to Amos, Elizabeth had run to her buggy. She'd clearly made her choice.

The betrayal by both his brother and his former girlfriend was gnawing away at him, despite the prayers he'd been saying daily for strength to forgive them both.

"You and Elizabeth planning your wedding?" Elias crossed his ankles and put his hands behind his head when Amos entered the room.

"*Nee.*" Amos pushed back his covers and got into bed. He snuffed out his lantern and fluffed his pillow.

Elias reached for his lantern on the nightstand and turned it up. "You ain't going to sleep, Amos. We're going to talk about this." He swung his feet over the side of the bed and held the lantern high.

Amos sighed, but he sat up on his bed and faced Elias. "Fine."

"How could you do this to me, Amos? I'm your *bruder.*" Elias dabbed at his swollen lip, not that his physical injuries were as important as the hurt in his heart.

"I-I'm sorry. I . . . really am." Amos hung his head, sighing again.

"*Ya*, well, that's all *gut* and fine, but I love Elizabeth. And you stole her from me." Elias put the lantern on the nightstand, struggling with the feelings of rage and love comingling in his heart.

"If she was really yours, then I reckon I couldn't have stolen her from you."

Elias grunted, locking his one good eye with his brother's. "What's that supposed to mean?"

Amos shrugged. "I-I'm just saying that if sh-she was so in love with you, she wouldn't have had anything to do with me."

"She thought you *were* me!" Elias spoke in an angry whisper.

"*Nee*. She d-didn't. Fern's herbs helped a l-little, but I still stuttered. She knew the first time that I saw her for lunch that I wasn't you."

"I don't believe you."

"It's true. And—and I know I hurt you real bad, Elias, and I'm sorry f-for that. But I love her too."

Elias let out an exasperated huff. "She wasn't yours to love."

"She flirted with me. A-All the time. I think she liked some things 'bout me, and she liked other things about you. But she couldn't have us b-both."

"When? When did she flirt with you?" Elias swallowed hard as he tried to keep his emotions under control.

"Anytime she could. A-After church sometimes when you—you weren't around. Other times too."

"Well, now you've got her, *bruder*. Congratulations."

Amos lowered his gaze. "She's not the right girl for me." He paused. "I—I figure she'd probably flirt w-with you behind my back." He looked up. "I ain't proud of the way I acted, but I've never had a girl really like me. I'm a-ashamed." He sat taller, chin lifted. "But no *maedel* should come between us."

Elias grunted. "She already did."

Amos shook his head. "*Nee.* I told her I ain't gonna date her, much less marry her."

Elias rubbed his chin, cocking his head to one side. "Are you saying you could have had Elizabeth, and you turned her down?"

As Amos nodded, Elias wondered if he would have done the same thing if the situation were reversed. If Amos was right, and Elizabeth did like some things about each of them, then things were as they should be. He extended his hand to Amos. "I'm sorry I threw the first punch."

"I'm s-sorry too."

For the first time in days, Elias felt like he might get a decent night's sleep. He snuffed out his lantern and crawled underneath the covers. His heart still hurt over Elizabeth, but Amos's heart was hurting too. A huge knot formed in his throat, knowing what his brother had so unselfishly given up.

"Amos?"

"*Ya?*"

Elias dabbed at his eyes in the darkness. "*Bruders* forever."

"*Ya. Bruders* forever."

CHAPTER 15

"Two weeks have passed, and it still feels *gut* to wake up in *mei* own bed." Eve rolled over and gently touched Benny on the cheek.

"It feels *gut* to sleep in on a Saturday morning too."

Eve snuggled closer to her husband. "*Ya*, it does. We don't do it often, but when we do, it's nice."

"Are you going to Our Daily Bread today?"

"*Ya*." She poked Benny playfully on the arm. "And guess what? *Mei mamm* is going with me."

She was looking forward to going to the prayer gathering. She hadn't been in weeks. Today would be extra special since her mother had agreed to go, and Eve and her mother had something to share with the group.

"I'm glad Dr. Knepp's medications are helping her," Benny said. "You were right to keep pushing her to go to the *Englisch* doctor."

It had been two weeks since Eve had hired a driver and they'd gone to see Dr. Knepp. There'd been good news and bad news. *Mamm's* Parkinson's disease was progressing, but the doctor had said that with medication she could better control her shaking, and he'd also prescribed something to help with her mind. Eve's father had said just yesterday that *Mamm* was still putting her glasses in odd places, and sometimes she forgot things, but overall he could see an improvement.

Mamm had purchased a floor sweeper too, and Eve knew that was a big step—a statement, really, of not wanting to be so judgmental. It had taken a lifetime for them to see inside each other's heart, but Eve was hopeful that she and her mother had begun a journey toward a better relationship.

Eve glanced at the clock by the bed. "I bet the boys are starving. You know they won't get started on chores until they have some breakfast. It's almost six thirty."

. . .

Rosemary put on a freshly ironed *kapp* and one of her best Sunday dresses. For months she'd avoided going to the prayer gatherings at Our Daily Bread because she was self-conscious about all her shaking and twitching. Many times she would have stayed home from worship service for the same reason, but every time she was tempted, she reminded herself how much Jesus had suffered. Her aches and pains were of no comparison.

Today, however, was a good day. Very little trembling.

"You look pretty," Joseph said when Rosemary walked into the living room.

"*Danki.*" She smoothed the wrinkles from her black apron as she looked around the room. "It still seems so quiet in here with all the *kinner* back in their own *haus*."

Joseph pushed his glasses up on his nose and closed the book he was reading. "Been real nice having Eve over here so much, even after they moved back home. Good to see the two of you cooking together."

Rosemary smiled. "That's when Eve and I were always at our best. I guess it still is." She walked to the door and put on her black sweater and bonnet, glad the pre-spring temperatures had arrived. Peeking out the window, she saw Eve's buggy coming up the driveway. "See you soon." She kissed Joseph on the cheek.

. . .

Eve followed her mother into the white cinder-block building where the local women had been gathering since well before Eve was born. As they walked down the aisle with the fabrics, Eve was reminded that she needed material for some new shirts for Benny and the boys.

She followed her mother up the stairs to the upper room of the store. Familiar faces lit up when they entered. Eve swallowed back a lump in her throat as she watched her mother hugging some of the women. *What a blessing today is.* She silently thanked God for her mother's improved symptoms and that she and her mother were finally able to work on being closer.

After chatting in small groups for about fifteen minutes, the women settled into chairs and prayed for each other and their families. Then Ann Lapp offered prayers for all those who couldn't be with them today. Eve knew that she had been on that list the past few weeks, and her mother even longer. Eve was thankful for so many things today. A restored home, her family, and a newfound relationship with her mother. When Ann was done, Eve bowed her head and spoke aloud. "I would like to thank the Lord for our newly repaired home." She glanced around the room at the women.

"And please thank your husbands and *sohns* who took time when they could to help Benny, my boys, and *mei daed* work on the *haus*."

Ann clapped her hands together. "I think it would be nice if we all said what we're thankful for today." She waved her hand toward the window, bright sunshine streaming into the room and onto the wooden floors. "It's such a beautiful day in so many ways." She paused. "I'm thankful that Hiram is almost completely recovered from the flu he's been suffering from this winter."

All of the women nodded, and then each one thanked God for something they were thankful for on this glorious day. Eve was relieved that Elizabeth wasn't in attendance today. She would always wish Elizabeth well, but after what happened with the twins, she wasn't ready to face the girl yet. The feeling was probably mutual.

"I'm thankful for my first taste of love," Fern Zook said, her green eyes glowing. She reminded Eve of herself when she'd first fallen in love with Benny all those years ago.

Hannah King was the next one to speak up. "I'm thankful that God led Stephen to Paradise and our bed-and-breakfast." Her wide smile was indicative of more new love in the air, and Eve was extra thankful—if that was possible—that she and her mother were here today.

Eve's mother was the only one in the group who hadn't spoken up yet, and she raised a trembling hand to her chest, then reached for Eve's hand with her other one. "I'm thankful that *mei dochder* convinced me to go see Dr. Knepp for medication that helps with my shaking." She glanced at Fern. "Not that Fern's herbs weren't *gut* . . ." She smiled. "I just needed something a bit stronger." She squeezed Eve's hand. "Most of all, I'm thankful for the time I spent with my family while their house was being rebuilt."

Eve squeezed her mom's hand back, blinking her eyes. After a deep breath, she eased her hand away and reached into her apron pocket. She unfolded the piece of paper, recalling fondly the time she and her mother had spent together in preparation for this moment.

"*Mamm* and I have been cooking a lot," Eve began, smiling. "And we've been writing down all of our recipes so that future generations will always have them. On the back of some of the recipe cards, we wrote down fond memories we have of times we cooked together. And last week we created a recipe together that we would like to share with you." Eve glanced at her mother, who dabbed at her eyes. "It's a recipe for hope, and I'd like to read it to you." She read aloud:

LOVE IN STORE

VANNETTA CHAPMAN

For Jodi Hughes

GLOSSARY

daddi—grandfather

danki—thank you

dat—dad, father

Englischer—non-Amish person

fra—wife

Gotte's wille—God's will

gudemariye—good morning

gut—good

kapp—prayer covering

kinner—children

mamm—mom

mammi—grandmother

nein—no

rumspringa—running around; time before an Amish young person has officially joined the church, provides a bridge between childhood and adulthood.

schweschder—sister

willkumm—welcome

wunderbaar—wonderful

ya—yes

youngie—teenaged to young adult

"Whatever you do, work at it with all your heart, as working for the Lord . . ."
—COLOSSIANS 3:23

"How pleasant and good it is when brothers are peaceable, when their doings are in agreement."
—AMISH PROVERB

PROLOGUE

NAPPANEE, INDIANA
MARCH

David Stoltzfus didn't wake planning to save a child's life. He'd worked the first half of his shift at the Old Amish Mill and then walked over to the market building. In the back, past the Plain merchandise and the canned goods, was a bakery where he liked to sit and enjoy his lunch. The first bite of his sandwich tasted delicious. He was about to take a second when he heard a woman scream in alarm. Looking up, he saw her standing next to a child that was probably not yet a year old.

"Cough, Cami. Cough!" the older woman said.

The little girl's face was turning blue. David didn't hesitate. He hurried to the child's side, scooped her up, and held her facedown over his forearm. Holding her jaw with his left hand to support her head, he used the heel of his right hand to slap the area between her shoulder blades. With the third slap a grape popped out and rolled across the floor. The child pulled in a deep breath, pinking up immediately. David breathed a prayer of relief and handed the little thing back to her grandmother.

"I was cutting them in half." Tears coursed down the woman's cheeks as she clutched the child to her chest. "I turned around for a minute and I guess . . . I guess she managed to grab one off my plate."

Stella Schwartz had hurried from the register to the woman's side. "Would you like us to call an ambulance?"

"No. No, I think she's all right now."

"Let me bring you another hot tea—to calm your nerves. And perhaps a bottle of juice for your grand-daughter?"

The woman nodded and then suddenly seemed to realize that David was still standing there. "How can I thank you?"

"Not necessary. Glad I could help. You have a *gut* afternoon." David went back to his sandwich, but the rest of lunch was not to be the peaceful half hour he had envisioned. The manager of the Mill must have been called. He checked on the woman and child, and then he thanked David and Stella for their help.

"Quick thinking and calm in a crisis," Bobo McPherson said. "We need more employees like that."

David only nodded as he gathered up his trash. But his mind wasn't on the child as he made his way out of the restaurant. Instead David was thinking of Stella, the gracious way she had helped the grandmother, the tender way she had looked at the child, the look of pure gratitude she had shared with David before returning to her work and her normal, somewhat dour, disposi-tion. Stella was an enigma to David, as most women were. He'd been fortunate to have one woman by his side for most of his adult life. He still felt Beverly's love like a blanket that comforted him. He supposed he always would.

But what was Stella's story?

His daughter had told him that Stella had never married. Why?

And why the perpetual bad attitude? If David hadn't seen her with the child, he never would have believed she could be tender and compassionate. But he had seen her, and it wasn't a sight he would soon forget.

CHAPTER 1

Life took more turns than a country road. David Stoltzfus was currently navigating one of those turns, and he marveled that he could still feel peaceful about it. Then again, his parents had been an example of faith in daily living, not even worrying through the long Wisconsin winters. Yes, he'd had good people to bring him up in the faith, and faith was what would see him through this current crisis.

He nearly laughed to think what his *mamm* and *dat* would say about his living in Indiana. They'd already passed before his daughter had married and moved. Though David loved the area where he'd been born and raised, he also found these first few weeks in Nappanee, Indiana to be a pleasant change. Anywhere family resided was a wonderful place to be, in his opinion.

David walked toward the icehouse on the northern side of the property of the Old Amish Mill complex, known to locals as simply the Mill. The property had close to forty buildings, including a large gift shop, market, café, and theater. The majority of the buildings were historic in nature—either from the original farmstead or restored buildings that had been moved to the site. He whistled as he walked past each one. Why wouldn't he whistle? It was a fine spring day—the temperature in the forties but projected to rise to a balmy fifty-six. He had a job that he enjoyed, and he was now living with his daughter. He was grateful for the chance to help Rebecca during her time of trouble.

Yes, life was good. He thanked the Lord each night that in spite of their troubles, they were able to enjoy the small blessings of life.

"*Gudemariye*, David." Peter Yoder raised a hand in greeting. He worked in the maple-sugar camp, and their buildings were adjacent to one another.

Peter was a few years older than David, surely in his early sixties. David had recently turned fifty-two. Though they'd only known each other a few weeks they were fast becoming friends. In fact, Peter was the one who had mentioned the job opening at the Mill to Rebecca. The community had certainly rallied around Rebecca since the death of her husband. It had been a tragedy for sure and for certain, but now David was there to help her with the three children and provide a little extra income.

"It's a fine morning indeed," David said. "Reminds me of when we'd rise early to work in the fields."

"Only now our job is to escort *Englischers*, teaching them our ways."

David and Peter stood with their backs against the wall of what they called the sugar building and studied the fields that stretched to the north of the property. The sugar building was an old wooden structure that had been moved to the area many years ago. For the entire month of March, a sweet aroma would seep from its walls, as sap water was boiled down into maple syrup.

"Do you miss it?" David asked. "The farming?"

David could see, off in the distance, one of the younger employees farming five acres of the north pasture. Though the Mill was a tourist attraction, it was also a working farm.

"*Ya.* For certain I do, especially as I'm driving past the fields in the morning, watching the *youngies* out there driving the horses and plow."

"It's a satisfying thing indeed to work the land."

"My mind and heart misses it." Peter cast David a sideways look, his eyes crinkling as he smiled. "But my back and knees? Not so much. It is *gut* that we pass such work to our sons."

"Indeed. I'm thankful for this job. The extra money helps Rebecca."

"How is she?"

"Some days better than others."

"Young Jacob's life was complete, but I know first-hand that grief is a hard thing. We will continue to pray for her and the *kinner.*"

David nodded. He'd learned, in the few weeks he'd been in Nappanee, that the community was a close one and went to great lengths to support one another through seasons of trouble. By the time David had moved to Rebecca's, the spring planting was already underway, the barn had been repaired, and the livestock were being cared for—all by church members or family of Jacob's.

"How do you like the icehouse?" Peter asked.

"*Gut* enough. I don't mind showing the young children or even the old *Englischers* how we harvest the ice and store it. Such a simple thing, but they seem astonished when they learn the process."

"They're amazed because it's done with the work of our hands and the sweat of our brows, not by pushing some button."

Peter was getting wound up for one of his lectures against modern conveniences. He had that look in his eye and shake to his head. David needed to escape.

"Suppose I should be moseying over. I still need to check the rooms before the first tour group comes through."

"Pleasant day to you."

David walked across the dirt lane to the icehouse—what he was already thinking of as *his* house. Donning the coat he kept on a hook inside the door, he walked over to the cubby built into the south wall. It was where he kept his things. He stored his lunch and glanced over his supplies. Only the most basic of tools were required to care for the icehouse. There were work gloves and a clipboard, along with several sizes of ice picks and mallets to use in demonstrations. There was also an assortment of hooks to show the youngsters how to pick up the blocks of ice. Though only twelve by eighteen inches and twelve inches thick, each block weighed eighty pounds—always a surprise to the children who thought they could pick one up.

The clipboard contained an updated schedule of tours. Since it was a Friday, they would have three groups. Saturdays were even busier and he could only imagine what the summer crowds would be like. He'd only worked at the Mill for two weeks.

At the moment his job was to oversee the icehouse and the several hundred blocks of ice in it, which wasn't a difficult task. He enjoyed explaining to visitors how the ice had been harvested from area lakes and ponds, even the small pond the icehouse was positioned near. *Englischers* were always surprised that the ice didn't melt, even during the warm summer days, but the building had been constructed with that purpose in mind, and it was well built.

So he was flabbergasted when he began his morning inspection and found water standing throughout the building. Some of it had frozen and the place had become a virtual ice rink. He carefully made his way to the faucet at the back of the building, filled a mop bucket with hot water, and began cleaning up the mess. Water or ice on the floor might cause a visitor to slip. The Mill would be responsible, and David would probably lose his job. Fortunately the rooms were small and the cleaning only took a few moments.

When he was done, David checked to see if he needed to add any sawdust around the hundreds of blocks of ice, but there were only a few small gaps. He preferred to let one of their guests take care of it. There were always volunteers, and they seemed to enjoy helping—usually pausing so that someone could take a picture on their cell phones.

David had reached the back of the icehouse and was turning again to the front when he spied something red out of his peripheral vision. Moving back toward the corner, he stepped to the left and then the right trying to make sense of what he was seeing.

There was a rubber chicken—no doubt at all that it was not real—lying across one of the blocks of ice. A red substance had been dripped around the chicken, and an ice pick had been stuck into the chicken's neck. Why would someone leave such a thing? And who would do it?

Then he remembered—the day was April 1. Someone was pulling an April Fools' joke. The Amish didn't usually participate in Fools' Day pranks and jokes, but the *youngie* might and the *Englisch* certainly did. David grunted as he moved to where his tools were kept and retrieved a large ice pick, a mallet, and a bucket. He hurried to the scene of the mock killing and placed the chicken and small pick in the bucket. Then he set about chipping away the ice that had been stained. Lastly, he retrieved his mop and cleaned up the mess on the floor.

The chicken was a joke, for sure and certain. But the partially frozen water on the floor? Someone must have come in the evening before, for it to be frozen already. Had they dropped a bucket of water and not taken the time to clean up? Why would they need a bucket of water? Why would they even be in the icehouse to begin with?

By the time he had finished cleaning up the mess, a double tap came over his walkie-talkie. That would mean Stella Schwartz had begun her tour. She would be at the icehouse in roughly an hour. He had enough time to go next door and chat a little more with Peter Yoder. The two men lived in opposite directions, so they only saw each other at church meetings or between tour groups. Peter drove his own buggy to work—he lived to the east off Highway 6.

David lived to the west, and he rode to work with several other Mill employees. They hired an *Englischer* with a large van to transport them each morning and evening. He could have driven Rebecca's buggy, but she only had the one and he didn't like leaving her with no means of transportation. Riding with the *Englischer* was no problem and cost only twenty dollars a week, far less than the cost of another horse and buggy.

Earlier, David had stepped out of the van in the parking lot and then walked straight toward the icehouse. He hadn't seen anyone near the building, but perhaps Peter had. David didn't plan to reprimand the person, but he did want to remind him or her that a child could have found the pick and gotten hurt, or an older person could have slipped on the red juice. It hadn't been paint, because it washed off too easily. Jell-O, maybe.

Looking out across the property, David saw Stella and her group enter the Meeting House. He'd be back well before she made it to the icehouse. One thing was for certain, he did not want to start off his day irritating Stella Schwartz.

The woman had a sharp tongue and a bitter spirit.

And yet, something about Stella intrigued him. He couldn't help thinking that there was more to her. What, he wasn't sure, but he was interested in finding out. Time would tell whether that was foolish or wise.

CHAPTER 2

Stella Schwartz led her group of twelve guests past the Round Barn Theater and into the Meeting House. As she did, she happened to look up and see David Stoltzfus dash from the icehouse over to the sugar camp.

"Why can't he stay at his assigned post?"

Ethel Miller's eyes widened. In Stella's opinion the girl was impossibly young and terribly naïve. But then no one had asked Stella if she wanted seventeen-year-old Ethel as an apprentice. And what was the point anyway? The girl was already seeing one of the boys who worked on the grounds crew. By the time Stella trained her, she would be married and gone.

"Maybe he wanted to say hello to Peter."

"Work is not the time to socialize." Stella made a sound like *humph*, then wished she could take it back. She sounded like her mother who had died in her eighties. She didn't want to sound eighty or any age other than the fifty years she was.

She would have liked to remind young Ethel to pull her *kapp* forward—too much of her blond hair was showing. It was all about fashion and style with the young girls, but Stella thought they would do well to mind the ways of their elders.

She couldn't reprimand Ethel though, because her guests had all walked into the Meeting House and taken a seat on the long wooden benches. It was time to acquaint them with the history of the Amish in general and this facility in particular.

"*Gudemariye* and welcome to the Old Amish Mill. We are pleased that you have chosen to spend your morning with us. The Amish Mill encompasses seventy-two acres and is listed in the National Register of Historic Places." As she proceeded to tell them how Amish settlers had first come to the Nappanee area in 1839, she released some of the tension from her muscles and forgot about the sharp edges of her life.

Her regrets slipped away.

Her anger quieted.

For a moment, she gave rest to the bitterness in her soul and instead focused on the young and old in front of her.

They were a varied lot—from small ones who could barely toddle to an older gentleman who was using a cane. They had respectfully silenced their cell phones, and perhaps that helped to brighten her mood. The small group was friendly and attentive, and Stella relaxed in the knowledge that she was being useful. She was teaching others about the history of the area, important aspects of the past and the present. Something they hopefully would tell others about. Maybe they'd even learn to apply some of what they saw while on the grounds to their everyday, mostly urban, lives.

After she'd handed out maps and told them the tour would take nearly two hours, she nodded to Ethel. The girl was already in the small sound room at the back, and she pushed the button to start the film. The lights dimmed and the ten minute documentary began. Although Stella didn't abide television or picture shows, she thought the film was well done, and the guests seemed to enjoy it.

When it was over, they moved smoothly through the first forty minutes of the tour—seeing the orchard, which was just beginning to bloom, the blacksmith shop, and the sorghum press. When they reached the maple-sugar camp, Stella thought to ask Peter why David had been dashing over to see him.

She decided it was none of her business.

As long as he did his job, she had no interest in what David did.

She had been repeating that very thing to herself all week, but that hadn't stopped David Stoltzfus from popping up in her path when he had no business being there. Nearly every day he stopped into the bakery where she worked in the afternoons. He always purchased a small item—a pack of gum or sometimes a soda. She couldn't imagine why he wasted his money on such things.

Her mind flashed back to the little girl David had saved. He had scooped her up and patted her on the back like it was something he did daily. Perhaps he had some medical training. Or maybe he had learned to do so after someone in his community choked. She knew he was from Wisconsin, but other than that he was a mystery—a mystery that she had no intention of unraveling.

Guiding her group across the dirt lane to the front of the wooden icehouse, she refused to meet David's eyes. He had an unnerving way of smiling at her. Best to appear occupied with other things.

"*Willkumm*," he said robustly. David wasn't one to keep his voice down. He spoke as if he were preaching at the front of a church gathering. "I'm pleased that you have stopped by to visit my humble icehouse."

"It's not as if it belongs to him," Stella grumbled under her breath.

Ethel nearly giggled at that, which made no sense.

"Today I will explain to you how the building was constructed, how we cut and store the ice, and why it lasts all year long."

"We push a button and ice comes out of our refrigerator," a small *Englisch* girl said.

"Ah, *ya*, and is that so?"

David was playing stupid. Another child had said the same thing earlier in the week.

"Our ice does not come out of a machine, but from the ponds and lakes. For some Amish communities, like those in Wisconsin where I am from, it even comes from the rivers. Let's walk around to the back porch which stretches out over the pond, and I will show you what I mean."

David tugged on his beard, no doubt reminding the small ones of Santa Claus. The little girl who had mentioned her refrigerator reached up and snagged his hand as if it was the most natural thing in the world.

In that moment, Stella felt a pain in her chest that was akin to a physical ache. She'd grown accustomed to it long ago, yet such moments still had the power to steal her breath. She mourned for the children she never had, the bareness of her womb, and she wondered—once again—what was the point of her life?

Ethel's walkie-talkie squeaked, pulling Stella back to the present. The voice of their manager, Bobo McPherson, came over the device. Stella closed her eyes and tried to find a bit of patience from deep inside. There was much about Mr. McPherson that rubbed her the wrong way.

They both stepped away from the group while David continued with his demonstration.

"Hi, Ethel. This is Bobo."

Stella resisted the urge to roll her eyes. Bobo was not a proper name, and in her opinion Mr. McPherson would do better to remain on a more formal basis with his employees.

"Good morning," Ethel said.

"It is. However, we had an employee call in sick at the restaurant. Could you possibly abandon Stella and go lend a hand?"

"Abandon me?"

Stella glanced at Ethel, shoulders raised in a questioning pose.

"Fine. I can escort a group of twelve, including an infant and an old cripple, all by myself." Stella did her best to put a sarcastic tone in her reply, but Ethel didn't appear to notice.

"Ethel, I've asked David to fill in your spot," Mr. McPherson continued. "Peter will cover both the sugar camp and the icehouse. It'll only be for this tour and the next, then we'll have things all straightened out."

Ethel responded with something inane like she'd be happy to, and Stella stared left then right, hoping a different solution would pop out of the shrubs. Instead all she saw was Peter Yoder, making his way across to where they stood.

With a sinking feeling, Stella realized that her Friday had taken an abrupt turn for the worse. She'd be spending hours in the company of the one man she'd rather not be around—David Stoltzfus.

CHAPTER 3

Stella survived the morning tours.

During the afternoon hours she worked quietly in the market, lost in her own thoughts and speaking very little to the other workers. She couldn't put her finger on what it was about David Stoltzfus that bothered her so much. He was polite, did his job well, and was personable with the guests.

She thought suddenly of the old tomcat her sister insisted on feeding. The pitiful thing had part of one ear missing, continually showed up needing bandaging, and yet he lay in the sun content as a newborn kitten.

That was it.

David's contentment.

"Can you tell me if these potholders are actually made by Amish women?" The customer was holding eight in her hands.

Stella wondered who needed eight potholders, but she didn't comment on that. "*Ya*, they are made by a woman in my church, and they're hand stitched and hand quilted."

She rung up the woman's purchase and then returned to dusting shelves.

David's contented attitude was more than she could fathom, and it caused her soul to bristle. Why wasn't he railing against the injustices of life? She knew little about him, but of course she had attended Jacob's funeral. It was the first time she'd laid eyes on David, and even then—though he'd been properly somber— there was a peace about him that defied explanation.

His daughter was a widow!

His grandchildren fatherless!

Yet he stood next to them at the graveside, back straight and shoulders square as if he didn't feel the burden that had been passed to him.

"If you dust those shelves any harder you're going to take off part of the paint." Joan Neeley was Stella's age and had worked in the market nearly as long.

"Seems I just did this job yesterday."

"And we'll do it again tomorrow."

Joan hurried over to the register to check out another customer, and Stella continued the never-ending task of keeping the market clean. Her thoughts though, they returned to David Stoltzfus.

A real tragedy what had happened to David's son-in-law.

Her life was nowhere near as tragic, and yet she didn't feel the need to placidly accept it. *Nein*, when something was wrong, then it should be treated as wrong. Hadn't Job argued with God? Didn't they all have the right to struggle against the curves and turns their lives took? Acceptance and peace were all good and well when spoken by a preacher, but in Stella's opinion it went against human nature.

David Stoltzfus went against human nature.

She spent the rest of her shift ringing up orders for the customers who purchased fresh bread, pies, and cookies. Then she walked to the barn. Eli Strong had already fetched her horse and hitched it to the buggy. Eli was a good lad though not particularly bright. She had to check and make sure the harness was fastened correctly.

Satisfied that her buggy wouldn't come unhitched and kill her on the way home, she climbed up, nodded to Eli, and set out to the west down Highway 6.

She'd traveled less than a half mile when she spotted David walking along the side of the road.

What was the old fool doing now?

Rebecca's farm was a good four miles from the Mill. Against her better judgment, she pulled over to the side of the road and stopped. There was no need to get out of the buggy. David walked up alongside her window within a few minutes.

"Afternoon, Stella."

"What are you doing?"

"Ah, well, I'm walking home from work."

"You ride in the van."

"Most days I do." David smiled and the folds around his eyes crinkled.

"Then why are you walking?"

"Didn't quite finish my work in time. They left without me."

"How late were you?"

"Doesn't matter. Sandy has to pick up her daughter from gymnastics by five, so she can't wait. It was my fault, not hers."

There he went again, looking on the sunny side. It was enough to make Stella want to clap her hands over her ears or drive off without him. Of course, she did neither.

"Better climb in. Four miles is too far to walk for folks our age, especially after a full day at work."

David shrugged at that, but he did walk around the buggy and climb in.

She prayed they would ride in silence, but that was not to be.

"I enjoyed working with you this morning, Stella. You do a *gut* job leading the tour groups."

Stella didn't respond to that compliment, though she could feel her ears warming. No doubt they were also pinking up like a spring rose. Fortunately her *kapp* covered her ears, so David wouldn't see.

"Mr. McPherson would do well to have more standby employees for when there's an emergency. Ethel shouldn't be pulled in to whatever spot he needs filled. She has a regular spot—with me."

"Yet change is *gut* for us. Don't you agree? I certainly enjoy working in the icehouse, but it was nice to have a morning out on the property."

Stella made the *humph* sound. It was getting to be a habit. She needed to find a better way to express herself.

"I've only been here a little while—"

"Less than a month." Stella sniffed.

"But I can see that Bobo is a fair and competent manager. At least he seems that way to me."

Stella didn't respond to that. She wouldn't be baited by David into gossiping. Instead she focused on her driving and hoped that he would take the hint and ride in silence.

He didn't.

Instead he talked about the interesting people they had met in their groups that morning, pointed out flowers that were blooming on the side of the road, and regaled her with stories of his grandchildren.

His daughter, Rebecca, had a boy who was just starting school and twin girls who were still in diapers.

"Emma puts everything in her mouth, but Sophie holds anything she picks up next to her ear. They look completely alike, other than a tiny birthmark on the back of Sophie's neck, but in many ways they're different. It's an amazing thing, twins. Never had any in our family, but my wife's family—they had plenty. I guess that's why Rebecca had a set."

Stella could almost smell the baby powder. She wished she could tell David to stop talking, but she wasn't sure he was capable. He'd already moved on to describing the older boy to her.

"Teacher says he's *wunderbaar* with numbers. It's his reading that is poor. Any idea what would cause that?"

She realized with a start that David was waiting for her to respond.

When she didn't answer, David said, "I told Rebecca not to worry, but I suppose it's natural for a *mamm* to do so. Still, it seems to me that children will learn most things in time and it's best not to make too big a fuss."

"Glasses."

"Pardon?"

"The boy might need glasses."

David stroked his beard. Finally he asked, "Then how does he complete the math lessons so well?"

"Math is usually written a bit larger, at least in our school books. There's more white space on the page too. Reading on the other hand—the page is cluttered with print."

Now David was studying her. It made her decidedly nervous.

"Ask him to read to you tonight. See if he squints or tries to bring the page closer."

"I hadn't even thought of that," David admitted. "*Danki*, Stella. I'll watch young Adam, and I'll let you know if that seems to be the problem."

Stella had endured quite enough of David Stoltzfus's cheery conversation for one day. With a sigh of relief, she saw the corner of her sister's property.

"I'm afraid you'll have to walk the rest of the way. My *schweschder* doesn't like me to take the buggy farther than work and back."

"No problem at all. I appreciate the lift. Rebecca's is only a short piece from here." David wished her good night, waiting until she glanced his way before nodding and then moving out of the buggy.

Overall she was happy with the afternoon. She'd done her good deed by giving David a ride and now she was rid of him. Hopefully tomorrow everyone would show up for their assigned duties, and she wouldn't be bothered with his constant presence.

She ate a quiet dinner with Carolyn. They spoke of the inconsequential aspects of their day. Carolyn described the progress of their vegetables in the garden, how the baby birds situated in the barn eaves had begun to fly, and some silly thing the old tomcat had done. Carolyn started to mention a letter from her daughter, then changed the subject.

"You might as well tell me. What did it say?"

"It's nothing . . . nothing I want to talk about just yet."

"You're the one who brought it up, so you must want to talk about it." Stella waited, but Carolyn only changed the subject again.

It was later as Stella washed the dishes that she allowed her mind to comb back over the conversation with David in the buggy. Washing dishes always soothed her. It was a quiet task and easily done. Carolyn always cooked and Stella always washed up. But this evening she took longer than usual. She'd find herself holding a plate and wondering if she had washed it or not. When she was finally finished, she draped the towel over the dish drainer and glanced a final time out the window—westward toward Rebecca's farm. As she gazed at the last rays of light spreading out across the sky, she couldn't help wondering if David was sitting beside young Adam Hotstettler as he did his homework and whether or not the young boy was squinting at the text.

D avid wanted to go see Stella the next day and tell her about his grandson, but he had no time. The Old Amish Mill was closed on Mondays, except for the inn, which was always open. Most Amish employees worked Tuesday through Saturday. He knew Stella would be leading groups and working in the market, but he'd once again been pulled away from the ice-house. Actually, Bobo McPherson had come to visit him before the workday had begun. They'd stood on the back porch, looking out over the pond.

"I read your report about the prank yesterday." McPherson was probably in his midthirties. He was most certainly not Amish. His black hair curled at his neck and sometimes flopped into his eyes. And his clothing was somewhat casual—always blue jeans though he wore a crisply ironed cotton button-up shirt with them.

"Certainly I didn't want to get anyone in trouble," David said. "It was harmless enough as pranks go, but it worried me that someone might slip on the ice that had formed on the floor."

"Yes, well. What you couldn't have known is yours was the third report I've received in the last week."

"Did they all involve rubber chickens and red Jell-O?"

McPherson smiled and leaned against the porch railing. "No. As a matter of fact, your report was unique in that aspect."

He hesitated. "Someone switched out the Girls and Boys signs outside the bathrooms at the old schoolhouse last week. They also removed all the brooms from the broom shop and placed them on the porch of the Walnut Street House."

David ran his fingers through his beard. "Sounds like a teenager. Silly things, but nothing that would really hurt anyone."

"I agree. However, it doesn't present the Mill in the best light when visitors walk into a broom house with no brooms."

"Or step into the wrong bathroom."

"Exactly."

McPherson hadn't stopped by simply to chat, so David asked, "What can I do to help?"

"You're new here, so I think you could be objective. You don't have any ties or connections to any of the workers."

"Amish workers?"

"Or *Englisch*. You have no history at all here." Bobo had been studying the pond, but now he turned his attention to David. "You're also quick to respond to a situation appropriately. I saw that when you saved the girl from choking."

"Anyone would have done that."

"Some would have, I suppose. Some wouldn't have known what to do, and some might have stood there in a state of panic. A hesitation of even a minute might have cost that child her life."

David didn't respond. The thought was sobering, and he once again thanked God that he had learned the technique in the first-aid class back in his old community.

"What I'm saying is that I'd like to make you my grounds inspector. Your job will be to walk the property, become familiar with the employees, of course help where you're needed but also report back to me at the end of each day."

David had rather liked his simple job at the icehouse, but he could tell that McPherson was worried. David would hate to see tourism fall off at the Old Amish Mill. He might lose his job just when the income he was giving to Rebecca was needed the most. The crops had been planted by Jacob's brothers, but she was also missing the income from Jacob's side business of fixing broken farm tools. No, now would not be a good time for him to be unemployed. So, he looked at McPherson and said, "Sure, I'd be happy to help."

"Great. You'll start today. Now let's map out a strategy for catching our mischievous culprit."

"Have you alerted the police?"

McPherson hesitated and then said, "Not yet. All police reports make it into our local paper. I don't want the bad publicity."

"But you will, if the situation grows worse?"

"Yes, of course. But my hope is that we can stop whoever is doing this before it reaches that stage."

. . .

David spent the rest of the day walking the property and becoming familiar with areas he hadn't been in. The site had many historic buildings, plus the inn, which was actually more recently constructed but designed to blend in with the structures around it.

McPherson already had a decent plan—that David would check each building at least once a day, look for anything that might be out of the ordinary, and try to win the trust of the other employees. David only dissented in one respect.

"The term *inspector* makes it sound as if I'm checking up on them."

"You are."

"*Ya*, for certain. But perhaps they would take me into their confidence if they thought I was only there to help—which I will be so it's not dishonest."

"You don't like the job title."

David had glanced out toward the road. Stella was walking toward them with the first group of the day. It seemed as if he'd been talking to McPherson for hours, but in fact it had only been thirty minutes. As he watched Stella, he remembered what she'd said the day before— that there should be more employees who could fill in when needed.

"I could be your handyman. That sounds less intimidating, and actually you could use someone who can fill in the gaps, work in any position." He turned his attention from Stella to McPherson and waited.

"Handyman?"

"*Ya.*"

"Sounds like I can pay a handyman less than an inspector." Bobo thrust out his hand.

David shook it, and the deal was sealed.

So he'd spent the day walking the Mill property, talking to employees, and giving them his walkie-talkie channel. "If there's anything you need, call me."

No one did, until an hour before his day was to end.

Then there was a crackle on his walkie-talkie, and Frank Black's voice came over the line. "I'm at the mint distillery. You stopped by earlier today."

"*Ya*, I remember. How are things going, Frank?"

"Not so good, but before I call the police, I thought I'd call you."

"That bad?" David was already reversing course and heading toward the mint distillery, which happened to be across the pond from the icehouse.

"Bad enough."

"I'll be there in five minutes."

He saw Frank before he had skirted the pond.

David had noticed that approximately half the employees at the Mill were Amish—the other half were *Englisch*. He supposed this worked well, especially for filling Sunday shifts—though no doubt some of the *Englisch* wouldn't have wanted to work on the Sabbath either. From what he'd been able to gather, they alternated Sundays when they worked, and McPherson also closed some of the less frequented buildings in the Mill. This way there were enough employees to go around, but no one had to work who strictly did not want to. Again, it reminded David that McPherson was a fair and compassionate employer.

Frank Black was older than David, in fact—he probably could have been David's dad. The whiteness of his hair and lines around his eyes attested to his age. From their earlier visit, David had learned that Frank worked full time into his sixties and then took a part-time job at the Mill over ten years ago. At the moment he was standing outside the mint distillery, and he'd put a Closed sign on the front door. The building wasn't part of the tour, but guests were able to walk the property and stop in if they were interested.

"Thanks for coming so fast."

"It's no problem at all."

"There are fumes coming from the distillery."

"Fumes?"

"Yes, and they are not natural fumes."

David studied the building and sniffed the air, trying to detect anything unusual. His wife had claimed he wouldn't be able to smell a skunk if it walked into the house and sat under their sofa. That might have been an exaggeration. Rebecca had burned the oatmeal just that morning, and he'd certainly smelled that.

"You're certain?"

"Worked in Indiana's largest mint distillery for over twenty years. Yeah, I'm certain."

"All right. Well, let's go in and see what we can find."

CHAPTER 5

As soon as they walked into the main room, David's eyes began to water and shortly after that he felt rather light-headed. He waved to Frank that they should leave. Once outside, he pulled in several deep breaths of air.

"See what I mean?" Frank asked.

"*Ya.* Any idea what's causing it?"

"None." Frank fiddled with his glasses—behind them his blue eyes looked worried. "It's not a natural by-product of the distilling. I'd only just turned the machine on. Plus it's never happened before."

"Did you have a chance to look around?"

"No. By the time I recognized that something was wrong, the fumes were so strong that I had to leave."

At that moment Jimmy Cotton turned a corner round the pond and headed toward them on his riding lawn mower. Jimmy was an *Englisch* teenager who mowed the areas bordering the dirt path, as well as the walking areas around the pond and through the cultivated fields. He mainly worked after school and on Saturday.

David held up his hand, and Jimmy stopped.

The boy was all arms and legs with a good deal of acne thrown in. David didn't envy him that time of life, though he could have told him it wouldn't last. He had good years ahead of him.

Jimmy shut down the motor and pulled out the earbuds that he always wore. Perhaps it helped to shut out the noise of the mower, though the raucous music David heard coming through the small device sounded worse than a mower to him.

"Hi, Jimmy. Could I borrow your—" He put his hand over his nose and mouth to indicate that he wanted the mask Jimmy was wearing.

"This? We're not supposed to use each other's."

"*Ya*, that makes sense, but there's a problem in the mint distillery. I need to cover my mouth and nose . . ."

Jimmy wasn't listening. He'd hopped off the mower, pulled up the seat, and was digging through the items in the storage compartment. Finally he pulled out a package of face masks and handed a clean one to David.

"*Danki.*"

"No problem." Without another word, Jimmy replaced his earbuds, started the mower, and drove away.

"Want me to go in?" Frank asked.

For a moment, David almost said yes. But then he remembered Frank was closing in on his eightieth birthday. While he might know what to look for, the dangers seemed too great.

"I'll just take a look around and then come back and describe it to you."

"Should we call the police or Bobo?"

"Not yet."

McPherson had been quite adamant that he did not want the police involved if it could be helped. Obviously if someone was hurt, they would need to file a report. Otherwise, he wanted David to handle things on his own and report back to him.

"Let me take a look first."

David placed the mask firmly over his mouth and nose and then walked into the distillery. He really had no idea what he was looking for. His eyes once again began to water, but he didn't feel light-headed as he had before. Walking through the main room, he saw nothing out of the ordinary. Then he moved to the room where the actual still was located.

He didn't know a lot about the process, though there were a few distilleries back in Wisconsin. He'd never been involved in harvesting or distilling any of the plants, and he had never tried to grow mint as a crop. His wife had a few spearmint plants here and there in her garden—claimed they helped keep insects away. That thought made him smile. Always Beverly's sweet memory seemed to hover around the edges of his life, comforting him when he needed it most.

He was certainly out of his comfort zone now.

But looking at the machinery, it seemed simple enough to him. Water was added to the bottom chamber of the still and fresh herbs were placed in the middle chamber. Glass tubing collected the steam. The end of the tube emptied the oil extracted into a jar. David didn't know all of this instinctively. Someone had put a flow chart on the wall, no doubt for the guests to read.

So what had gone wrong?

If it happened as soon as Frank turned the still on, then the problem must be in the bottom chamber. There hadn't been enough time for any amount of oil to collect in the jar. He knelt next to the bottom chamber, pulled a handkerchief from his pocket, and dipped it in the liquid. By that point, tears were pouring from his eyes. He knew if he waited much longer, he'd be walking out unable to see a thing. He reached over, shut off the machine, and then hurried outside yanking off the mask as he pulled in a deep breath of the clean April air.

Frank waited while David flushed his eyes from an old hand pump located next to the building.

"Worse than peeling onions," David muttered.

"I thought Amish women did all the cooking." Frank's mouth twitched into a smile as he handed David a clean rag to blot his eyes.

"Often that's true, but during canning season? Any person not busy was fair game. My Beverly could be very persuasive on that point." David reached into his pocket and pulled out the handkerchief he had dipped into the bottom compartment of the still. "What does that smell like to you?"

David took a strong sniff, then held the cloth at arm's length, staring at it incredulously. "Vinegar. No doubt about it."

"I thought so. When you're close to the bottom chamber, the odor is quite strong."

"But I put water in that chamber not an hour ago."

"Explain to me your process."

"Each day after the last of the tourists come through, I fill the pail up with water. Then I do a test run for the next day's visitors. Once I see that everything is working as it should, I shut it down."

"But today everything wasn't working as it should."

"No. No, it wasn't."

"Someone substituted vinegar for your water. It must have happened sometime between when you filled the pail and when you started your test batch."

Frank adjusted his glasses, a look of worry on his face.

"What is it? What are you remembering?"

"I don't think I filled the chamber. I ushered the last visitor out, then hurried over to the barn for a bottle of water. There's a small refrigerator there where we keep drinks and such. My throat was dry from talking, and Bobo doesn't mind if I take a short break when needed."

"I'm sure he doesn't."

"When I returned, I went to put the water into the chamber, but it was already full." Frank shook his head. "I thought I must have done it before I left, but now I'm wondering . . ."

"Maybe someone did it for you. Only they used vinegar instead of water."

Frank glanced left and then right. "But why would anyone do that?"

"Couldn't say. Is there a lock on the door?"

"Yes. I don't use it unless I'm leaving for the day."

"Until you hear back from me, start using it whenever you're gone."

"All right. Thanks, David."

"No problem. I'm glad you called me."

David turned and headed toward the Mill's offices. His reports to McPherson were always verbal, as the

man didn't want any records of what was going on—
not yet, he had said.

His mind cataloged the events of the last few days.
What was bothering him was not what *had* happened,
but what *might* happen next. It seemed that their
prankster had been working solely on the northwest
side of the property, but he was now out of buildings.
If he wanted to attempt new destruction, he'd have to
move toward the center of the property.

And that could spell trouble for their guests.

CHAPTER 6

Stella couldn't remember a Sunday morning when she had felt so unsettled. It had all started when David Stoltzfus greeted her with a wide smile and a rousing *"Gudemariye."* She'd nodded uncertainly and turned to hurry away, but not before she heard David telling his daughter, "Stella is *wunderbaar* with the tour groups. You should see her!"

What had gotten into the man?

Everyone knew that she led the tour groups and no one thought she did a *wunderbaar* job. At least no one had told her that before. David was new to the community. Maybe he didn't realize that she was the black sheep.

That thought popped into her mind before she could pull it back. Black sheep. Was that how she saw herself? It didn't help that the Scripture they read was Isaiah 53:6, "We all, like sheep, have gone astray," and then the sermon focused on hearing God's voice, for "He is the good shepherd."

It was David's fault that she was distracted throughout the entire service.

Did she see herself as a black sheep?

Because she couldn't have children?

They rose to sing. Stella's voice joined those around her. She tried to focus on the words, the tune, the rhythm of the praise to God. But still her mind wandered.

Certainly she wasn't the first woman with a barren womb, though perhaps most women didn't receive the news as young as she had. When she was seventeen and still showed no signs of having her monthly time, her mother had taken her to the doctor. He'd confirmed what Stella had already suspected—she was different. She would never be able to conceive children.

Though she'd barely begun seeing boys, she immediately stopped. What was the point? No Amish boy would want a barren wife. Perhaps *Englischers* could overlook such a thing. Over the years she'd noticed *Englisch* couples who had simply decided not to have children, but among the Amish, having a home full of children was very important. Who would be willing to marry her? *Nein.* She could not put someone else through such tragedy and disgrace. Or so she had thought then.

She sat as the singing ended, though she couldn't remember if they'd sung all the verses. Her sister looked at her curiously, but Stella simply shook her head and stared down at her open Bible.

Later, she'd received some attention from widowed men in the community, but she'd become set in her ways by that point—and perhaps hardened by some perceived rejections. Looking back, she'd never given anyone the chance to reject her.

She'd accepted her fate and decided she was to spend her life alone.

Had she been wrong?

Had she refused to listen to the voice of the Shepherd?

She brushed such foolish thoughts aside as they stood for the final singing. The next hour was spent helping to serve the food, and then suddenly she found herself sitting among the women, eating and listening to the chatter.

Tidbits were shared about their children, their grandchildren, even their nieces and nephews. Yes, the Amish life certainly centered on children. With a start she realized that Rebecca Hotstettler was talking to her, or about her.

"*Ya*, we never realized that Adam wasn't able to see. It was Stella who suggested *Dat* watch him read."

All eyes turned to Stella. She'd just popped a large bite of ham into her mouth and she had to chew around it and swallow before she could answer.

Finally it was Helen Miller, Ethel's mom, who said, "How curious that you would think of it, Stella."

"Yes, well . . ." She stared at her hands and then looked up, surprised to see several women smiling at her. "The guests at the Mill, sometimes the little ones will wear glasses. I saw one last week who couldn't have been three years old, sporting a bright pink pair that was fastened around her head with an elastic strap."

"You don't say?" This from her sister, Carolyn.

"*Ya*, surprised me too. Now and again I'll see one of the older guests peer at our pamphlets and then say they'd forgotten their glasses. I guess my mind put the two things together."

"I'm glad that you did." Rebecca wiped the mouth of

one of the twin girls—was it Sophie or Emma? David had said that Sophie had a small birthmark on the back of her neck. Stella had an urge to ask to hold the child and check. She didn't of course. She rarely held children and probably wouldn't know how to do so properly.

The conversation had turned to happenings at the local schoolhouse, and Stella's mind drifted to other things. She finished her meal, then hurried over to lend a hand with the cleanup. She helped every week, since she had no family to tend other than her sister who was perfectly able to take care of herself. Carolyn was ten years older than Stella. Some days it seemed as if it had always been only the two of them at the old farmstead.

"If you're done wiping that already clean table I thought we might take a walk."

Stella looked up into David's blue eyes. He was holding one of the twins in each arm and had a diaper bag slung over his shoulder. She found herself at a complete loss for how to answer the man. All her usual sharp retorts simply deserted her. "Pardon?"

"The table—" David nodded at the makeshift table, a board that had been set across two sawhorses. "Looks clean."

"*Ya*. I suppose it is." She flicked the dishcloth across the plyboard one last time and tried to regain her composure.

"Would you care for a walk?" He juggled his twin granddaughters, who stared at her with wide blue eyes. "I thought I'd give Rebecca a bit of a break, but it doesn't seem to work unless I leave her immediate area. Otherwise she's wiping their faces, checking their diapers—"

"Being a mother hen."

"Exactly."

Before Stella could think of a reason to say no, David had thrust Emma into her arms. Certainly it was Emma as there was no birthmark below the hem of her *kapp*, and she could see Sophie's strawberry mark from where she stood.

"There's an old blanket stuffed in the diaper bag. I thought we could set the girls down under the shade of the maple tree—should be safe from the breeze there, too, since the barn will block the northern wind."

Stella nodded, completely distracted by the heavenly weight in her arms.

As they walked, she focused on holding the baby correctly. What she wanted to do was smell little Emma's neck, take off her socks and examine her toes, hold her close to her bosom. But she hadn't taken complete leave of her senses, so she chattered with David about the service and the food and then they were standing under the tree.

"Can you hold both while I—"

"Certainly." The two girls stared at each other and then at their grandpa. Sophie waved a pudgy hand at David while Emma proceeded to chew on Stella's *kapp* strings.

David spread the blanket on the ground and then turned to take Sophie. "All right. That should do it. Down you go, baby girl."

Stella sat on the blanket and placed Emma beside her sister. The girls lay on their backs, staring up at the new green leaves of the trees. Emma reached for her foot and attempted to pull it toward her mouth. David gave them each a toy from the bag he was carrying. Emma immediately tried to chew hers; whereas, Sophie pressed hers against her ear.

"I told you," David said, smiling. "It's as if Emma is exploring the world through taste—"

"And Sophie through sound."

"Exactly." David leaned back on his elbows.

Though Stella had spent a lot of time arguing with David Stoltzfus in her mind, she hadn't actually allowed herself to study him much. Now, with him preoccupied with the grandbabies, she did. His blue eyes were the color of the sky—clear and serene, if eyes could reflect such things. His beard was mostly gray, owing to his age, which he had told her was fifty-two, but his hair looked like that of a younger man. There was still more brown than gray. He was a few feet taller than Stella, probably topping her five-foot-six height by a good three inches. And although he wasn't thin, neither had he gained the large belly that many older men did.

There was a scar above his lip, and somehow it kept him from being too good-looking. It made him seem like a normal guy. She wondered how he'd come by it, but then felt foolish. She had no business asking David about his scars.

Out of the blue, David said, "Rebecca tells me you've never married."

"*Nein.*"

"It's a shame."

"I . . . I couldn't have children," she said, and then she wondered what had caused her to share such a thing.

"You would have made a *gut fra.*"

Stella shrugged and retrieved the rattle that Emma had tossed to the side. Perhaps it was because she was holding the little child's toy, or it could have been the way the sun was slanting through the leaves, but suddenly she wanted to know about David. She wanted to know his past, his joys, and his heartaches.

"Tell me about your *fra.*"

"Beverly?" The smile on David's face widened until his eyes were nearly closed. "We met when I first moved to Wisconsin, a lad of nineteen. Our family is originally from the Ohio area, but I set out looking for something different."

Stella nodded as if she understood.

"I suppose I found it, as Beverly was about as different as you could imagine. She had red hair for one—"

"That explains Rebecca's strawberry blonde."

"It does. Our boys—all five of them—"

"You had five boys?"

"*Ya.* A big group around the table, especially as they grew older and started to bring friends to dinner. Each of them, even Rebecca, had the reddish tint, which they inherited from their mother. Not a common sight in an Amish community."

Emma began to fuss, so Stella reached forward and picked up the babe. Such a simple thing to do, but she couldn't fathom that it came natural to her. She had helped with her nieces and nephews, but that had been years ago.

"Beverly was a *gut* wife, and I loved her dearly."

"What happened?"

"Cancer . . . of the ovaries. It's been five years now."

"I'm sorry."

"So am I. When one dies we say their life is complete, and I suppose hers was. She was happy and content, even through the final months." David leaned forward and caught Emma's foot causing her to laugh. "I think it helped that she was surrounded by her family—all of our *kinner* were home when she died. Their love comforted her, like a quilt on a cold winter's day."

Stella didn't respond. She could picture it—a redheaded Amish woman, burrowed under a quilt and surrounded on all sides by her children.

"Your family has experienced its share of tragedy."

"I suppose, but then haven't we all?" David ran his hand over the top of Sophie's head. "I would never wish for my *doschder* to walk this road of single parenthood. But her husband's untimely death has brought me closer to these two."

"I'm surprised she didn't move back to Wisconsin."

David laughed at that. "Rebecca never was fond of the outhouses we still use."

"Understandable."

"It is. But more than that, I think she has come to see this community here in Nappanee as her home. She'd rather not take the twins away from Jacob's family, who have been a real help to her."

"And yet you felt the need to move here and help."

"I wanted to be with her during this time."

"How long will you stay?" The question popped out of her mouth before she could snatch it back.

"As long as I'm needed, I suppose."

Stella realized that was no answer at all. It could be a month or until the children were grown and married.

David was watching something over Stella's shoulder. He stood and said, "Rebecca's trying to get my attention. I suppose it's time to get these two gals home for their naps."

As they carried the babies and blanket and diaper bag back toward the main group, Stella thought of what a strange day it had turned out to be. She'd started the day feeling out of sorts, but now her mood was curiously relaxed—even after passing an hour with David Stoltzfus. Truly surprising, but then life had taken more curious turns. She supposed that the two of them could go back to being adversaries when they returned to work on Tuesday.

CHAPTER 7

Since the Old Mill was closed on Mondays, Stella spent the day at home helping Carolyn with the laundry and cleaning.

As they hung their clothes and sheets on the line, Carolyn said, "I noticed you enjoying some time with David."

"He needed help with the twins."

"I'm not criticizing you, Stella. It was *gut* to see you relaxing."

Stella sniffed. By the time she'd returned home from church, she'd come to her senses. No doubt folks were talking about what a fool she was—sitting alone with David on a blanket! Of course the twins had been there, but still, she wasn't sure it was entirely appropriate. What had caused her to say yes? She wouldn't fall for his smooth charm or blue eyes again. No, she'd be on her guard and keep a good, healthy distance from the man in the future.

But as she hung laundry, changed their bed linens, and scrubbed the bathroom, her mind kept returning to the feel of Emma in her arms, Sophie's sweet smile, and how David was completely smitten with his granddaughters. Even the young boy . . . what was his name? Adam. Even Adam had come up to her as she was leaving and given her a plate of cookies that his *mamm* had kept in her buggy.

"I go to the eye doctor next week," he said.

"Is that so?"

"*Ya. Daddi* says it will help me to read."

"I imagine it will."

"Have you ever worn glasses?"

"*Nein.*"

The boy frowned and stared at the ground.

"But my nephew does. He lives over in Goshen, and he's worn them for many years now."

"Can he still play ball?"

"Well he's a *dat* now and not quite as good with a bat and ball as he once was . . . but yes, he does still play with the *youngie.*"

Adam's expression changed to one of relief. He thanked her and ran off toward his mother. She'd replayed the conversation in her mind several times and found herself praying that the boy's vision was easily corrected.

As she carried the mop to the back porch, she noticed Carolyn sitting at the kitchen table, the day's mail spread out before her.

"A letter from one of the girls?"

"*Ya.*" Carolyn regularly received letters from her children. The two girls wrote the most—they had married and moved to Pennsylvania. One son had purchased a farm in Goshen, and four other sons were in Ohio. Her family had spread out like so many leaves in the wind.

Usually she shared the letters, but today she quickly folded the page and stuffed it under the pile of circulars. "Rebecca's cookies are *gut*—oatmeal and chocolate chip."

Stella poured a glass of milk and sat down across from Carolyn.

"Are you looking forward to work tomorrow?"

"I suppose."

Carolyn leaned forward. "You don't have to continue to work, Stella. Not if you don't want to."

"I'm not shirking my responsibility."

"But it's not needed—not strictly speaking. We'd get by fine with what we make off the fields. The King boy—"

"He's past thirty, Carolyn."

"Yes, well, he tells me the yield will be *gut* this year. If you don't want to work you shouldn't."

Stella felt prickly again. It felt good, like putting on a pair of shoes that were worn out and comfortable. "And what of next year? If I quit my job and then we need income—"

"The Lord provides." Carolyn reached for another cookie. "As He has since we've been here alone."

How had that happened? Not so long ago the house had been filled with the sounds of her parents, Carolyn's husband, and their seven children. Carolyn's husband died of a heart attack—late one fall afternoon they'd found him in the fields, lying among the tall stalks of corn, his expression one of utter peace. Their parents had passed within a few months of each other. Now they were alone. So much for Amish families remaining close.

That was an uncharitable thought and she knew it.

The children had been faithful to send money and they visited as often as possible.

It wasn't their fault that they had a widowed mother and an old-maid aunt living back at the farmstead.

Some days it seemed to Stella that she had been a burden to others all of her life. She sighed and pushed away from the table. "The last of the laundry should be dry. I'll fetch it."

"Before you go . . ." It wasn't like her sister to hesitate when she had something to say. The oldest child in their family, Carolyn seemed more like a mother to Stella than a sister in many ways. They had four brothers between them—all now living in Ohio. How had their family become so scattered?

"I had heard there was some trouble at the Mill."

Stella felt her spine stiffen. "It's not like you to listen to gossip—"

"Honestly, Stella. You can be so sensitive sometimes." Carolyn broke her cookie in quarters and popped a piece in her mouth. "No one was gossiping. One of the women mentioned a chicken in the icehouse."

"A childish prank."

"And the switching of the restroom signs."

"I didn't see it myself."

"Also some nonsense with the brooms?"

Stella sighed. "I don't know. Maybe someone has spring fever. Maybe one of our boys is indulging their *rumspringa*."

"You think it's an Amish person?"

"Or maybe . . ." Stella clasped her hands and stared down at them. "Maybe it was an *Englischer* who doesn't like the horse droppings on the road or waiting behind a buggy driver."

"I know there have been some complaints, but nothing recently."

"No, it's been a while since the proposition to diaper our horses came before the city council."

"And it failed as it should. Our city leaders might not be Amish, but they seem to have a reasonable head on their shoulders." She finished her cookie and then asked, "So you have no idea?"

"I only lead the tours, Carolyn. I don't run the Mill."

"You're bright though, and you listen and pay attention. I'd think if anyone knew, you would."

Stella shrugged. She'd received more compliments in the last week than she'd been given in the last ten years. Or was she just now noticing them?

"*Danki,*" she said belatedly.

"Did you know about David's new job?"

"New job?" Stella's heart kicked into a faster rhythm. Was David leaving the Mill? Wouldn't he have mentioned it the day before?

Carolyn proceeded to tell her how he had joked about his "handyman" title and that he would be working in various positions as needed.

Stella didn't know what to make of that, so she repeated that she hadn't heard a thing and headed outside to retrieve the laundry.

She glanced back when she reached the door. Carolyn had pulled the letter out from the stack of mail and was once again lost in its contents.

What was in the letter that was of such interest to her?

And why would Bobo McPherson have given David a new job? He hadn't been at the Mill long enough to warrant a promotion. And anyway, handyman didn't sound like much of a promotion.

No, she suspected something else was going on. David's job had changed at the same time that the incidents were increasing. That couldn't be a coincidence. So had McPherson asked David to spy on the other employees? And had he said yes?

The thought bothered her. She'd finally let her guard down. If she were honest with herself, she was beginning to like and trust David Stoltzfus. Now she didn't know what to do with this new information.

Of course it was none of her business—but then again in a small community, what affected one affected another. With that thought in mind, she determined that the next day she would begin her own private search for an explanation for the strange happenings occurring at the Mill.

CHAPTER 8

David was surprised when he looked up and saw Stella hurrying toward him. The day had turned cool for April and a light rain was falling.

He stepped onto the porch of the Oak Street House and waited for her. There was no doubt she was walking in his direction, unless she'd felt a sudden need to take a tour of the one-room schoolhouse, which was directly across from him. He couldn't think of a thing she'd want to see there or in the Oak Street House, which was a representation of one of the local homes from the 1800s.

"David, I wasn't sure I'd find you. Seems I was destined to lag ten minutes behind wherever you were—"

He was actually pleased that she was looking for him. Perhaps she had softened toward him after their walk on Sunday—though on Tuesday she'd refused to even return his greeting.

"*Ya*, they've had me quite busy today. A squirrel loose in the soda fountain shop, molasses spilled in the blacksmith shop . . ." He pulled off his hat and scratched his head. That last one still made no sense to him.

"Word is that you have a new job title."

"Oh, that." David wondered how much McPherson would want him to share, but then this was Stella. Surely she needed to know what was going on. She led morning tours all over the property. Besides, nothing would remain a secret for long with so many employees. It was probably best she heard the details from him. "It's true, though I'm not sure how much help I am. Trouble seems to pop up in a different corner of the property faster than I can clean up after it."

"Trouble? What kind of trouble?"

They were standing near the porch rail, but now the light rain had turned to a downpour, and they stepped back at the same moment, their shoulders brushing up against one another. Stella took two steps away and repeated, "What kind of trouble?"

He told her about the previous incidents, and McPherson's idea that he might be able to fend off real trouble.

"He wants you to spy on employees?"

"*Nein*. That's not it at all. It's only that he thought I could see things more objectively. Honestly, none of what has happened makes any sense to me. It's all very random. My guess would still be the *youngie*."

"Amish?"

"Or *Englisch*. I couldn't say."

Stella folded her arms across her chest. "I'm glad I asked. It seems to me that you need the insight of someone who has lived here awhile, someone who could make connections you couldn't possibly know about. I might be able to help."

"Help is one thing I can always use."

"I'll keep my eyes open on my tours."

"And during your shifts in the bakery. Perhaps our culprit has a sweet tooth."

Stella gave him a reproving look. He wasn't surprised that she was taking the situation seriously. He tended toward a more casual outlook. Other than the vinegar in the distillery, it didn't seem to him that anyone was causing any real harm. There were certainly plenty of worse things that could have happened.

As if to prove his line of reasoning wrong, the day took a drastic turn. At that very moment, shouts and cries rang out from across the lane.

He and Stella both stepped forward and saw young Ethel Miller standing inside the schoolhouse with her face pressed against a pane of glass in one of the schoolroom windows. She was hollering and waving her arms, apparently trying to get their attention.

Without another word, they both began running through the rain. Stella ran up onto the front porch of the schoolhouse. David hurried to the side window where Ethel continued to holler. He ignored the rain that was falling in sheets, soaking him through to the bone.

"What's wrong?" he shouted.

"The doors. They're stuck! We can't get out."

"Front door?"

"Won't budge."

"How about the back?"

Ethel shook her head. Now that he was closer, he could see the guests behind her. Some stood in groups, looking perplexed. Others were trying to open some of the windows, but the humidity had caused the old wooden casings to swell.

He hurried back to the front porch. Stella was rattling the door. "It seems to be stuck."

"Not stuck, jammed." David knelt in front of the lock. "Look. Someone has locked the mechanism and then broken off a piece of metal inside of it. We'll need a locksmith."

"How are we going to get them out?"

David shrugged. "I'll check the back."

What he found there caused his blood to boil. Someone had taken a rope and tied one end to the doorknob, the other end to an old water pump that was beside the porch but toward the front of the house. The result was a tension in the rope that couldn't be lessened without disconnecting the rope. No wonder they couldn't open the door. David pulled out his pocketknife. It took several moments to saw through the rope, which was new and stiff. By the time Stella had joined him at the back door, the rope had surrendered to his knife's blade.

The door opened easily, and he stepped inside.

Ethel hurried over to speak with them. "I don't know what happened. We came in and everything was fine."

"This is not acceptable." One of the male guests stepped forward and interrupted them. "My name is Ethan Avery, and you can be sure I will be contacting the city and possibly the police about this."

Two more families approached him, and from the corner of his eye, David saw an older woman walking in through the back door.

"I was in the outhouse. What happened?"

"We were locked inside, if you can you imagine that."
This from an *Englisch* grandmother who wore a T-shirt
that said *I'm a grandma. What's your superpower?*

"It's nothing to worry about, Mrs. Benson." Stella
hurried over to the older woman with long gray hair
pulled back with a simple band.

David noticed she was a small thing, rather like a
bird. He also noticed the thin scar along her neck. His
aenti back in Wisconsin had one of those from when
her thyroid was removed.

"I didn't know you were visiting us today," Stella said.

"Is that a crime? I suppose I can visit any day I want."

"Yes, of course you can."

"Why would anyone do such a thing?" Mr. Avery
was still standing directly in front of David, as if to
block his exit. He pulled out his cell phone and began
to tap away. "And why would you allow it?"

"I can't say as we're allowing it." David worked to
keep his tone pleasant.

"Hoodlums probably. You can't win against people
like that." This from Mrs. Benson. "I only went to visit
the outhouse—which you have remodeled nicely, I
might add. Still, I could have been locked out from the
group, and you all could have been locked inside for
hours. The world is a dangerous place."

Stella attempted to reason with the guests, but David
stepped to the front of the room and held up his hands.
"We're sorry for any inconvenience and hope that you
have enjoyed your time here at the Mill."

"We were locked inside a one-room schoolhouse. I
wouldn't call that enjoyable, and I still want to know

how such a thing could have possibly happened." Mr. Avery finished tapping on his phone and stuck it back into his pocket.

David began to answer, though he had no idea what to say, when he looked outside and saw that the motorized trolleys had arrived. They were only used during the rain or when they had a handicapped guest who needed transportation assistance. "Your ride is here and will take you back to the shop and bakery, and I'm happy to inform you it's a covered vehicle—so you'll be able to remain dry. Be careful as you leave that you don't slip in the mud."

The rain had lightened, but everyone still seemed appreciative for the ride. No doubt they were ready for hot coffee and pie.

David pulled out his walkie-talkie and called maintenance. When he finished speaking with them, he was surprised to see that Stella was still there. He joined her at the window, watching the trolley make its way along the wet but still hard-packed dirt trail.

"These incidents—they're all connected," she said.

"Probably."

"Then we need to catch whoever is doing them. The Mill doesn't need this kind of publicity." She paused, tapping her fingertips against the windowsill, as if she needed to buy time. Finally she said, "Most people in Nappanee enjoy and support the Mill, but not everyone. We've had our fair share of battles over the years. I would hate to see this facility close over these sorts of incidents. More than half the employees are Amish. The jobs help our community."

"Why would we close?"

"The public's opinion is fickle and nothing stays the same in this life."

"The older woman you were speaking to—" David traced a finger across his throat, indicating her scar.

"Mrs. Benson."

"She seemed particularly upset. What's her connection to the Mill?"

"We used to see her a lot here on the property, but in the last few years, not as much. She's old and widowed. Perhaps she's bored."

"Idle hands—"

"Are the devil's playground. *Ya.* I heard that one too. But Mrs. Benson doesn't strike me as being capable of such things. No, I think it's being done by a person with a plan. Maybe someone wants to purchase the property to put up a new hotel. It seems I read about them wanting highway property. It could be that they offered to buy the place and the owners said no."

"Huh."

"Or maybe someone would like to build a golf course."

"Golfing?"

"There was a developer a few years back, he offered one of our farmers three million dollars for his eighty-acre property, but the farmer—who was Amish—turned him down. The developer did not accept losing gracefully."

David ran his thumbs under his suspenders. "I haven't thought about it to that extent. We didn't have much tourism in our Wisconsin community."

"Well it's big business here. Amish are big business whether we like it or not. Sometimes that's okay and we can live in harmony. But sometimes there is dissension between Amish and *Englisch*. Whenever that has happened—we always back off."

"Because we want to remain separate."

"*Ya.*"

They were both silent for a few moments. When Stella turned and looked up at him, David felt something stir in his heart. There was a certain quality about Stella, a strength which might be disguised as bitterness. He thought that beneath the exterior shell was a beautiful and caring woman.

"I want to help," she said. "I care about this place and I want to help you catch whoever is doing this."

And so they became partners in solving the crimes at the Old Amish Mill.

CHAPTER 9

Stella met with David each day at lunch. He would share with her any odd events that had happened in the previous twenty-four hours, and they would try to discern any connection between them. It became the favorite part of her day, the hour that she looked forward to most.

The day after the schoolhouse incident the lights went out suddenly in the gift shop. Guests and employees were plunged into darkness until the breaker box could be located. They couldn't determine what had caused the breaker to flip.

"It might have been an accident," David said.

"Doubtful since we haven't had this many accidents in ten years." She felt as if a clock were ticking somewhere, ticking down to a terrible event that she couldn't imagine.

Things were quiet for the next three days. Though Stella remained worried, David began to think perhaps they'd imagined a conspiracy when there had been none.

"Perhaps it has simply been a run of bad luck," he said as they sat on a picnic bench sharing cheese and sausage and crackers.

She didn't answer him then. She was thinking how her life had changed since David came to work at the Mill. She found herself humming as she went about her tasks, and she was certainly less irritated by young Ethel. She had even sewn a spring dress to replace one of the old worn ones she should have cut up for quilt squares years ago.

She began to hope that perhaps her life had found some peaceful, natural pattern and maybe the problems at the Mill would disappear.

But the following week dispelled any possibilities of that.

The animals were let out of the hog house.

Bees were stirred up and chased one man across the property. Some of the bees had to be moved to a different hive as the first had been bludgeoned with a bat. They'd had to call in a beekeeper to relocate the queen.

The wooden hand pump, which connected the open well with the milk house, was broken in two. The basement of the house was flooded and one guest slipped on the steps, spraining an ankle.

"Perhaps it's time to file a report with the police," she suggested.

David stared down into his cup of coffee. "That's McPherson's decision. I don't know that we need more folks traipsing around watching us work though. There are city officials here nearly every day now. You can't walk ten minutes without tripping over someone with a city badge and a clipboard."

David's mood was sour, which was unusual. She

wanted to reach out and touch his shoulder, to comfort him somehow, but she didn't.

Instead she said, "We simply need to look over all of your reports one more time."

"Sure. You're right." He looked at her and smiled, and all was right with her world in spite of the mysterious happenings.

"I'll bring them tomorrow, to lunch. Maybe you can spot something I haven't been able to see."

That luncheon was destined not to happen though. They had barely sat down to eat the next day when David's walkie-talkie suddenly squawked and a grim voice came over the line. "David, I'm at the back of the wetlands." Sixty-five acres had been set aside for a Federal Wetlands Reserve. Several times a week, Joe Briar led a group of bird watchers along a trail through the area.

"We have a fire here. I've contacted the fire department. I need you to get the trolleys over here so we can evacuate these folks. Do it fast."

David began to run toward the maintenance building where the trolleys were kept. Already Stella could hear the sirens of the fire engines coming down the road. She stood there, helpless, and watched David jump on one of the trolleys and begin to drive it toward the fire. It wasn't natural to run toward a fire—that was something you ran away from. Why did he have to be the hero? Why couldn't he have sent someone else?

Though they'd had rain recently, the grasses were high on that portion of the property. She'd once seen a grass fire, and it had burned incredibly fast. Already

David was a mere dot in the distance as folks began to come out of the building to see what the sirens were about.

A part of Stella's heart ached even as her pulse raced.

Why had she let herself care about this man?

What if something happened to him?

What if she was once again plunged into the loneliness and bitterness that had defined her life before?

Stella hurried to the bakery, assured customers that the fire was on the other side of the pond and they were safe. She filled orders and made change and wiped down shelves. She did her job, and as she worked she allowed doubt and fear to seep in and control her outlook.

She'd made up her mind by the time she walked to her buggy. Employees were abuzz with news of the fire, which had been put out by the local fire department. No one was hurt, but Ethel had heard one of the city officials tell McPherson that if another incident occurred, the place would be shut down. They cited all sorts of city ordinances as well as a few OSHA regulations. Stella didn't even know what OSHA was until someone pointed out the poster in their workroom. Occupational Safety and Health Administration. She wondered if OSHA would help them find new jobs.

Another nail of fear slammed into her thoughts.

Another part of her heart turned back toward expecting little from life but trouble and heartache.

It was then David caught up with her, as she was about to climb into her sister's buggy—her *sister's*. She'd never even owned her own horse. Her entire life had been possible solely because of the charity of others.

David had soot smudged across his face. Dirt marked his sleeves and pants. She could make out a small blister on the back of his right hand. And still he smiled.

That smile sealed their fate.

She understood in that moment how different they truly were.

"I wanted to catch up with you. Let you know everything is fine."

She nodded but didn't answer, didn't trust herself to speak.

"One more thing to add to our analysis of events, which I suppose we'll have to postpone until tomorrow."

"I can't—"

He stopped talking, cocked his head, and studied her.

"I'm busy at lunch tomorrow." She wasn't but she could be. It wasn't exactly a lie.

"Oh. Maybe afterward then."

She shook her head. How could she explain to him what she'd been through the last four hours? He'd been fighting a fire and she'd dismantled her life, seeing what a fool she had been to think that she could start over.

"What's wrong, Stella?" David stepped closer.

Stella stepped back, bumping into the side of the buggy. "I have to stop seeing you."

"Seeing me?"

"The lunches . . . the shared rides home . . . the walks after church. It all has to stop."

"Stop?" He took off his hat now and ran his fingers through his hair.

She'd noticed it was something he did when he was stumped. The look on his face almost made her relent, but she closed her eyes and resolved to hold firm. "I have to go, David."

He reached for her arm, and she practically batted him away.

"If you have to go, okay. But tell me what's wrong. Tell me what's happened since I saw you four hours ago."

Tears stung her eyes, and when she tried to speak, words caught in her throat.

"I can see you're upset. Let me help."

"You can't help me. Don't you understand? I'm hopeless." When he tried to argue, she held up a hand. "I'm not one of your projects, David. I'm not a puzzle you can solve. I'm a woman, and though my life might not be good, it is my life. It's what I have, what I've always had, and I was foolish to think that things could change now."

"But they can change—"

"They cannot!" Her voice rose in anger, and she fought to bring it back down. "You are an old fool, and I almost followed you down some reckless path. We're not *youngie*. We're old, David. Now I don't want to talk about it, and I don't want to see you again unless it's in passing. Please, just leave me alone."

Stella hopped into the buggy, released the brake, and called out to the mare. As she made her way across the property and out onto the two lane, she swiped at the tears running down her cheeks. Pain was something she was used to. It was hope that was difficult to bear.

She stared straight down the road and didn't give David even one backward glance.

CHAPTER 10

A week later David still had no idea why Stella wasn't speaking to him. He gave her space, as it seemed that was what she wanted. But he thought of her constantly. He wondered if he had said or done something to hurt her. He prayed that God would soften her heart.

On Friday he was once again late leaving work. They were all under increased pressure from city officials, and he had been called a dozen times to different buildings by disgruntled employees. Mostly people wanted assurance that they were following the city ordinances to the letter, and in the majority of cases they were.

But the officials that he and McPherson had spoken with weren't concerned with the intent of their laws. They were in full defense mode, and they were combing over the ordinances carefully, looking at anything that could possibly be perceived as noncompliance.

An Exit sign with a flickering bulb.

Emergency exit plans that had grown a bit faded or were not displayed as prominently as a fire chief might suggest.

A step that wasn't marked with caution tape.

Any of several dozen rules could sink them. The

sad part was that David had been into other establishments that didn't do half of what they had done to ensure employee and guest safety. But the other establishments weren't the ones under the microscope. The Old Amish Mill was. If they had any hope of staying open, then they had to persevere through this difficult time and do so together.

He stopped to drop off his report for the day—they were now filing everything on triplicate paper forms so that they would have back-up evidence of all they'd done to comply with the city regulations.

He neatly wrote down the day's activities, then signed the sheets and put them in McPherson's mailbox. His own box was typically empty, as folks usually just called him on the walkie-talkie. But when he glanced over at it, he saw a single envelope with his name scrawled in black ink on the outside. Turning it over, he was surprised to see it was sealed.

He broke the seal, pulled out the paper, and then sank into a chair as he read the seven lines.

> *I told you that you couldn't win.*
> *Go home, David. Go to New York.*
> *Immerse yourself in your plain and fancy life.*
> *Even Joseph Stein can't rebuild what has been destroyed.*
> *It is time for these acres to lie fallow.*
> *It is time for a genuine jubilee.*
> *It is time for the soil to rest.*

He read the note again, but it made no sense. Perhaps

Stella could make sense of it. Though she still remained angry at him, more like her old self than the woman who had been helping him these last few weeks, he felt a strong desire to show it to her and to ask her opinion.

He glanced out the window. Sunlight faded across the fields and darkness pushed its way over the land. The day had slipped away. He would be walking home again, and his route happened to go directly by Stella's farm.

He tucked the letter into his pants pocket and hurried out into the night. The miles fell away as he thought of the words written on the sheet of paper. Why address it to him instead of McPherson? The first line, "I told you that you couldn't win," made it sound as if he knew the person. Could he have met the person responsible for the recent destruction at the Old Amish Mill?

He turned down Stella's lane and nearly changed his mind. A single light shone from a back window. Perhaps she'd gone to bed early. Maybe she was sick. Should he be bothering her? She had said she didn't want to see him anymore except in passing.

But this was different.

Even as his mind struggled with the wisdom of visiting Stella, his feet hurried down the lane and up the steps of the front porch. He knocked softly on the door and waited. A lantern was lit in the front room, and then the door opened, but it was Carolyn who answered.

"David. Is something wrong?" She held up another small battery-powered lantern to get a better look at his face.

"Yes. Maybe. Is Stella here? I'd like to speak to her."

Carolyn glanced over her shoulder and then back at David. "She's here, but . . ." Carolyn pushed the screen door open and then stepped onto the porch.

She walked to the railing, set the lantern down, and stood facing out toward the night. Carolyn was in her sixties and her skin was wrinkled from years of being in the sun, of being a farmer's wife. There was a softness about her though. She seemed a gentle soul. David wondered about their life here—two women living alone. Were they content? Did they have other options?

When David joined her at the railing, she glanced up at him. Her arms were crossed but a smile played across her lips. David thought her expression was tinged with sadness, but he could have been imagining it.

"Stella's life has been difficult."

David didn't know how to respond to that, so he remained silent.

"She told you why she never married?"

He nodded, and then added, "Weeks ago. That first Sunday she sat with me and helped with the twins. Such a thing though—it doesn't matter at our age."

"Indeed. And yet after she learned that she couldn't have children, when she was only a young woman, she withdrew from life. Stella practically embraced being alone, and she cultivated a bitter attitude." Carolyn ran her hand back and forth across the porch railing. "Perhaps that was my fault. I was already married with a houseful of *kinner*. I must have been a daily reminder of what she'd never have."

"*Gotte's wille*," David said softly, because he felt he should say something.

"I suppose. And yet a difficult path, especially for one so young. She lived with my parents—here. Then as they grew older, my husband and I moved here to help with the land. We'd been leasing a place on the other side of town."

Carolyn's voice had grown soft, and David knew she was remembering that other place, her husband, and the sound of small feet running through the house.

"For many years, this house was full of life and laughter and even some sadness. But we had each other to lean on. The last few years—well, they have been filled with loss. First my husband, then our parents. By then, my daughters and sons had married and moved to farms of their own. And so it's been just me and Stella."

David's mind and imagination easily captured the scenes that Carolyn was describing, but another part of him was thinking of the letter in his pocket. He needed to speak with Stella.

"I've enjoyed Stella's friendship," he said. "She's a special woman, and I do . . . I do care for her. I thought maybe she cared for me, but the last few days she has been—"

"Afraid. She has been afraid, David."

Any response stuck in his throat. He finally managed to ask, "Of what?"

"Of being left alone again. Of caring too much. Of seeing yet another life slip through her fingers." Carolyn's head bowed for a moment, perhaps in prayer. Finally she turned to him, patted his arm, and then asked, "Are you sure you want to come in?"

Her eyes sparkled with good humor, and David found himself smiling and following her into the house.

They walked through a sitting room that was immaculate, something he could see even though the lamp was set to low and cast shadows across the floor. He thought of his daughter's house, of the chaos and liveliness there. Of the laughter and tears and small arms clasped around his neck. Would Stella want to share that life with him? Would she be willing to trade this for that? The thought should have surprised him, but he knew in that moment that he had been considering it for weeks. He'd even gone as far as to speak with his daughter. She was keen on him pursuing the relationship. David had been on the verge of doing just that when Stella had broken off their friendship.

Maybe she'd been able to sense his growing feelings for her. She was a perceptive woman. Maybe his feelings had frightened her.

What did he actually have to offer her?

And how could he banish her fears?

Then they entered the kitchen, and Stella looked up from her needlework. Perhaps she hadn't heard his knock. Maybe she didn't realize her sister had stepped outside. For whatever reason, her expression was one of complete surprise and even joy at seeing him. Then her mind caught up with her heart, and it was as if a shade was quickly pulled down over her features.

David knew in that moment that if he was to win Stella's heart, it would not be easy. In fact, only God could cut through such deeply ingrained fear and heartache. Their road might be tough. But then, much of what was worth having was difficult to come by. Fortunately, David was a patient and persistent man.

CHAPTER 11

Stella carefully stored her needle into the pillowcase she was embroidering for her niece. She didn't look up at David again. She couldn't find the courage to meet his gaze.

Carolyn said, "I'll be in the sitting room if you need me."

And then Stella was left alone with the man who had filled her thoughts for days.

Her cheeks burned with embarrassment. "Why are you here?"

"Because I needed to see you." He hesitated and then motioned toward the chair across from her.

She nodded, though she still had trouble meeting his eyes. Instead she glanced around the kitchen, her sister's kitchen. Her eyes landed on the dish drain. It held two plates, two forks, and two knives. Suddenly she remembered something her mother had often said. "Mistakes are like knives—they serve you or cut you, depending on how you use them."

She remembered her mother—her kindness and wisdom. She thought of how much she cared for David, and how embarrassed she would be to apologize. But what was more important? Her pride? Or her future? She knew what she should do, and she prayed God would give her the courage to say what needed to be said.

"I'm sorry. I'm sorry I spoke to you as I did. I was cruel and ungrateful, and I wish that I would learn to hold my tongue." She stopped, wondering if she'd said too much.

But David merely smiled, reached across the table, and covered her hands with his. "We're all allowed a bad day, Stella. I want us to be friends, to be more than friends if you want the truth."

Her eyes widened, but David only laughed. "And if you cannot be honest with me when you're having a bad day, then who can you be honest with?"

She shook her head. "But that doesn't excuse—"

"You apologized, and I accept your apology. What more is there to say?"

She only stared at him, her heart tapping out a too-fast rhythm. Then David's face turned serious, and he pulled an envelope from his pocket.

"But tonight I came here for a different reason. There's something I want to show you."

She studied the outside of the envelope as well as the note. She read it twice, then a third time. Finally she pointed toward the first line.

I told you that you couldn't win.

"Perhaps this person has spoken to you before."

"Maybe. I can't remember. There's something in the back of my mind, but I can't put my finger on it."

"And this—" She tapped the second line.

Go home, David. Go to New York.

"It's curious since you're not from New York. Everyone knows you're from Wisconsin."

"Maybe not everyone."

"Our community isn't so large," she reminded him. "But look . . ." She turned the page around so that he could better see it and she was reading upside down.

"This next line—*plain and fancy life*—has to be speaking of the musical. The writer is speaking of the show that is performed in the Round Barn each evening."

"And Joseph Stein?"

"The author of the original book—*Plain and Fancy*."

"I haven't read it," David admitted.

"The show is a big success in *Englisch* circles."

"Is it now?"

"*Ya*. Auditions for the cast are actually held in New York City."

"Now you're pulling my beard."

"I'm not. The casting auditions have always been in New York. They bring in some of the best talent in the country."

"To perform at our little Round Barn?"

Stella laughed. "It's odd, I'll admit, but as we know, Amish tourism can bring big money to a community."

She tapped the words *New York* on the note. "Perhaps the play explains the reference."

David sat back and ran his fingers through his beard. "I haven't seen the play myself, but these last four lines— they don't seem to be referring to a play. They seem to speak of something else entirely."

Stella stood, murmured, "Wait here," and hurried from the room. When she returned she was carrying a well-worn Bible. "It's in Leviticus. I'm sure of it, but I can't remember the chapter or verse."

"The year of jubilee."

"*Ya.* Exactly."

He moved next to her, his fingers following hers down the page until they both paused over the tenth verse of the twenty-fifth chapter. "Consecrate the fiftieth year and proclaim liberty throughout the land to all its inhabitants. It shall be a jubilee for you; each of you is to return to your family property and to your own clan."

Stella sank into the chair beside him. For a moment neither of them spoke, and then she asked, "Do you usually check your mailbox at night?"

"*Nein.* Most days, I do so first thing in the morning, but I was late turning in my report, and then as I put the report into McPherson's box I noticed the letter in mine."

"So whoever did this, whoever left it, didn't expect for you to find it until tomorrow morning."

They stared at one another, realization dawning in Stella's mind at the same time that David stood, nearly knocking over his chair.

"We have to get to the theater."

"We can take my buggy."

"I'll go and hitch it up."

Carolyn said she'd stay up until they returned and spend the time praying for their safety.

It was with her sister's words of comfort echoing in her mind that Stella climbed into the buggy beside David. Though it was Carolyn's buggy, David drove.

And when they reached the end of the lane, she pointed in the opposite direction of the Mill.

"There's a phone shack only a quarter of a mile down the road."

David nodded in agreement, but when they'd reached it, he didn't call the police. It didn't seem they had enough to go on yet—only suspicions and weakly drawn conclusions. Instead he dialed McPherson's number, which he'd memorized the day he'd first taken on his new job as handyman.

"What did he say?" Stella asked as they hurried back to the buggy.

"He'll meet us at the theater. He knows someone on the police force, a friend of his. Said he'd ask this man to meet us there as well."

As the mare clip-clopped down the road, forcing them to slow down when Stella would have liked to run, she again remembered her sister's words. "*I will pray until you return.*"

She would do well to follow Carolyn's example. So she did. As David drove the buggy she prayed for their safety, for the well-being of the guests watching the play in the Round Barn Theater, even for the misguided person who was causing such trouble. Finally she prayed for David and Mr. McPherson and his officer friend and herself.

David pulled the buggy to a stop at the side of the theater. By the time Stella hopped out and shut the door, feeling remarkably younger than her fifty years, he had already wound the horse's lead around the hitching post.

"Wait here for McPherson."

"*Nein.* I'm going with you."

"Stella, I need you to wait here." David put his hands on her shoulders, and then he did something she did not at all expect. He leaned forward and brushed his lips against hers. When he spoke again his voice was husky and tender. "Wait for McPherson. Tell him I went inside to search for this person. I need you in my life, Stella. Promise me you won't go inside and confront this man."

She nodded mutely, the blood rushing to her ears and her heart hammering faster than the wings of a hummingbird in flight.

David squeezed her hands, and then he turned and walked into the theater.

CHAPTER 12

Within minutes Stella came to her senses. She'd let herself be swayed by a kiss! Why had she promised to stay outside? What good could she do out here?

She paced back and forth beside the buggy, and then McPherson pulled his car to a stop next to her. He was followed by a Nappanee officer who was in uniform but driving his personal vehicle. The two men hurried over to her.

"Where's David?"

"Inside. We think, that is to say, we're certain someone is going to interrupt the play, maybe even hurt some of the guests in the process. There was a letter, and—"

"I trust your and David's judgment." McPherson turned to the officer.

Stella could see his name tag now that he'd walked closer under the eaves of the building where there was soft lighting. Dark-skinned with a perfectly bald head, Officer Parris was approximately the same age as McPherson. He nodded at Stella in greeting, then said, "I suggest that we pull the fire alarm and get everyone out of the building."

"But what if . . . what if we're wrong?"

"If we find no danger, then the show can continue. But we err on the side of safety."

McPherson was already moving toward the front door when the sound of a small explosion boomed from inside, followed by gasps from the audience. All three of them ran into the building.

"What was that?" McPherson asked an usher.

"Fireworks, sir. Apparently they've been added to the play."

"No. They haven't."

McPherson opened the inner door to the theater and strode inside.

Parris stepped closer to Stella. "Go back to the front door. Hold it open and help usher people outside."

Then he walked over to the red fire alarm handle on the wall and pulled it down. Immediately the building was filled with a bright strobe light and a piercing siren. Stella clapped her hands over her ears and rushed to the front door.

By the time she pushed it open, people were already streaming out of the building. She was relieved to see they remained fairly orderly. The workers in the theater must have been trained to handle just such an emergency. Some helped the guests. Others were already standing a good distance away, waving flashlights and directing people to stand behind a fire lane. Stella was so focused on the scene across the parking lot that she almost missed the man carrying some sort of messenger bag.

Why would someone carry such a large tote bag to a play?

Why was he wearing a floppy waterproof hat when the weather had been clear?

She watched him clutch the bag to his chest.

As Stella watched, he looked left, then right, and then pivoted and moved back into the building, working his way against the throng of people. Stella glanced around, hoping she would see David or McPherson or Officer Parris. But there was no one—only a mob of guests and employees who were helping them outside.

She couldn't let this man walk away.

What if he was going back inside to finish what he'd started? If she didn't stop him now and he *was* the person bent on the destruction of the Mill, he'd just move on to his next plan, and it could be worse than this one. She thought of her promise to David, but if she stayed outside someone could be hurt. Wondering if she'd taken complete leave of her senses, she stepped away from the door and followed the man back inside.

He moved toward the south side of the building where the actors changed costumes and applied their makeup. There were no crowds here. She waited until she saw him go through the door that led to a staircase. Stella had been to the theater many times, sometimes filling in for someone who couldn't work their shift. The staircase led up into the rafters. It was where the stage crew worked on any lighting problems.

Giving him a head start so he wouldn't see her, she followed him through the door and then crept up the stairs. As she reached the top, she saw him drop the bag he was carrying onto the floor and then unzip it. It seemed to be filled with packages of fireworks. As she watched, he pulled out two, and proceeded to light them with a lighter from his pocket. He peered over the balcony to make sure no one was looking up at him, and then he dropped the lit fireworks onto a seat beside him where they began to smolder, small flames licking up. Quickly he pulled two more from his tote and began the same process again.

"Someone help! He's up here trying to light the place on fire," Stella screamed.

The arsonist turned to look at her, and Stella stumbled backward, unable to believe what she was seeing—the man they had been chasing wasn't a man at all. The arsonist was a woman, and someone that Stella knew. Regaining her balance, she rushed forward and attempted to knock the fireworks out of the seat and onto the floor. She was terrified the floor would catch fire, but certainly it wouldn't combust as quickly as fabric. She stomped on them, wondering if they would burn through the soles of her shoes.

At that moment, David burst through the door.

The arsonist attempted to run past him, but David was bigger and quicker. He blocked the exit, snatched the firecrackers away, and began to stomp on them. If he was surprised to see the arsonist was Mrs. Benson, he didn't show it.

"Watch her!" he called out as he took off his jacket and slapped it against the seat cushions, which had continued to smolder. "Don't let her leave."

Stella wasn't sure how she was supposed to stop her. The woman had fallen into a seat when David snatched the fireworks away, but now she had righted herself and was attempting to flee. Unsure what else to do, Stella began to scream and wave her arms. She must have looked positively crazy, for Mrs. Benson backed away and looked around furtively for another exit.

The area filled with the smell of singed upholstery and carpet. Unable to escape, Benson was attempting to light yet another firecracker, but now McPherson and Parris were rushing through the door. They quickly assessed the situation, strode over to the culprit, and snatched away the rest of the explosives.

As the older woman reached for her nefarious supplies, the hat fell off and gray hair straggled down around her face. She scowled and pursed her lips, accentuating the roadmap of wrinkles. Raising her chin in defiance, Stella could clearly see the scar on Mrs. Benson's neck as the red emergency lights continued to pulse.

"Get your hands off me. You're ruining everything. Stop. Just stop."

"You're under arrest for violation of the city fire code, among other things." Parris pulled a set of handcuffs from his pocket and slapped them on the older woman's thin wrists. "You have the right to remain silent when questioned. Anything you say or do may be used against you in a court of law. You have the right to consult an attorney . . ."

His voice faded as he marched her down the stairs.

Stella collapsed onto a stool.

"You were going to stay outside," David said, but the smile on his face told her he was proud of her actions.

"I promised I would, and I meant to. Then I saw him . . . I mean to say her . . ."

"The woman from the schoolhouse."

"*Ya*. Mrs. Benson."

"The woman with the scar?"

"The same. She used to be a regular around the Mill, but I hadn't seen much of her in the last few years."

"Until recently."

"Yes, she'd begun showing up again, like she did the day at the schoolhouse." Stella paused, shook her head, and said, "After Parris pulled the fire alarm, I saw her sneaking back into the building. Who goes into a building that might be on fire?"

"It's a good thing you followed her," McPherson said. "Parris and I found the firecrackers on the stage— the ones that the guests thought were part of the show."

"Apparently they were meant to be a distraction." David shook his head in disbelief. "The real damage was going to be done up here."

"If she had succeeded in lighting more of them . . ." McPherson wiped at the sweat on his face. "This is a sixty-foot, self-supporting wood dome, and it's a historical treasure."

He glanced from Stella to David. "I don't know how to thank you."

"Keep the Mill open," David said.

Stella nodded in agreement. "That will be thanks enough."

CHAPTER 13

David drove Stella home that night, and even took Carolyn's buggy on to his daughter's house when Stella insisted. "You shouldn't be walking down the road this late in the evening. What if . . . what if something happened to you?"

He'd kissed her again, like he had outside the Round Barn Theater, and he'd taken the horse and buggy on home. He also made sure he returned it the next morning in plenty of time for her work shift. Driving her to the Mill was a pleasure, and David could imagine doing it every day. He realized anew that Stella had captivated his heart.

But he took things slowly.

The Mill had temporarily closed while the police processed the crime scene. Within forty-eight hours of the incident, the Mill reopened. The number of visitors had risen drastically in the days following Mrs. Benson's capture. Especially at the theater. No doubt the news stories had fanned the flames of curiosity.

David waited a week before asking Stella to share a lunch with him.

Ten days after that, he invited her to dinner at Rebecca's.

Within six weeks it was common to see them walking together after the church service.

Always he remembered Carolyn's words, her description of Stella's fear. "Of being left alone again. Of caring too much. Of seeing yet another life slip through her fingers."

He prayed that such fear would leave her heart and that she would be filled with God's peace. When he couldn't sleep, he pulled out his Bible and turned through its pages, searching for guidance. Often he found himself reading the first book of John, chapter four verse eighteen. "There is no fear in love. But perfect love drives out fear." He prayed that he could offer Stella the kind of love that would drive out a lifetime of fear. He prayed that she would lean on God's love, which was perfect.

And he continued to wait.

One night, while they were eating dinner with Carolyn, he shared the status of the case against Mrs. Benson. "As you know, the police have charged Gwyneth Benson with trespassing and intent to cause bodily harm."

"She's lived in this area all of her life," Carolyn said.

"I don't understand why she would do such a thing. What was she hoping to accomplish?" Stella stirred her bowl of stew, but didn't eat. Finally she placed her hands in her lap.

"She previously owned the southeastern portion of land, where the inn was built."

"That portion was purchased years ago," Carolyn

said. "I don't remember the woman, but I do remember that we couldn't imagine what the Mill owners would do with so much land. We didn't envision the many buildings McPherson has added over the years."

"Her husband actually sold the land—something about back taxes that were owed. Over the years, she became convinced this was the reason for her financial problems. She has been a widow these past ten years, and apparently struggling both financially and emotionally."

"Why the reference to jubilee?" Stella asked.

"The fact that she left a note at all has convinced the district attorney that she isn't in her right mind. From what McPherson has told me, Mr. and Mrs. Benson moved here and purchased the land for a farm fifty years ago when she was a young woman of twenty-nine. The approaching anniversary was what made her decide to act now."

"What did she hope to accomplish, David?" Carolyn helped herself to another piece of cornbread.

"The closing of the Mill, I suppose. Somehow in her mind, she envisioned herself owning that land again."

"Will she go to jail?" Stella fiddled with her *kapp* strings.

"Due to her age and mental issues—which may be dementia of one sort or another—the prosecutor is recommending parole. Several of the local churches are reaching out to her, helping her with the home she's in—which has fallen into disrepair. They also are providing financial assistance to help her with groceries and utilities."

"But why did she focus on you? Why did she address the letter to you?"

David shrugged. "According to her statement to the police, she confused me with the man who had negotiated the original sale of the property. I suppose her dementia mixed everything up in her head. She thought if she could convince me to leave and reduce the flow of tourists, life would go back to the way it had been."

Silence followed for a few minutes, and then the conversation turned to crops and harvests and fall festivals, which were just around the corner. In one sense, it was hard for David to believe that he'd been in Nappanee for six months. In another sense, it felt as if he'd always lived there.

David continued to be patient, until he was certain that Stella was ready. He waited another month, which seemed to him like several months. Autumn arrived and the leaves began to fall. David waited until his heart wouldn't allow him to wait any longer.

And so it was that one evening, when the moon was high and the air held a pleasant coolness, that David asked Stella a very important question.

They were sitting on Rebecca's front porch, rocking Emma and Sophie, both girls wrapped in well-worn baby quilts.

The sun had set, leaving the sky softly colored with pink, purple, and gold. Behind him, in the house, David could hear Rebecca speaking with Adam as they washed dishes together.

"The glasses have helped?" Stella said.

"They have, and since two of the older boys in our district are now wearing them, he doesn't feel self-conscious about them."

"He'll have a *gut* school year."

"I think so."

Their rockers made a soft murmur against the wooden porch floor.

"All three of the children look forward to your visits. They've even taken to calling you *Mammi*."

Stella's smile widened. "Never a *mamm*, but now I'm a *mammi*. Sounds like a story from the Bible, even though it's not official."

"Let's make it official."

"What?"

"Marry me." David stopped rocking, moved Emma to his right arm and reached out with his left to claim Stella's hand. "Marry me, Stella. You know how I care for you, and Rebecca would be happy to have you here with us."

Stella slipped her hand out from under his, pretending that Sophie needed to be better covered. "Wouldn't she resent me? No one wants their mother replaced."

"You wouldn't be replacing Beverly." David paused. He'd learned it was best not to rush Stella, best to give her time.

Finally she asked, "Are you certain you want to marry again?"

David's laughter echoed through the night. "If you asked me that a year ago, even six months ago, I would have said no. I never planned to marry again, but then I also didn't plan to meet you. It seems that *Gotte* had different ideas for my future than I did."

"Six months ago, I never would have dreamed . . ." She stopped midsentence, shook her head, and stared down at the babe in her arms.

"For some widows, it would be the wrong thing to remarry," David admitted. "Some are quite content in their solitude."

"Like Carolyn."

"Yes, I suppose." David thought of the letters Carolyn had received from her daughter, asking her to move to Pennsylvania. She had not shared them with Stella, didn't want her sister to feel pressured to make any kind of change. He knew that Carolyn was content to be widowed, but she longed to be with her children and grandchildren. It was only her sense of duty to Stella that kept her at the old farmhouse.

"We may have strayed from the path I'd hoped this conversation would take." David stood and pulled his rocking chair around so that he was facing Stella. "I love you, Stella. And I would be honored if you would marry me."

When she looked up, David saw that his prayers had been answered. The expression of fear was gone, and in its place was one of joy.

Then she said "yes," and David shouted in celebration, waking both of the girls and causing them to fuss. Which was fine. The joys and trials of life made it rich, and he would be sharing them with the woman he loved.

When he'd come to work at the Mill, he never supposed that God would have a new life in store for him, but that was exactly what he'd received—a new life and a new love. He'd thought that stage of his life was over. Stella's smile assured him it wasn't. As to what would come next? He didn't have to worry about that. He'd learned that God held the future in the palm of His hand. All David had to do was prayerfully navigate each day.

BUILDING FAITH

KATHLEEN FULLER

To James. I love you.

GLOSSARY

ab im kopp—crazy, crazy in the head
daag/daags—day/days
daed—dad
danki—thank you
dawdi haus—small house used for in-laws/parents/
    grandparents
familye—family
geh—go
grossdaadi—grandfather
gut—good
gute nacht—good night
haus—house
kaffee—coffee
kapp—white hat worn by Amish women
maed—girls
mamm—mom
mei—my
nee—no
sehr—very
sohn—son
ya—yes
yer—your
yers—yours
yerself—yourself

CHAPTER 1

Faith Miller ran her palm across the smooth, cherry wood surface of the bread box, then blew sawdust off the top. The cherry was fancy for something as simple as a box to hold bread, but the wood had belonged to her grandfather, and she wanted to use it. Fine particles of dust floated in front of her, dancing in the air of her grandfather's woodshop. This was her sanctuary. She had loved being here as a small child, helping *Grossdaadi* with his various woodworking projects. It had been a hobby for him, a serious one. He would have rather been a carpenter than a farmer.

Like her grandfather she loved the smell of the wood, the feel of the sawdust on her hands, the precision of measuring to one fifteenth of an inch. She stood back and inspected the bread box, a birthday gift for her mother. A little more light sanding, a few coats of varnish, then a clear coat, and the box would be finished.

She ran her fingers across the sleek, soft wood again and listened. Her grandfather used to tell her the wood talked. Not in words, of course, but it spoke to him on a soul level. Wood had never spoken to her, but she didn't have the deep connection with carpentry and woodcrafting her grandfather had. She yearned for it and spent as much of her spare time as she could increasing and perfecting her skills.

She stood up and stretched. It was late—very late. She should've gone to bed hours ago. She had to get up early in the morning to go to her job at Schlabach's Bulk Food store with her younger sister, Grace. But as each hour had passed, she kept telling herself just a little bit longer, a little bit more work, and then she would stop. She needed to sand down the top of the bread box until it was glass-like smooth. She eyed it critically. The surface still wasn't perfect but it would have to do, at least for tonight.

Faith pushed back the stray strand of hair that refused to stay in her *kapp* and glanced out the shop window at the inky darkness. She didn't accomplish everything she had wanted to, but she was tired, a feeling she'd been increasingly familiar with. It had always seemed that way lately—so much to do, but not enough time to do it. At twenty-two she'd learned the hard lesson that life was precious and time was short. She didn't want to waste a single minute.

She turned off the lantern and walked out the door, stepping into the night air, cicadas and bullfrogs punctuating the dark silence. The house where she lived with her sisters and parents was a few yards away. Everyone would be asleep by now. *Like I should be.* She could barely make out her footsteps as she stumbled to the back door, but she didn't dare turn on her flashlight. If her father knew she was out so late, she'd get another lecture, another reminder that "early to bed, early to rise makes a man wise." Perhaps working on a bread box well past midnight wasn't the wisest decision, but it was worth it.

She crept into the house and slipped off her shoes, then carefully made her way up the stairs and opened the door to the bedroom she shared with her twenty-year-old sister, Grace. Her other sisters, Charity and Patience, were in their bedroom down the hall. They were still in school, and in the morning the family would be bustling to get to their jobs and to the schoolhouse, all under the supervision of her mother.

As soon as Faith shut the door, Grace turned on the battery-operated lamp. Faith jumped. "Grace," she hissed, squinting her eyes in the bright light. "What are you doing up?"

Grace folded her arms and leaned back against the pillow, her ash-blond hair in a long braid that hung over her shoulder. "You woke me up."

"Sorry. I was trying to be quiet."

"Not quiet enough. Where have you been?"

Faith unpinned her *kapp* and set it on the dresser. "I was out in the woodshop."

Grace glanced at the small clock on the bedstand. "It's almost one a.m." Her grin turned sly. "If I didn't know any better, I would have thought you snuck off to *geh* visit somebody."

Faith grimaced. "I would never do that."

Grace arched a dark-blond eyebrow. "Never?"

Faith's cheeks heated but she didn't look at her sister. "That only happened one time. Now, turn off the light so I can put on *mei* nightgown."

Grace chuckled. "Guess I hit a nerve," she said before turning out the light.

Faith heard the rustling of covers as her sister settled in bed. She quickly changed into her nightgown and got into the twin bed on the opposite side of the room. She closed her weary eyes to say a quick prayer.

"I was worried about you." Grace's soft voice lilted in the darkness.

Faith's eyes opened, even though she couldn't see her sister. "Why would you be worried about me?"

"You're spending a lot of time in *Grossdaadi*'s woodshop. More time than you used to."

Faith closed her eyes again. "I have work to do."

"You have work to do during the *daag*. Work you get paid for. That should be *yer* priority."

Holding in a sigh, Faith bit her tongue before she said something she would regret. *Nothing like getting a lecture from my little sister.* "I take *mei* job at Schlabach's seriously. So far there hasn't been a problem."

"Then why did I have to wake you up yesterday morning to get ready for work?"

Oh. Faith had forgotten about that. "So I slept in a bit. Usually I'm up before you. Now, quit talking so I can get some sleep or you will have to wake me up again come sunrise."

"See, you're already crabby."

"*Gute nacht*, Grace."

"'Night, Faith."

Faith closed her eyes again, but she wasn't near sleep like she'd been moments ago. Her sister was right. She had been spending a lot of time in the woodshop. But Grace didn't understand. Nobody understood. She needed to be out there. She needed to work on her projects. They gave her purpose, much more purpose than working in a bulk food store, cashing out customers and straightening shelves of flour and salt and baking supplies. If she knew there was a way she could sell the small projects she made so she could do woodworking full time, she would. But no one in her church district took her work seriously. The one time she had suggested taking a small birdhouse to Schlabach's to see if it would sell, her father had given her a look that could melt ice cubes. "You have a job," he'd said. "One that is appropriate for a woman." Then he'd gone back to reading his paper. End of subject.

This time Faith couldn't keep herself from sighing. She flipped over on her side. There was something else nagging at her. Or rather *someone* else intruding on her thoughts. She blamed Grace for bringing him up. Thanks to her sister, Faith couldn't stop thinking about the time she actually *had* snuck out of the house to meet someone. Silas Graber.

They had just started courting, and one Saturday evening last fall he came over after everyone had gone to bed. It had been pitch-dark outside, much like tonight. He'd tossed pebbles at her window until she met him in the backyard.

"You're going to get us in trouble," she'd snapped. "It's a miracle you didn't wake up Grace."

"*Kumme* on." He put his hands on her waist. "Nothing wrong with having a little fun."

"This isn't fun." But her heart thrummed with excitement. "It's risky."

"I'll take the blame. If *yer daed* discovers us, I'll tell him you found me irresistible."

"Ooh." She lightly batted his shoulder with her fingers. "What am I going to do with you?"

"You can kiss me, for starters."

She'd found out later that Grace had only pretended to be asleep and knew exactly what Faith was doing. She should have known then that her relationship with Silas wouldn't work. She'd always followed the rules—with the exception of that night—and Silas played by his own rules.

She pressed her lips inward, forcing the memory out of her mind. Which wasn't easy. She had been willing to marry him at one time. Thankfully she had realized the kind of man he really was. Irresponsible. Selfish. Undependable. She'd come so close to making the biggest mistake of her life almost a year ago when she'd become engaged to him. Then tragedy had struck, revealing his real character. Breaking up with Silas had been the best decision she'd ever made.

Still, she felt a pinch in her heart. Like her memories, she tried to ignore it. She was over him—for good.

· · ·

Silas ran his hand through his hair and pulled on the ends. He looked at the paperwork on the kitchen table. A stack of bills to the right and the accounting book to the left. It was late, nearly one in the morning, and his brain was swimming with numbers that didn't make sense. He didn't have much of a head for figures. Never had. It had taken him years to learn how to measure accurately, which was a necessary skill for his job. He'd been happy to eyeball things, but that always ended up ruining whatever project he was working on. At first his father had been patient in teaching him. But eventually he accused Silas of not paying attention. There had been a nugget of truth in that, especially when he was younger. Silas would eventually take over his *daed*'s carpentry business at some point. Unfortunately, that time had come sooner than either of them had imagined.

He stared at the bills again. They needed to be paid. Some were even overdue. He had work lined up for the next couple of weeks, but no new orders after that. Normally he would be happy for the break, which would give him a chance to go fishing. He hadn't been near a creek or river in weeks, and he missed the quiet peace he always found when casting his line into the water. But fishing didn't pay the bills and he needed more work. It didn't help that a new carpentry shop had opened up a few miles away, further diluting what was already slow business.

He needed to go to bed. He had to open up the shop in the morning, and he'd already worked four hours after closing today. For the past two months he'd been handling most of the work himself. His father helped out when he could, but for the most part Silas had the responsibility of running the shop, filling orders, taking care of accounts, and making sure the business—and their family—didn't go under.

All that required organization—and he had never been organized. Another one of his downfalls, one that used to drive his father crazy. But now his *daed* didn't say anything about Silas's lack of focus, which had improved recently out of necessity. He didn't say much lately, not since *Mamm* . . .

Silas pushed away from the table and stood. He arched his back, then went to his room upstairs. He was tired. Bone weary, really. But he wouldn't let his father down. He'd done that before. He'd let too many people down, Faith most of all.

He shook his head. He needed to stop thinking about her, stop nursing the pain that had been in his heart since she ended things between them. They had been apart for nearly half a year after dating for two, and he needed to move on. Some days he thought he had. But when he was tired or lonely or . . . anything . . . he missed her.

Yet how could he move on when they lived in the same church district and saw each other every other Sunday? They didn't speak, but just seeing her was enough to remind him of the good times . . . and the bad. Near the end the bad had outweighed the good.

He fell into bed, closed his eyes, and was instantly asleep. The next morning he rose early, fixed coffee, and started on breakfast. He'd finished cooking the sausage links by the time his father came into the kitchen, bleary-eyed.

"Rough night?" Silas asked, his tone heavy.

"*Ya.*" *Daed* sat down.

Silas nodded and took a sip of his coffee. Then he poured a cup for his dad and set it in front of him. "Breakfast?"

"*Kaffee* will be fine. Make *yer mamm* a plate, though. I'll take it to her."

He did as he was told, adding one sausage link to the scrambled eggs and toast he had at the ready. He set the plate in front of his father. Giving Silas an appreciative smile, *Daed* said, "I'll be out later this morning to help you in the shop."

"I've got it under control." Silas ignored *Daed*'s skeptical look. "Really, I do."

"I need to work, at least when I can."

Silas nodded, relenting. But he knew his father may or may not be able to work today. And Silas needed to be prepared for that. It was time for him to grow up, to be responsible. He was twenty-two years old but he'd spent his entire life acting like a kid. Then the diagnosis came, changing his life and his parents' lives forever.

His father picked up the plate. "I'll see you in a little while."

Silas nodded as his father left. He downed his coffee, inhaled the eggs and toast, washed and dried the dishes, then went out to open up the shop. He started mixing up the mahogany wood stain he would apply to a china hutch that needed to be ready for a Yankee customer by tomorrow afternoon. He'd barely finished preparing the stain when the bell above the door jingled. He turned to see his friend Melvin Weaver walk in.

"Hey," he said, putting down the container of stain. "What brings you here so early this morning? I figured you'd be at the harness shop already."

"I'm on *mei* way. I've been meaning to come by before,

but we've been so busy with the *haus*, time got away from me."

"I know how that is." Silas put his hands on his hips. "What can I do for you?"

"We've got the kitchen framed in and drywalled," Melvin said. "I'd like to hire you to build the cabinets and do the flooring."

Silas had to keep his jaw from hitting the floor. Melvin was getting married in a couple of months, and he was working hard to get his future home ready. Silas mentally calculated how much money he'd profit from making and installing cabinets and installing flooring in the spacious house. The cash would go a long way toward paying the bills. He couldn't believe his luck. No, not luck. God was answering his prayers. Maybe that's why business had slowed. God knew Melvin would need a carpenter, and the Lord was dropping the opportunity on Silas's doorstep. "Wow," he finally said, at a loss for more words.

"I know it's a big project, but you do great work, Silas. I want these cabinets to be perfect for Martha. You're the best there is, next to *yer daed*."

"He taught me everything I know." Silas was pleased by the compliment. He did have natural skill, an intuition about how to create something beautiful out of raw materials. His father had admitted that several years ago, which had only added to *Daed*'s frustration with him. "You're wasting the talent God gave you," he'd said more than once. "You need to focus instead of daydreaming."

But his father hadn't realized that daydreaming and

imagining were part of the process for him. In *Daed*'s defense, Silas hadn't realized how important focus and discipline were. He was learning that lesson now. "Martha will have the best cabinets in Middlefield," he promised.

"*Gut.*" Melvin grinned. "I'll pay top dollar too."

Silas almost leaned against the counter with relief. The Lord provided the opportunity. All Silas had to do was not mess up. "I'll have to work on the installation during the evenings and weekends though, for the next couple of weeks. *Mamm* . . . she hasn't been feeling well. I've been taking care of things here at the shop while *Daed* is . . . helping her." *Daed* insisted on keeping *Mamm*'s condition a secret as long as possible. The man could be so stubborn. They could use the community's help. But he wouldn't argue with him. *Daed* was suffering as much as *Mamm*, and Silas would let his father deal with the pain in his own way.

Fortunately, Melvin didn't pry. "Can you get the work done before the wedding?"

Silas did a few calculations in his head. Then he redid them just to make sure they were right. "*Ya*," he said. He'd get it done. "I'll stop by and take some measurements after work today."

"Sounds *gut*." Melvin looked at the clock on the carpentry shop wall. "Speaking of work, I need to get to the harness shop. Martha's *daed* doesn't abide lateness." He turned to leave, then paused. "The *haus* is unlocked," he said over his shoulder, "so feel free to go right on in."

"I will." Once his friend was gone, Silas let out a whoop of joy. Finally, some good news. Now he was seeing—and feeling—some hope. *God, You are good.*

CHAPTER 2

A few hours after she arrived at Schlabach's, Faith was surprised to see her cousin Martha walk into the store. She smiled, happy to see her. "It's the middle of the *daag*," Faith said. "Are you off work already?"

"I'm on lunch break." Martha's smile brightened her pretty face. She and Melvin Weaver were engaged to be married, and even though they hadn't announced their engagement at church yet, it wasn't a secret. The entire district knew the wedding would be soon.

Martha was not only Faith's cousin, but one of her closest friends. Yet this past year they hadn't spent much time together. Faith could blame Melvin for that, since Martha did spend a lot of time with her fiancé. But to be fair, Faith hadn't exactly made herself available to Martha either, not when she spent all her free time in her grandfather's shop. But now that Martha was here, Faith realized how much she had missed her friend.

"Do you have some time for a bite to eat?" Martha asked. "I brought us lunch."

"Definitely." She gestured to the empty store. "We haven't been very busy today. Let me tell Grace that I'll be back in a bit."

A short while later Faith and Martha were sitting behind the store at a small picnic table the owner of the store, a Yankee named Mr. Furlong, had put outside for the employees. Early spring days like this were the perfect time to enjoy the warmer weather. Martha pulled out a paper sack from her large tote bag and put it on the table. "Roast beef sandwiches okay?"

"Sounds delicious."

Martha took out the sandwiches and two apples, then handed one sandwich and an apple to Faith. They bowed their heads in silent prayer before they started eating.

"How's business at the harness store?" Faith asked, glancing at her sandwich. She usually cut her sandwiches in two equal pieces, but since she didn't have a knife—

"Here." Martha handed Faith a small knife.

Faith beamed as she took it. "You remembered."

"Of course. You're the only person I know who insists on cutting her sandwiches."

"They're easier to eat that way."

Martha picked up her whole sandwich. "Work at the shop is fine, although *Daed* is wondering who's going to take *mei* place in the office after Melvin and I get married."

Carefully cutting her sandwich, Faith said, "I guess he'll have to look outside the *familye* to find someone."

"*Ya*, although he said every time he hires someone new they end up marrying one of us." Martha tore off a small piece of crust from her bread. "You know Jonah is single now."

"He and Rachel broke up?"

"A couple of weeks ago. *Daed*'s keeping a close eye

on him now. He's the only person at the shop other than Melvin who's not related to us, and Fanny is marrying age. I guess *Daed*'s not ready to see his youngest daughter tie the knot anytime soon. Not that he has anything to worry about. Jonah's been working with us for so long, he's like the brother we never had. But he would be a *gut* catch for someone else."

Faith wasn't sure if Martha was making small talk or if she was hinting at something. "Doing a little matchmaking, are you?"

Martha's eyes grew round with fake innocence. "Me? Of course not." Her expression turned serious. "That didn't turn out too well the last time."

Another heart pinch. Again, Faith ignored it. "It's not *yer* fault Silas and I didn't work out."

"I really thought you would," Martha said in a soft voice.

Faith took a bite of her sandwich so she wouldn't have to respond. She tried to enjoy the juicy roast beef and spicy horseradish, but she couldn't, not while Silas was fresh on her mind. Again. She swallowed. "How are the wedding plans going?" she asked, desperate to change the subject.

"*Gut. Sehr gut*, actually. I've had a lot on *mei* mind lately, though."

"I imagine getting ready for a wedding is a lot of work when you're the bride." She tried not to think about how close she came to finding out firsthand how much work was involved.

"But on the subject of the wedding," Martha said, "I have a question for you."

Faith prepared herself for what she knew was coming. She would love to be one of Martha's wedding attendants. Or even her maid of honor. She opened her mouth to say so, when Martha surprised her for the second time that day.

"I would be so happy if you would make the cabinets for our kitchen."

Faith shut her mouth. Surely she heard her wrong. "What?"

"I know how much you enjoy woodworking and you're really *gut* at it. I would love to have something of *yers* in *mei haus*. I thought the cabinets would be perfect, and I know you would do an excellent job."

"I'm not sure what to say."

"Say *ya*." Martha frowned. "Unless you can't. If you're too busy with work, I'd understand—"

"*Nee*. I'm not too busy." Faith clasped her hands together. She couldn't believe this was actually happening. She would be able to make something bigger than a bread box. This was a real job, one that was complex and challenging. The fact that she was making something for her dear friend and cousin was a bonus. "I'm so pleased you asked me."

"Of course I'll pay you."

Faith shook her head. "I won't hear of it. This is *mei* gift to you and Melvin."

"That's a generous gift," Martha said.

"*Grossdaadi* has a lot of wood in the shop. He was always doing different projects."

"I remember. It will be nice to have something of his in our *haus*."

Faith looked at Martha intently. Martha hadn't been as close to *Grossdaadi* as she had, but they had both loved their grandfather. "You know he would have wanted the wood to be used for a *gut* purpose. So if you're okay with oak cabinets, then they will be my wedding present. I can stain them any color you like."

"You can decide on the stain. I trust *yer* judgment."

Excitement bloomed inside Faith. "I'll have to come by and take some measurements. Would tonight be okay?"

"*Ya*. The *haus* is unlocked since there's nothing in it. Melvin will be putting in the plumbing soon, but right now it's basically rooms and walls." She looked at Faith, her brows knitting. "Are you sure I can't pay you at least for *yer* time?"

Faith held up her hand. "*Nee.* I want to do this for you."

Martha's eyes grew soft. "*Danki*, Faith." She paused. "I've missed you. I don't want us to grow apart after Melvin and I get married."

"We won't." She wanted the words to be true, but she wasn't so sure. Once Martha and Melvin married, they'd have their own house and their own lives. They'd still be part of the church and Faith would still see them, but they wouldn't have much in common anymore. And once they had children, Martha would be busy and become closer with the other young mothers in their community. The thought saddened her. She didn't want to lose her friend. *I'm so tired of losing people I love.*

But she wasn't going to mourn, not when she finally had a project that was not only challenging, but meaningful. "I can't wait to come up with the plans," she said.

"And I can't wait to see what you come up with."

"I won't let you down, Martha," Faith said, smiling. "I promise."

. . .

That evening Faith was so eager to get to Martha's new house she didn't want to bother eating supper. As her mother was putting the meal on the table, Faith slipped on her light jacket. The warmth of the day had turned cool. "Where are you going?" *Mamm* asked. "Supper is almost ready."

"To see Martha." A little lie, which could turn into the truth if Martha happened to be at her future home tonight.

"Now?" *Mamm* set a bowl of cabbage salad on the table. "I'm sure her *familye* is starting supper too."

"I won't be gone long."

Mamm lifted one eyebrow. "All right. Tell her parents I said hello."

Faith walked out the door as Grace, Charity, and Patience came into the kitchen. When Faith was outside, she blew out a long breath. She didn't want to explain to her mother what she was doing for Martha. *Mamm* didn't approve of her spending so much time in her grandfather's workshop, either.

She did have to get her measuring tape and possibly some tools, so she darted inside the shop, found the items, then went to hitch up her buggy.

Thirty minutes later she arrived at Martha's house. She went to the front door and opened it. Martha was right; it was little more than a shell. The layout of the house was simple and she found the kitchen right away. It was empty, too, and the floor was still plywood. A single window was on the south-facing wall, the perfect height for a sink to be placed under it. It was a fairly large space, which didn't surprise Faith. Martha had always wanted a lot of kids. She said a quick prayer that the Lord would bless Martha and Melvin with as many children as their hearts desired. Then she went to work measuring, thinking about the type of cabinets Martha would like.

"What are you doing here?"

She turned at the familiar voice, her heart stopping in her chest. Then it skipped a beat when she saw Silas standing there. She immediately put her heart in check, although she wished it didn't need so many reminders.

But her heart had other ideas, because her pulse started to hammer as she and Silas stood in the same room alone for the first time since their breakup. It was one thing to see him at church. Among the community they could avoid each other. Here, there was nowhere to hide.

He tilted his head, then crossed his arms over his chest. "I didn't realize you were giving me the silent treatment."

She frowned, confused, then realized she hadn't answered his question. She lifted her chin and stared him down, determined for him to know he didn't affect her. "I'm measuring," she said.

"I can see that." He put his hands on his hips.

She saw the tool belt around his waist, and a knot formed in the pit of her stomach. "Why are *you* here?" Although by the sinking sensation in her stomach she suspected she already knew the answer.

He paused, looking at her with equal intensity. "Measuring."

They continued the standoff, their gazes locked. He was still gorgeous. He always had been, with chestnut-colored hair that curled at the ends, thick eyebrows above brown eyes that always held warmth and a twinkle of mischief. Faith tried not to think about the two years they'd spent together. The plans they had made. The plans she had made, to be a wife and a mother. He had ruined all that. "What, you ran out of fish to catch?"

His gaze narrowed. "Why are you here?" Silas asked again, this time slowly, as if she didn't understand what he was saying. He also didn't respond to her cutting remark. Then again, he didn't have to. They both knew she had always come in second to stupid fish. Sometimes third . . . or not at all.

Dread formed in her stomach as realization dawned. Martha was her cousin, but Melvin was Silas's good friend. Surely, no . . . "Martha asked me to build their kitchen cabinets."

Silas scoffed. "Martha must have made a mistake, because Melvin asked me to make the cabinets and put in the kitchen flooring."

"She didn't make a mistake. Martha asked me a few hours ago."

"Melvin asked me this morning."

They stared at each other, and Faith wasn't sure what to do. "This must be a miscommunication."

"Must be."

"We'll have to talk to them about it."

"Might as well do it now," Silas said, turning to leave. "I'll *geh* talk to Melvin."

"I'll *geh* talk to Martha." Clearly he didn't want to be around her. Which shouldn't bother her, but it did . . . a little. Okay, a lot. Yet she should have known he had moved on from her.

Silas stopped. He looked at her again, and she searched his eyes for the softness, the love she used to see there. Instead she saw something rare for Silas. Seriousness. "Just to let you know," he said, his voice stronger and more confident than she'd ever heard it, "this job is mine. Melvin wants a proper carpenter to do the work."

That made Faith's blood boil. "I *am* a proper carpenter."

"You're a hobbyist. There's a big difference."

"You never respected the fact that I am as *gut* a carpenter as any man."

"That's not true." He paused. "I know you're *gut*."

She ignored the tiny bit of satisfaction his remark gave her. "Don't think I don't know what you're doing, trying to put me off guard with sweet talk."

Silas huffed. "Think what you want. You always do. I was just letting you know I am *not* giving up on this job."

Faith looked at him. "I'm not giving up on it either. Martha is *mei* cousin—"

"Melvin is *mei* friend—"

"And she asked me to do this and I will do it."

"We'll see about that."

She watched Silas walk out the door, held her breath, then exhaled when she saw him disappear. She turned off both lanterns and heard the sound of Silas's horse and buggy leave. How had she not heard his buggy approach? Then again, she always became engrossed in her tasks, enough to block out everything around her.

A stab of grief hit her. It always did at unexpected times, often the worst times. She had been so focused that day in the woodshop, using a bevel-edged chisel to practice her carving skills on an old piece of wood. If she had paid more attention, maybe she would have heard her grandfather cry for help just outside the door of the shop. She would have been there in time—

She drove the thought away. She wasn't about to let Silas take this opportunity from her. It wasn't as if he needed the extra work. He and his father had their own carpentry shop. Why would Silas need to take on an extra job? Faith thought about that for a moment as she got into her buggy, then shook her head. It wasn't any of her business what Silas did anymore.

That was how she had to live her life now. Not get involved, not entangle herself, not risk her heart.

CHAPTER 3

Silas, I don't know what to say." Melvin held out his hands and shrugged his shoulders as they stood in the living room of Melvin's parents' house. "I had no idea Martha was going to ask Faith to make those cabinets. We've been so busy dealing with work and wedding plans and other things that have to be done to the *haus*, I guess we didn't talk about it."

"It's okay, Melvin. I just want to get everything cleared up." *And to set Faith straight.* She hadn't changed a bit since she'd broken their engagement—and his heart. She was still hard, still brittle, still jumping to conclusions . . . and still hurting. He could see the pain in her eyes, hidden behind a mask of pride. Although she was an Amish woman and in good standing with the church, she was the most prideful woman he knew. But she didn't have to be. He hoped she'd realize that someday.

He gave himself a mental shake. Faith wasn't his concern anymore. She had made that clear six months ago. But this job was his concern, and he wasn't going to let her, or anyone else, take it from him.

"I'll have to talk to Martha about it," Melvin said, derailing Silas's train of thought.

At first Silas wondered what there was to talk about. Wasn't Melvin in charge of building the house? Then again, while he knew marrying Faith would have been the biggest mistake of his life, if they were married, would he make a decision like this without her input? Even if she wasn't so stubborn and headstrong, he would never decide something so important without involving her. Which made him understand why Melvin wouldn't do that to Martha either. "That's fine," Silas said. "Just let me know." *And let Faith know too.*

That brought about a twinge of guilt. More than a twinge. Faith was a good carpenter. Her grandfather had taught her well. But she wasn't experienced. She'd never done a project as big as a whole kitchen. She only helped her grandfather in his woodshop.

"How about Martha and I meet you at the *haus* tomorrow evening? That will give us time to straighten this out."

"I appreciate it, Melvin."

"*Nee* problem. I'm sorry for the mix-up."

"I'm sure you and Martha will work this out." Silas left, confident that by this time tomorrow the kitchen job would be his, and his alone.

. . .

"Faith, I had *nee* idea," Martha said when Faith stopped by her house on the way home. "Melvin and I . . . I guess we talked about the kitchen. I can't remember."

Martha put her fingers to her forehead. "Things have been so busy."

"I understand," Faith said as Martha sat down on the couch. "And it's okay."

"*Nee*, it's not." Martha looked distressed. "Of all the people in Middlefield Melvin had to ask, it had to be—"

"Silas." Faith sighed. "But I understand why he did it. I'm sure he wants the best for you and Silas is very *gut*." She had to admit that. It wouldn't be fair to him not to. He was really talented. But he was also irresponsible and so lackadaisical about work and life that he drove her *ab im kopp*.

At first his carefree attitude appealed to her. He was spontaneous, like the night he'd come over and they'd kissed under the stars. He'd made her feel special, even loved. But love was more than midnight kisses and charming smiles. Love was putting the other person first. Choosing to honor a commitment—like a relationship—instead of treating it as an afterthought. Love was about being there during the worst time of her life. Which he hadn't been.

"I'll tell you what," Martha said, her face brightening. "I know Melvin and I can work this out. We'll discuss it and come to a decision. I'm sure he'll see *mei* point of view and how much I want you to be involved in this. Melvin and I will talk tonight and then I'll meet you tomorrow at the *haus*. Does that sound *gut*?"

"Perfect," Faith said. She was sure Melvin would see Martha's side.

As she drove home, she couldn't stop wondering why Silas was taking on extra work. Was there something wrong at his father's carpentry business? She hadn't heard anything. Then again, she always tuned out any mention of Silas. No, this was a simple misunderstanding. Melvin and Silas were friends, and it would be like Silas to want to do the work as a favor to Melvin. Just like Faith wanted to do for Martha. Silas was kind like that. He was the kindest man she knew.

She straightened in her seat, lifting her chin and steeling her resolve. Blood was thicker than water, at least in this situation. She had no doubt that Martha and Melvin would make the right decision, and that by this time tomorrow, Faith would be able to start working on making the most beautiful kitchen cabinets anyone in Middlefield had ever seen.

• • •

When Faith arrived at Martha's new house the next evening after work, she was more tired than usual. She'd spent last night in the woodshop drawing diagrams and searching through the large stash of her grandfather's wood. Just as she had told Martha she would, she found a lot of beautiful oak, and after some quick calculations, she realized that if she was careful and didn't make any mistakes, she'd have just enough to build the cabinets.

Once again she'd stayed out in the shop longer than she should, and when she finally went to bed, she couldn't fall asleep. Not because she was excited, but because for the first time, she started to have doubts. She'd never worked on a project this extensive before.

She'd helped her grandfather repair a few cabinets, but she'd never planned an entire kitchen. Silas was right. She was a hobbyist. She couldn't deny that. He was a professional. She couldn't deny that either.

But she also couldn't spend energy doubting herself. For years she had wanted to prove herself to someone other than her grandfather. Now she had that opportunity, and she wouldn't let self-doubt eat away at her. She could do this. Martha had confidence in her. More important, she had to maintain confidence in herself.

Faith parked next to Martha's buggy, then tethered her horse. The April air was a little chilly tonight, and a stiff breeze blew the skirt of her dress around her knees. She tucked her chin farther into her lightweight jacket and went inside. As she crossed the threshold, she froze. Martha wasn't there, but Silas was. "Oh *nee*," she said before she could stop the words from coming out of her mouth.

"Glad to see you, too, Faith," he said.

"*Yer* sarcasm is not appreciated." She looked around the empty room. "Where's Martha?"

"She and Melvin left a few minutes ago. They had more to talk about."

Faith frowned. "I thought this was already settled."

"So did I." He was still wearing his coat, and she realized she hadn't seen his buggy outside.

"How did you get here?" she asked.

"I walked."

Her frown deepened. The distance between this house and Silas's wasn't that far, but it made for a fairly long walk. And she knew what it meant when Silas took walks.

She noticed tiny lines of strain at the corners of his dusty brown eyes. "What's—" She stopped herself. It wasn't her business what was wrong with him. Not anymore. She lifted her chin. "You made a wasted trip," she said. "I'm telling you right now that I'm the one who has the job."

"We'll see about that." He nodded toward the door.

Faith heard the sound of horses' hooves outside on the driveway. She gave Silas a cool look before folding her hands together.

The door opened and Martha walked in. Faith started to smile but her smile slipped as soon as she saw her cousin's solemn expression. Melvin was right behind her, looking just as grim.

"This can't be *gut*," Silas muttered behind Faith.

"Hi, Faith." Martha's smile was forced. Melvin kept his gaze on the crude floor.

Silas stepped forward. "Have you come to a decision?"

Faith looked at him, her brow wrinkling. Again, there was something different about Silas. He'd always been so laid back. Too laid back, in her opinion, although he was the one person she could fully relax around, who with one look or word could make her smile. At least he had been. Now he was serious. Determined.

Melvin and Martha exchanged a look. "We've been talking," Melvin said hesitantly.

"We know," she and Silas said at the same time.

"And we're having a bit of a problem," Martha added.

"What kind of problem?" Silas asked.

"Well . . ." Melvin looked at Silas, then at Faith, then back at Silas again. "We can't choose between the two of you."

Silas folded his arms over his chest much like Faith had her arms crossed over hers. "What do you mean you can't choose?"

"We both agree that each one of you would be good for the job," Melvin said, sounding a little more settled now. "We want to hire you both."

Faith shook her head. *"Nee—"*

"Nope," Silas said.

Faith nodded. At least she and Silas could agree on something. "That would be a disaster."

"Bigger than a disaster."

"Now wait a minute." Melvin held up his hand. "Look, I know you two have a . . ."

"Past," Martha said gently.

"And I realize Martha and I made a mistake by not being on the same page about this. But building a kitchen is a big project. Both of you work during the *daag.* Martha and I think the job would go faster and be easier on you two if you cooperated and did the work together."

This was ridiculous. How could they even think she and Silas could work together? They could barely stand to be in the same room with each other. She also wondered if Melvin and Martha were telling the whole truth. "Can I talk to you for a minute?" she asked her cousin. Then she glanced at Melvin and Silas. "Privately?"

Martha nodded, the grim look on her face returning. She headed out the door and Faith followed her.

A blast of cold air swirled around them. Spring was always so unpredictable. It wasn't much warmer inside

the house but at least there they had protection from
the howling wind. "I can't work with Silas," Faith said,
seeing no reason to be tactful. "You know why. Besides,
I thought you had confidence in me."

"Oh, Faith, I do. So does Melvin. But we also know
Silas does good work. Melvin and I would like to get the
haus finished as soon as possible. It only makes sense
to hire two carpenters." Her expression turned stern. "I
understand if you can't work with Silas. But we aren't
changing our minds. If you and Silas can't come to an
agreement on this, we'll hire someone else. I'm sorry."

Faith's teeth started to chatter. What was she going
to do now? She was tempted to tell Martha to forget
it, but reined in her thoughts. She still wanted to do
something special for her cousin. Wasn't that one of
the main reasons she wanted to work on the kitchen?
She could do that, and still prove herself while working
with Silas. Then another thought came to her. "What if
he doesn't agree to work with me?" Which was a likely
possibility.

"Then we will hire another carpenter to work with
you." Martha tucked her hands into her coat. "Faith,
it's cold out here and frankly I'm tired. Melvin's tired.
We've both been a little stressed."

Faith became concerned. "Is everything okay between
the two of you?"

"Oh, *ya*, everything is fine. It's just that he and I
have different ways of doing things, and if we don't
consult each other on the important stuff, then misunderstandings happen. Like this one."

Faith could relate to what her cousin was saying.

Wasn't that one of the problems she and Silas had? They were different people. Polar opposites.

"But Melvin and I also complement each other," Martha said. "That's the beauty of our relationship. He's strong where I'm weak, and vice versa. Plus," she said with a grin, "we love each other and we always work things out. That's what couples do."

Resisting a frown, Faith nodded. In the past she and Silas couldn't work out their issues. And now they were both expected to come to an agreement about collaborating on the kitchen. She didn't know if that was possible.

"Now can we go inside?" Martha asked.

Faith nodded and followed her cousin. While she was glad Martha and Melvin had a strong relationship, they had what Faith and Silas lacked. They had love.

CHAPTER 4

Silas, I'm really sorry," Melvin said, shuffling his feet against the plywood floor.

Silas held himself in check. What had been an answer to prayer was turning into another disappointment. "Was this Martha's idea?"

"No, it was both of ours. We had to compromise and this was our solution." His gaze was stern. "If you and Faith can't work it out, then we'll find somebody else. But we want both of you for the job."

Silas rubbed his forehead with his callused fingers. Melvin wasn't giving him much of a choice here. And Silas couldn't afford to be emotional about the situation. "I'm willing," he said, barely able to say the words out loud. So much for not being emotional. "But I doubt she will be."

"Maybe she'll surprise you."

He let out a bitter chuckle. "Surprise? Faith doesn't know what that word means. She plans everything, down to the tiniest detail."

Melvin shrugged. "People change."

Silas was about to make another sarcastic comment, but held off. Change was possible. He ought to know.

He'd been forced to change. But Faith was different. She was predictable and liked it that way. He had to acknowledge he'd always been drawn to her stead-fastness. Then he thought about Faith's grandfather's death. How her predictability had turned into inflexibility. Yes, she had changed too.

The door opened and Faith and Martha came in. Silas noticed Faith's lips were a little blue around the corners and Martha was visibly shaking. If he'd been thinking straight, he and Melvin should have gone outside and let the women stay in the house to talk. He started to take off his coat to give to Faith. But when she shot him a frigid look, he changed his mind. No, this wasn't going to work out. He was going to either lose this job or have to work with another carpenter. Faith wouldn't yield. That word wasn't even in her vocabulary.

Melvin moved to stand beside Martha. "Well?" he said, sounding hopeful.

She put her hand on Melvin's arm. "I think we should go." She looked at Faith and then at Silas. "You'll let us know tomorrow what you decide?"

Faith nodded.

"*Ya*," Silas added.

"We'll see you tomorrow, then." Melvin opened the door, and he and Martha left.

Silas looked at Faith, waiting for her to talk. She pressed her teeth on her bottom lip, something she did when she was deep in thought. The gears were turning in her mind like they always did.

He turned away, that small gesture making him

think of the first time they kissed. He'd gotten a wild idea soon after they started dating that he would coax her out of her house in the middle of the night. She wasn't happy with him, but she had met him in her backyard. There wasn't even a sliver of moonlight, and she made sure to tell him all the reasons they shouldn't be out there and all the rules they were breaking. Then he had joked about her kissing him, and to his surprise she had obliged. From that moment on he was a goner.

He shoved the memory from his mind and whirled around. She was still thinking, tapping her finger against her chin. She was very deliberate, often annoyingly so. Like now. "So?" he said, unable to keep the impatience out of his tone.

Faith cut her gaze to him. "Is this how we're going to start our working relationship? With you snapping at me?"

He pushed his hat farther back on his head. "Sorry. You've made a decision, then?"

"*Ya*. I'm willing to set aside our differences to help Melvin and Martha." She lifted her chin. "Can you?"

"Done." Then he paused. This time it was his turn to be deliberate and thoughtful, something he wasn't used to. But they couldn't jump into this job and expect things to run seamlessly, not without talking about it first. "We should set some ground rules."

She tilted her head, looking at him suspiciously. "What kind of ground rules?"

"No dredging up the past."

Faith nodded. "I think that's fair."

"Number two, no criticizing of each other's work. Or how each other works."

A pause. "All right," she said, "although I don't see how constructive feedback can be considered criticism—"

Silas held up his hand. "See? That's exactly what I'm talking about. All we have to do is work together to make this kitchen the best it can be for our friends. We both have our own ways of doing things. Somehow we'll have to figure out how to make that work."

Faith opened her mouth as if to say something, then she closed it.

He shook his head and let out a sour chuckle. "You were going to say something about the past, weren't you?"

"Nee." Her eyes shifted downward.

"You're an open book." Silas leveled his gaze on her face. "I know exactly what you're thinking." Why couldn't he stop looking at her? She was so pretty. More than pretty. He loved the light brown freckles that dotted her nose, the tops of her cheeks, and her chin. Her hair was a mix of light brown and blond, like the sun had gently kissed the strands. She was a few inches shorter than him, enough that he could lean his chin on top of her head with ease.

"You only *think* you know what I'm thinking." Her caramel-colored eyes lit with indignation. "And you always made assumptions."

"Ha!" Silas pointed his finger at her. "There you *geh*, bringing up the past."

Faith's eyes widened. "You tricked me."

"Tricked. Right."

She huffed and scowled at him. "Why don't we prepare

a schedule of when we're going to meet, how we're going to work, what we're going to do, who's going to order supplies—"

"Wait a minute." The thought of every minute and detail being scheduled made his skin itch. "Let's take this one step at a time. How about we meet here tomorrow after supper instead? Then we can go over *yer* endless list of things we have to do."

"It's not an endless list and it's very important. You can't just show up here with tools and wood and make something."

"Actually you can. I've done it a lot, as you well know."

She folded her arms against her chest. "If we're going to do this together, then we need to do it according to a plan."

Silas took a step toward her. "*Yer* plan, I'm assuming?"

"Unless you have a plan, which would be a first in *yer* entire life."

He had to put a stop to this now or they would never get started on the kitchen, much less finish it. Doubts started creeping up again. "We'll come up with a plan together, one that will work for both of us."

She gave him a small nod. "Agreed."

"Then I'll see you tomorrow," Silas said.

Faith headed for the door. "Tomorrow it is." Then she left.

Silas took in the empty space. He removed his hat and rubbed the top of his head. They hadn't even started working and already they were arguing. *Lord, this will take a miracle.* But he had to make it work. He put his hat back on and turned off the gas lamp. As he left for home, he hoped God was still in the miracle-making business.

. . .

When Faith got home, she didn't go directly into the house. Instead she went into her grandfather's wood-shop and slammed the door. She turned on the lantern, then slumped onto the wood bench in front of the long, sawdust-covered table and let out a long sigh.

All the good intentions in the world wouldn't help her and Silas come up with a way to collaborate. And she still couldn't stop wondering why he was willing to work with her, even though it was clear that it would be an uphill battle for both of them. Silas wasn't known for sticking around when things got difficult. He had to have another reason for wanting this job, other than his friendship with Melvin. Just like she had her own reasons for not giving up.

She rose and picked up a small plank of oak, then set it on the table. Maybe she should back out. She ran her hand across the top of the wood, careful not to press too hard so splinters wouldn't burrow under her skin. Her hands were already rough, probably rougher than a woman's should be. But she didn't care. She'd earned the calluses on her skin, spending hours working and practicing her craft, first with her grandfather and then alone.

She had as much right to this job as Silas did.

Somehow she'd have to make this work, and she knew she couldn't do it on her own. "Lord, help me." Then she swallowed. "And Silas too. Help us work together without making each other crazy."

CHAPTER 5

The next evening Faith arrived at Martha and Melvin's new house well before the appointed meeting time with Silas. She had taken part of the day off and had stopped at Martha's to tell her about her and Silas's decision, saving Melvin and Martha another trip out there. She'd planned to do some quick measuring before Silas arrived. Yet right away, she noticed Silas's buggy was there. She frowned. He was never early. She renewed her determination. There was no reason she couldn't get the measurements she needed.

When she walked inside the kitchen, she stopped at the sight of Silas lying on his back on the plywood floor. His eyes were closed. He wasn't moving. He didn't even appear to be breathing.

Panic rushed through her, the image of her grandfather's collapse slamming into her with full speed. She knelt beside him. "Silas!" She touched his face, his chest, his arm. "Silas! Can you hear me?"

He opened one eye. "Of course I can hear you. You're screaming in *mei* ear."

Faith groaned and sat back, her heartbeat slowing

while her irritation mounted. "I can't believe you'd scare me like that."

His lips lifted in a smile as he looked at her. "Nice to know you still care."

She sniffed. "I'd care about anyone I found lying in the middle of the floor." She scowled. "What are you doing, anyway?"

"Visualizing." He jumped up from the floor, dust coating his dark blue pants. "And waiting for Melvin and Martha to arrive."

"They're not coming." She stood and crossed her arms.

"Why not?"

"I informed Martha about our decision."

He cocked his head to the side. "I see. You did this without consulting me?"

"I already consulted you. We decided last night to work together. I thought I'd spare Martha and Melvin the trip here. They've been very busy with wedding plans, you know."

"I know. And it's nice that you thought of them. But did it cross *yer* mind that I might have wanted to talk to them? To get an idea of the type of cabinets and flooring they want?"

Faith waved her hand. "I already know."

"Martha told you?"

"*Nee*. She said to use *mei* judgment. She trusts me to pick out what she would want."

"Does Melvin get a say in any of this?" Silas asked. "Do I?"

"Of course you do. And I'm sure Martha and Melvin will talk about it—"

"Like they discussed who was building their kitchen?"

He had a point. "Do you think Melvin really cares that much about the kitchen cabinets?"

"Knowing Melvin, he just wants to make Martha happy."

"And I know what will make Martha happy."

"So I don't have any input? I just take orders from you?"

Faith pulled a measuring tape out of her bag. "I'll take any suggestions or visualizations you'd like to offer."

"How generous of you."

She shot him a hard look. "You know I can't stand sarcasm."

"And I don't like being dismissed." He took a step forward. "This is supposed to be a collaboration, Faith. That means we each contribute equally."

Once again she got the sense that Silas was different. They were both twenty-two, but she'd always felt older than him, mostly because he was more interested in having fun than taking life seriously. But now, with him gazing at her in absolute solemn determination, they were on equal ground. "I'm sorry," she found herself saying, and meaning it. "I didn't realize I was shutting you out."

His brow lifted. "An apology? Never thought I'd hear one from you."

"What's that supposed to mean?"

"*Nix.*" He heaved a sigh. "Now it's *mei* turn to be sorry. You know how *mei* mouth gets ahead of *mei* brain sometimes." He gave her a lopsided grin. "How about we discuss our ideas now? Get them all out in the open so we can develop a plan."

"You want a plan?"

"Honestly, *nee*. But I realize that planning is important, especially on a project this size. Plus I know you like to have things in order."

She'd expected to have to fight him on that. She reached in her bag and pulled out her sketchbook, then handed it to him.

Silas thumbed through it. "What kind of wood were you thinking about using?"

"Oak. *Grossdaadi* has a lot of it in his woodshop."

"Enough for all these cabinets?"

"*Ya*," she said. "As long as we don't make any mistakes."

Looking up from the book, he said, "So you don't have enough."

"I just said as long as we don't make mistakes—"

"Faith, we will make mistakes. It's inevitable."

"With proper planning and measuring, we won't."

He handed the book to her. "*Nee* one's perfect, Faith. Not even you." He walked to the center of the room and lay back down, gazing up at the ceiling.

"I knew it. You don't believe in me."

Silas folded his hands over his middle. "I never said that. What I said was you weren't perfect." He turned his head slightly toward her. "Which is true." With that he gazed up at the ceiling again. "Stop being so touchy."

"I'm not touchy."

"*Danki* for proving *mei* point." He lifted his hands and started tracing imaginary lines in the air.

Faith watched him for a moment, fascinated. In the two years they'd dated, she'd never seen him at work. She'd seen the carpentry shop and projects he'd finished, but this was the first time she'd witnessed him visualizing. "Do you do this a lot?"

"Lie on the floor and draw in the air? *Nee*. Then again, I've never stocked a kitchen with cabinets." He closed his eyes and traced again.

Unable to resist, she lay down on the floor next to him and stared at the ceiling. "I don't get it," she said. "What are you looking at? Why are you doing this?" She flailed her arms in the air.

His hands covered her forearms. "You look like you're directing traffic," he said. "Close *yer* eyes."

"Silas, we don't have time for this."

"There's always time for imagination." He turned until their eyes met and their noses were nearly touching. "Carpentry isn't just cutting and nailing boards. There's an art to it."

Now he was sounding like her grandfather, which made her heart ache. A second, different kind of ache joined her grief. Being this close to Silas was activating butterflies in her stomach, a sensation she hadn't felt in a long time. She shouldn't be surprised. He'd been the only man who'd made her feel . . . giddy.

She didn't want to feel giddy. She didn't want to feel anything, especially about Silas. She pulled her arms away from him and scrambled to her feet. "Did you like *mei* ideas or not?" she said, brushing the dust from the skirt of her dress and refusing to look at him. Or to acknowledge the heat rising from her neck to her cheeks.

"I did." He sat up and spun around to face her, still sitting on the floor. "They're . . . adequate."

"Adequate?"

"That's not an insult, Faith. You sketched out some very utilitarian cabinets."

"Which is what Martha needs."

"True. But I think she'd like some with a little character."

Faith rolled her eyes. "You know we can't make fancy cabinets. She wouldn't want that anyway."

Silas stood and held out his hand. "May I?"

She hesitated, then handed him the sketchbook. He took a pencil from behind his ear and started drawing. Less than two minutes later he handed back the book.

Faith looked over what Silas had sketched out, and she had to admit she was impressed. He had taken her drawing and added details—he had drawn grooves in her plain doors to make a rectangle within each door. He added dark circles, and she realized those were knots on the wood. He also added lower cabinets with a mix of drawers and doors. It wasn't fancy, but it wasn't boring either. It was . . . inspired.

"Does it meet with *yer* approval?" he asked.

"*Ya*," she said, studying his additions. "Martha will love this." She looked up at him. "You got all that from lying down on the floor?"

"Nah. I'd been thinking about that last night." He grinned. "I was just lying on the floor to see if you would join me. Which you did."

"Ooh!" She started to toss the sketchbook at him, then remembered it was hers. "You haven't changed one bit!"

"Is that what you wanted?" he asked, his grin fading away. "For me to change?"

She paused. "I . . . I don't know."

He stepped back from her. "Well, *gut* thing we're not together anymore. And once we're done with this kitchen, you won't have to be around me again."

"Silas—"

"I've got to get home. I'll be over tomorrow evening to look at that wood." His eyes narrowed. "I know you said we'll have enough, but I'll be the judge of that." He brushed past her and walked out the door.

Faith didn't move. She couldn't, not when she was tingling from the top of her *kapp* to the tips of her stockings. She hadn't expected this. Hadn't planned for it. But she couldn't deny she was more attracted to Silas than ever before. Somehow she would have to deal with it.

. . .

The next morning Silas woke up in a good mood, something that hadn't happened for a long time. The fact that he'd dreamed about Faith last night might have had something to do with it. A good dream, where they got along, enjoyed each other's company, and the sadness that seemed to always be in her clear caramel-colored eyes had disappeared.

He'd seen a bit of that sadness diminish when he was teasing her last night. When he'd heard the buggy approach Melvin's house, he'd peeked out the window and saw it was Faith . . . and decided to have a little fun. He wasn't surprised when curiosity got the best of her and she joined him on the floor. He'd anticipated that. For all of her stuffy, stiff-as-a-board ways, she was insatiably curious.

What he hadn't anticipated was how strong his attraction to her still was. That had worried him for a split second as their faces were close enough that all he had to do was lean forward a fraction of an inch to kiss her. And despite everything that had happened between them, how she had cut him to the core by breaking off their engagement, he had to stop himself from stealing a kiss. He couldn't let himself get that close to her again. Predictably she'd gotten up and destroyed the moment between them. A good thing, for both their sakes.

But none of that affected his dream last night or his good feelings this morning. He whistled as he walked into the kitchen. Maybe he'd make pancakes for *Mamm*'s breakfast. She'd made them at least once a week for him when he was little, and even when he was not so little. He smiled as he reached for the cast-iron skillet in the cabinet next to the stove.

"Tommy?"

Silas froze, the skillet heavy in his hand. He set it on top of the stove and forced a smile as he faced his mother. "*Nee, Mamm.* It's Silas. Do you want some pancakes?"

"You look like Tommy." *Mamm* went to Silas and gazed up at him. Then she put her hand against his cheek. He hadn't shaved yet, and he felt her fingers brush his whiskers as she spoke. "I've missed you, Tommy."

He swallowed as he took her hand in his and gently

moved it away. "I'm not Tommy, *Mamm*," he repeated, willing her to understand him. "I'm Silas. I'm *yer sohn*."

"*Mei sohn?* I have a *sohn*?"

Pain pierced his heart. He had no idea who Tommy was. *Daed* didn't know either. But when *Mamm* was in one of these states, she kept talking about him. "*Ya*. You have a *sohn*. And I love you very much." He kissed her cheek. "Now, how about I make us those pancakes?"

"Pancakes." She frowned. She was still wearing her nightgown, her grayish-brown hair in a messy braid down her back. "Pancakes," she repeated. "Do I like pancakes?"

"You like *yer* pancake recipe," he said, trying again to smile and lighten the mood, which was becoming harder to do the more disoriented she got. "I'm not so sure you'll like mine, but maybe you'll give them a try anyway."

She tilted her head, her eyes filled with confusion, then she nodded. "I'll try them, Tommy."

"There you are," *Daed* said as he came into the kitchen. He looked at Silas, asking him an all-too-familiar silent question. *Is she all right?* Silas gave a quick shake of his head and started toward the pantry to get ingredients for pancakes.

"Emma," *Daed* said, going to *Mamm*'s side. "You need to sit down. Silas is going to make us breakfast."

"He is?" She looked at *Daed*. "Oh, *ya*. He is. I didn't know Silas liked to cook."

And just like that, she was back to normal. "I'm learning to like it," he said, grabbing the flour and baking powder. He shut the pantry door. "I'm just not very *gut* at it."

Mamm started to get up. "I'll make the pancakes."

Silas met his *daed*'s gaze. They both knew that wouldn't be a good idea. Until her condition was stabilized, she was unpredictable. "Silas can do it," *Daed* said, sitting next to her. He took her hand. "He doesn't mind."

"Nope. I don't mind at all. Besides, it's *gut* for me to learn how to cook."

"*Yer* wife should be doing that for you," *Mamm* said. "Where is Faith, anyway?"

"Emma, Silas and Faith aren't married."

"Oh." *Mamm* looked at Silas. "That's right. But you were going to get married, *ya*?"

"*Ya*." Any good mood he'd had before had completely vanished. Cold reality set in. He had a little fun with Faith, but that wouldn't last. There was too much pain between them. Too many misunderstandings. Which made him more determined to finish Melvin's kitchen as soon as possible.

Daed quietly talked to *Mamm* as Silas made pancakes. They were a little tough because he'd stirred the batter too much, but they were edible. At least *Mamm* was eating this morning. Last night *Daed* said she wouldn't touch her supper.

"I'm tired," *Mamm* said, putting down her fork. "I want to *geh* to sleep."

Daed finished chewing and stood. "I'll be right back, Silas," he said as *Mamm* got up from her chair. "Don't open the shop until I get back."

Silas nodded, then started cleaning the kitchen while his father took care of his mother. He sighed, his heart feeling like an anvil was dangling from it. *Why* Mamm,

Lord? Why does she have dementia? It wasn't the first time he'd asked those questions, and it wouldn't be the last. He was an only child, and his parents had had him late in life. But the doctor said *Mamm* was on the young side to have such an advanced case. And when *Daed* had asked for the prognosis, the doctor refused to give one.

Since that time two months ago, Silas's world had been turned upside down. He knew it would never be the same again.

"She fell right asleep," *Daed* said when he came back. Silas had just finished washing the dishes.

"She didn't sleep last night?"

Daed shook his head. "Not much." He looked ready to collapse.

"Why don't we get some help?" Silas put his hand on his *daed*'s shoulder. "You don't have to do this alone. The doctor said there are people who can stay with her during the *daag*, even at night if we need them to."

"*Nee.*" *Daed* shrugged Silas's hand off his shoulder. "We take care of our own."

"All right, then why don't we ask some of our neighbors and friends to help? I'm sure the older ladies in church—"

"I said *nee!*" *Daed* walked to the table and sat down. "I'm not ready for people to know about her. Not yet."

"They're already wondering." Silas sat down next to him. "I can't keep making excuses at church, and you can't keep sending people away when they stop by to visit her."

"I just thought . . . this new medicine, it's supposed to help." *Daed* sat up straight. "It will help. We have to give it more time. Then she'll be back to her old self." He smiled, but the smile didn't reach his eyes. "You'll see, Silas. We'll have *yer mamm* back soon."

Silas felt a crack form in his soul. His father was in denial. "What if we don't?" he asked quietly.

His father looked at Silas, tears in his eyes. "Then it's God's will. And we'll have faith that He'll see us through." He stood and put his hand on Silas's shoulder. "I better check on her. Make sure she's still asleep."

Silas sank into his chair, then leaned forward and rubbed the stabbing pain in the back of his neck. While he believed God would get them through whatever happened with *Mamm*, that didn't mean he shouldn't be prepared. He let out a bitter laugh. Now he sounded like Faith. That was her motto. Be prepared. Have a plan. Stay in control. But Silas didn't have control over his mother's illness, or anything else. *God is in control.* The reminder gave him some comfort.

CHAPTER 6

Y ou're out of sorts."
Faith looked at Grace, who was standing next to her as they refilled the candy bins in the back of the store. She picked up a dipper full of black licorice drops and poured them into the plastic bin. "I'm fine." She glanced at her hand holding the dipper, aggravated that it was shaking. She'd been unnerved all day, not only because of her reaction to Silas yesterday when he left Martha's new house, but because she would see him again this evening. How did everything get so complicated? She thought the hardest part of working on the kitchen would be making the cabinets. She didn't imagine it would be fighting her feelings for Silas.

"The gumdrops *geh* in that bin," Grace said, tapping Faith on the arm, then pointing to the plastic container next to the black licorice.

Faith looked down and groaned. Now she had mixed up the colorful spice drops with black licorice pieces. Fortunately she was wearing clear plastic gloves, so she could reach in and fish out the gumdrops. The mistake wasn't a big deal, but her carelessness was uncharacteristic. She couldn't afford to be distracted while she was woodworking. That could cause an accident or injury. She let out a sigh as she pulled out two red gumdrops.

"Faith."

Grace's serious tone got Faith's attention. "What?"

"Something's bothering you. I know you're tired—"

"I'm not tired."

"You haven't gone to bed before one a.m. for the past four *daags*."

"Neither have you, since you've been keeping track."

"It's hard *not* to when you keep waking me up. It's *mei* room too." She closed the top of the butterscotch bin. "Maybe you should move out into the woodshop," she said, her tone filled with sarcasm. "You spend more time there than at home."

"Maybe I should."

"Faith, Grace." Mr. Furlong was walking toward them from the end of the aisle. His thick gray eyebrows flattened above square, brown glasses. "I can hear you bickering from the other side of the store. I don't know what you two are fighting about, but it will stop now."

Faith and Grace both nodded, neither of them saying anything. Mr. Furlong gave them one last warning look before walking away. Faith blew out a breath, relieved that since she and Grace had been speaking *Dietsch* at least Mr. Furlong and the Yankee customers hadn't understood their ridiculous argument. "Sorry," Faith said, closing the licorice bin and opening up the spice drop container beside it.

"I'm sorry too. I know you don't like to talk about

yer feelings much." Grace tied up the large bag of butterscotch pieces. "I just wanted to help."

"I know." Faith sighed, pausing before she dug the scoop into the gumdrops. "I promise, there's *nix* to talk about. And I promise I won't come in so late anymore. I shouldn't have been so thoughtless about waking you up."

"I appreciate it. After all, I need *mei* beauty sleep." Grace winked at her and walked away.

Faith smiled. Her sister never failed to make her feel better. She and Silas were similar in that way. She gripped the scoop again. Silas. What was she going to do about him?

After she finished filling up the candy bins, she took her afternoon break. She went outside and pulled out her sketchbook. But instead of drawing, she wrote out a schedule. If she did most of the cabinet building in her grandfather's woodshop, then she and Silas wouldn't have to work together. He was putting in the flooring, so he could focus on that while she made the cabinets. Then when he was done she could install the cabinets, which wouldn't take her more than a day or two. When she was finished, she had made sure she and Silas wouldn't see each other until the end of the month, except for tonight.

Satisfied, she put her sketchbook away and went back to work. The rest of the day went smoothly, and when she and Grace went home, they helped *Mamm* with supper while Charity and Patience were outside working with *Daed* as he tilled the garden. It wouldn't be long before they would start planting vegetables and flowers.

During supper, Faith glanced at the clock on the

kitchen wall. It was six thirty and Silas would be here soon. His house was within walking distance. She realized she needed to tell her parents he was coming over. "Silas is stopping by tonight," she said, then shoved a scoop of mashed potatoes into her mouth.

Mamm's brow rose so high it nearly touched her hairline. "He is?"

Faith had to hide a frown at the enthusiasm in her mother's voice. She glanced around the table and saw that her three sisters were looking at her with curious expressions. Only her father seemed more interested in food than Faith's announcement. She choked down the potatoes. "He's going to look at the wood in *Grossdaadi*'s woodshop."

That got her father's attention, as it always did when his father was brought up. "Why?"

She sighed inwardly. There was no reason to lie. "Because we're working on a project together."

"Oooh," Charity said.

Faith gave her a look. Since she was thirteen, Faith would excuse her immature teasing.

"Oooh," Patience and Grace added.

"It's not like that." Faith put down her fork.

"So you're helping Silas build something?" *Daed* said.

"That's nice of him to include you," *Mamm* added. "Especially after . . . well, you know."

"I'm not helping him." Faith crossed her arms over her chest, well aware she was not only losing patience but maturity. "We're working on the project together."

"What project is that?" *Daed* cut into his meat loaf with the side of his fork.

"We're making kitchen cabinets for Martha and Melvin. Together. Equal partners."

Daed scratched his head. "You don't know how to make cabinets."

This was what she was afraid of, that she'd have to defend herself. "I helped *Grossdaadi* refurbish Katherine Troyer's cabinets."

"That's not the same as building them."

"I've read up on how to make cabinets. And tables, chairs, rockers."

"Whose idea was this?" *Mamm* wiped the corner of her mouth with a napkin. "Surely not Silas's."

Faith explained with as few words as possible about Martha and Melvin hiring both her and Silas. "That's why he's coming over and we're picking out the wood."

"Sounds boring." Charity took a drink of milk.

"Or it could be romantic." Fourteen-year-old Patience put her chin in her hand. "You two might even get back together."

"That will *never* happen." Faith pushed away from the table, irritated that her face was heating as she thought about the jolt of attraction that had gone through her last night when she and Silas were together. "We're two different people."

"You're not as different as you think." Grace's voice could barely be heard above Charity and Patience's discussion of how they were sure the wedding would be back on within the next few months.

Faith looked at her, wondering if her sister knew something she didn't. Grace wasn't teasing. Instead she looked stern and serious, which was unusual for her. "I've got to *geh*," Faith said. "Silas will be here any minute."

"Oooh," Patience and Charity chimed.

"Will you stop that!"

"*Maed*," *Mamm* said. "That's enough." She looked at Faith. "After you and Silas are finished in the workshop, make sure you invite him inside for some cake and coffee."

"In other words, be polite," Grace said.

Faith gave her a quick nod and turned, snatching her sketchbook off the counter before walking out the kitchen door. She gulped the fresh evening air, breathing in the sweet, rich scent of mown grass and tilled earth from the garden patch to the left of the house. She didn't want to invite Silas in for cake and coffee, even though that would be the hospitable thing to do. All she wanted was for him to look at the wood, tell her she was right about having enough to make the cabinets, and leave after she gave him their schedule. She went to the woodshop and turned on the lantern.

She sat down on the bench and waited for Silas to appear. And waited. And waited. Then she paced back and forth, opening the door and checking outside. The sun had gone down, which meant she had been out here for nearly forty-five minutes. Where was he?

Frustration rose within her. She shouldn't be surprised that he was late. He had always been late when they were dating. She was a punctual person, and when he would show up half an hour after he said he'd pick her up for a singing or a ride in his buggy, she had to force herself not to lose her temper. He always had an excuse—he lost track of time, he had to work extra at the shop to get a project done because he hadn't realized how long it would take to finish, he'd fallen asleep on the couch. And she was expected to accept these excuses with a smile and forgiving spirit. Initially, she did. But then she got tired of it.

She waited a little longer, her anger growing stronger with each passing minute. Then she couldn't stand it anymore. She grabbed her flashlight, turned off the lantern, and headed for Silas's. He wasn't going to do this to her. They had a job to do, and if he couldn't be responsible enough to show up on time to pick out wood, how could she rely on him in the future? *I can't rely on him at all.* She knew that firsthand, and him proving that to her again cut her deeply.

. . .

"Tommy? Tommy? Why am I here, Tommy?"

Silas clenched his jaw and went to his mother's side. She was sitting on the couch, pulling on the skirt of her dress, looking scared and bewildered. "You're home, *Mamm,*" he said, trying to take her hand.

She snatched it from him. "Who are you?" she said, backing away from him.

"I'm Silas," he said, for the tenth time in the past hour. He glanced at the front door. Where was his father? At supper *Daed* said he needed to take a walk. Silas understood why. *Daed* needed a break. *Mamm* had been agitated all day, and it had gotten worse when the sun went down. Now Silas wasn't only worried about his mother, but his father too.

"Silas? Where's Tommy?"

"I don't know," Silas said absently, glancing at the small clock on the mantel of their fireplace. *Daed* had given *Mamm* the clock as a twenty-fifth wedding anniversary present almost ten years ago. It was nearly eight thirty. He gritted his teeth. Faith would be furious with him for being so late, but it couldn't be helped. He couldn't leave his mother alone, not even to go find his father. "*Mamm*," he said, lowering his voice and speaking softly like he'd heard his father do. "It's bedtime. You must be tired."

"I'm not tired." She stood and walked away.

Silas followed her. She went into the kitchen and started throwing open drawers. Silas shut them behind her. The medicine wasn't working. This was the worst he'd seen her. "Tell me what you're looking for and I can find it for you."

"Spoons," she said, opening the drawer that held the silverware. She stared at it, then walked away.

"The spoons are right here." Silas grabbed a handful and showed them to her.

She pushed his hand away and sat down at the table. Then she stared straight ahead.

"Lord, please," Silas whispered, his voice cracking. "Please help her."

He heard a knock on the front door and froze. His mother didn't move, just gazed straight ahead with an empty expression. Should he answer the door? If his father were here, he would send whoever stopped by

away, especially with *Mamm* being like this. Could
Silas even leave her to answer the door? He decided to
ignore it, even when the knocking grew louder. When it
stopped, he breathed a sigh of relief and leaned against
the table. *"Mamm?"*

She didn't move or say a word.

"If you think I'm going to put up with *yer* irresponsibility, think again Silas Graber!"

He spun around at the sound of Faith's shrill voice,
then groaned. He didn't need this right now. "How did
you get in?"

"Yer door is unlocked." She narrowed her gaze. "I
knew you were ignoring me."

Silas went to her, hoping he could calm her down.
She had a right to be mad, but unlike in the past, he
hadn't not shown up out of carelessness. "Faith, it's not
a *gut* time—"

"It never is, is it? You always have an excuse for going
back on *yer* word. This is a job, Silas. One you said you
would take seriously. I'm not going to be pushed aside
or ignored because you can't be bothered to—"

"Tommy? Tommy?"

The fear in his mother's voice made him forget about
Faith's tirade. He went to her side, about to tell her that
he was Silas. Instead, he said, "I'm here."

"Oh, Tommy." She took his hand and put it against
her cheek. "I've been looking everywhere for you." She
glanced up at him, tears in her confused eyes. "I want
to *geh* home."

"You are home." He couldn't stop the tears from spill-
ing from his own eyes. "I wish you could understand that."

She jumped up from her chair and turned on him. "I want to *geh* home!"

"Silas," Faith said. "What's wrong with *yer mamm*?"

"*Geh* to the phone shanty and call an ambulance." He was in over his head. His father would be angry, but his mother needed a doctor. He expected Faith to give him a hard time, but she immediately dashed out the door.

He spent the rest of the time until the ambulance arrived alternately calming down his mother and trying to get her to see reality. She had a few lucid moments, but she was growing more agitated. Just as the ambulance pulled up, *Daed* walked in the door.

"What's going on?" he said, hurrying to *Mamm*. "Emma, talk to me."

But she had gone into another speechless state. Silas looked at his father. "She's got to *geh* to the hospital."

He nodded. "I'm sorry, *sohn*. I was walking and I got so tired. I sat down under the tree by the pond near the Troyers'. I guess I fell asleep."

"It's okay," Silas said as the paramedics arrived.

"We'll take it from here," a short, stocky woman said.

Silas stepped back and watched as the woman talked gently and quietly to *Mamm*, while the other paramedic, a tall, thin male, spoke with *Daed*. The female paramedic somehow convinced *Mamm* to go with her to the ambulance. "I'm riding with her," *Daed* said.

"I'll meet you at the hospital," Silas said.

But *Daed* shook his head. "Stay here, *sohn*. I'll take care of this."

"But—"

"I said stay here!"

Silas nodded, and it was only after the ambulance left with his parents inside that he remembered Faith was still there—and she had seen everything.

CHAPTER 7

Faith couldn't speak when Silas turned around and faced her. All she could do was stare at him, her heart breaking, not only for him but for his mother and father. Then the pain she saw in Silas's eyes spurred her to action. She went to him. "What happened?"

He brushed past her and walked to the kitchen without saying a word. Faith followed him. There were a few kitchen drawers open, and Silas went around and closed them. "Silas," she said, "is *yer mamm* all right?"

He whirled around and glared at Faith. "You saw her. Did she look all right? Did she act all right?" He shook his head. "*Geh* home, Faith."

But she wasn't budging, not after what she saw, and not when Silas was so distraught. She went to the stove where the percolator sat. "Let me make us some *kaffee*—"

"For once in *yer* life will you listen to me?" Silas shouted. "I don't want *kaffee*, and I don't want you here. Get . . . out." His chest heaved as he spoke, and his voice cracked on the last word.

His words hurt her, but she stood her ground. "I'm not leaving until I know you're okay."

"Then you're gonna be here a long time." He sagged

into a chair and his head fell into his hands. "Forget what you saw."

"I can't." She sat down next to him. "How long has she been like that?"

He shrugged. "It started a couple of months ago. She's on medication but"—he lifted his head, his eyes haunted—"you can see for *yerself* it doesn't work. She's actually gotten worse since she started taking it. She's got dementia . . . and there's *nee* cure."

"Oh, Silas."

"Don't." He shot up from the chair. "Don't you dare give me *yer* pity." He glared at her. "Now I know why *mei daed* didn't want any help. Didn't want to tell anyone. We don't need you feeling sorry for us."

"I don't." But it was a lie. She was still shaking a little bit from the shock of seeing Silas's sweet mother having a complete breakdown. She didn't know a lot about dementia, but she vaguely remembered that she hadn't seen much of his mother lately, and she wasn't in church at the last service. Faith had to admit she also hadn't paid much attention. Avoiding Silas had meant avoiding his parents too.

"I've got to get to the hospital," Silas said, storming out of the kitchen.

Faith followed him. "*Yer daed* said to stay here."

"I'm not going to leave him alone." Silas spun around in the middle of the living room, his shoulders slumped. "I'm not . . ."

She couldn't stand seeing him like this. She went and put her arms around him. "It will be okay, Silas."

He leaned his cheek against the top of her *kapp* but

didn't return her embrace. "*Nee*, it won't. She's only going to get worse, until we won't be able to take care of her." He sniffed. "I'm not sure we'll be able to take care of her anymore after tonight."

She stepped back and took his hands. "Listen to me, Silas Graber. You're not giving up. I won't let you. We're going to pray for her, and for *yer daed*."

His gaze met hers. "Don't you think I've been doing that?"

"Then we'll do it again. And we'll keep praying." She squeezed his hands, closed her eyes, and prayed.

• • •

Silas was so tired. Every bone in his body ached. His heart ached. His soul even ached. But there was something sweetly peaceful about Faith holding his hands while she prayed with absolute confidence for his mother.

Without thinking, he tightened his grip on her hands. He hadn't held her hand in months. He felt the rough skin, the calluses so similar to his own. For that brief moment while she prayed, he did believe everything would be okay. Then again, she always had that effect on him when they were together. She was calm. Steady. And deeply emotional, even though she tried to hide it.

"Amen." She let go of his hands and stepped away, then looked up at him and smiled.

He nearly melted inside. Her smile made her face shine like the sun on a cloudless summer day.

"Should I let Martha and Melvin know you can't work on the kitchen?" Her voice was soft and . . . hopeful?

It also broke his trance. "You'll what?"

The smile faded. "You can't possibly work on the kitchen when *yer* mother is so ill."

His mouth fell open. "Unbelievable."

"Silas, I'm trying to help you."

"You're helping *yerself*." He pointed at her. "I knew you were still mad at me about the past. I have *nee* idea why, though."

"*Nee* idea?" Her tone turned shrill, the way it usually did when she was ticked off. "I told you why I was angry."

"Because you can't count on me, *ya*, I remember." He leveled his gaze on her. "And now I know I can't count on you. You would use *mei mamm*, after seeing how sick she is, to make sure you get what you want. So you'll have all the money from the job *yerself*." When her eyes widened, he huffed. "Don't act like that's not what you're doing." He turned and stalked off, then spun around again. "You're a piece of work, you know that? A selfish, spoiled brat who only thinks of herself."

Her lower lip trembled, and he almost took the words back. But he couldn't. First she shattered his heart, breaking off their engagement with some lame excuse about how she couldn't handle his irresponsibility. Which wasn't completely inaccurate, but she didn't even give them a chance to work things out. Now she wanted the kitchen job all to herself. She'd get all the money—money he and his father needed. And to think he actually believed she cared about his parents . . . about him. He was such a fool.

Yet as she stood there looking shocked, her lips quivering and her eyes filling with tears, his heart ripped even more. Unable to face her, he turned his back. Seconds later he heard the front door slam shut.

He looked up at the ceiling. "You know what, Lord?" he said, shouting. "She can have the job. I'll figure some other way to pay the bills. I'll take care of it myself." He fell into a chair, tears flowing again. He was helpless to do anything. He couldn't fix his mother. He couldn't work with Faith. He couldn't run the carpentry shop by himself, and he couldn't do the kitchen job. She was right about that. Not when his mother was so unstable. Not when he was sure he was going to lose her sooner than he'd ever thought.

. . .

Faith felt numb on her way home from Silas's. How dare he accuse her of taking advantage of the awful situation with his mother? Couldn't he see she was being practical? That she was trying to ease his burden, one she didn't know about until tonight? Instead he took her offer all wrong. Called her selfish. How could he say that to her after she had prayed so fervently for his family?

Yes, she should be angry. But she felt nothing. Nee, *not nothing. I'm hurting.*

She went inside, not bothering to be quiet. It wasn't that late, even though everyone was already in bed.

When she got to her room, Grace was sitting on the edge of her bed, brushing out her hair. Faith sat down on her own bed, not saying anything.

"Faith?" Grace put down the hairbrush. "Did Silas come over? Did you two get into a fight?"

"He didn't come over. But we did get into a fight."

"What does that mean?"

Faith looked at Grace. "I can't talk about it." She rose from the bed to get her nightgown, still in pain from Silas's words, and worse, the expression of stark betrayal on his face. He really did believe she was selfish and spoiled. Had he always felt that way? If so, why had they dated in the first place? Why had he asked her to marry him? Why had he once told her he loved her?

"Faith," Grace said, coming behind her. "Did you *geh* see Silas?"

She nodded, unfolding her nightgown.

"Does this have something to do with his *mamm*?"

Faith whirled around. "What do you know about Emma?"

Grace's eyes filled with sadness. "I know she's sick. She was at the store a few weeks ago and she was acting strange. First she forgot why she was there, then she couldn't remember *mei* name. I told her who I was, but when she left she said, 'Good-bye, Faith.' I'm not the only one who's noticed she's been behaving a little off recently. And the past two weeks *nee* one has seen her, and Silas's *daed* won't let anyone stop by."

Faith frowned. "You knew all this?"

Grace nodded. "You would, too, if you paid attention." She stepped back. "I don't want to hurt *yer* feelings, because it looks like you and Silas went at it pretty hard, but you've spent so much time isolated from everyone since *Grossdaddi* died. Even when you're not in the woodshop, *yer* mind is there . . . or somewhere else." She ran her finger under her nose. "You're not the only one who lost someone. I miss him too. I know you were his favorite—"

"I wasn't his favorite."

"*Ya*, you were. We all knew that. And it was okay, just like we understood that his death was the hardest on you. But that doesn't give you the right to stay isolated from the rest of the world. You're being—"

"Selfish." The word hit her to the core. Silas was right. She was selfish. She'd been so wrapped up in her grief—and yes, her pride—that she hadn't even noticed what was going on in her own community. Then she remembered Silas had mentioned money. *"So you'll have all the money from the job* yerself." He had no idea she wasn't getting paid for making the cabinets. But now his desperation to have the job made sense. Undoubtedly the medical bills for his mother were mounting up.

Faith sank down on the bed, feeling horrible. "I'm a terrible person."

Grace settled beside her. "*Nee*, you're not. You're hurting, though. And in *yer* typical independent way, you're not letting anyone help you."

"He didn't want *mei* pity," she whispered, remembering something else Silas said. And she understood that. He wanted to be strong, to show everyone else he was strong. Like she had after her grandfather died.

She'd used his death as an excuse to push Silas away—just like Silas had accused her of using his mother's illness. "I have to apologize to him," she said. She turned to Grace. "But I don't know how."

"You'll figure it out." Grace took her hand and squeezed it. "But not tonight. Sleep on it. Maybe something will come to you in the morning."

They both got into bed and Grace turned out the light. "*Danki*," Faith said as she turned on her side. "And I'm sorry if I've been acting like a spoiled brat."

"You haven't." Grace yawned. "I don't know where you got that idea."

Faith shut her eyes. *I do.*

CHAPTER 8

Silas's head popped up from the kitchen table as he heard the front door open. He blinked and looked down at his arms, which were folded in front of him. When had he fallen asleep? He stood as his father walked into the kitchen, his boots thudding heavily on the floor.

"Where's *Mamm*?" Silas said, going to his father.

Daed gave Silas a weary smile. "She's okay, *sohn*. She's still at the hospital." Then his smile grew. "They misdiagnosed her."

"What?"

"She doesn't have dementia."

Silas's brow furrowed. "But she's been forgetting things. And the hallucinations, and the combative behavior, and calling me Tommy . . . what else could it be?"

"Something with her thyroid." *Daed* sat down at the table. He pulled a scrap of paper out of the pocket of his pants. "Hashimoto's ence . . . encepho . . ." He handed the paper to Silas. "Here, you read it."

"Hashimoto's encephalopathy." Silas frowned. "What is it?"

"The way the doc explained it, her thyroid gland"—he pointed to the center of his neck, pressing his finger against his salt-and-pepper beard—"is acting up. It's a rare disease, but one that can be managed with medication. The right medication."

Silas joined him at the table. "So all those symptoms her other doctor thought were dementia were really from this?"

Tears welled in *Daed*'s eyes. "*Ya.*" He clasped his hands together and started to weep. "Silas, I wasn't ready to lose her. But I thought I would. And I thought I would be okay, knowing that if she died, it would be God's will." He wiped his eyes with a handkerchief. "I've been so scared."

"So have I." Silas swallowed around the lump in his throat. "She's been so sick the past few *daags*."

"Even that's a blessing. If we hadn't gotten her to the emergency room when we did, she could have gone into a coma. The doctors want to keep her for a couple of *daags* to make sure the thyroid medicine works, but they're sure it will. You did the right thing by calling for help." He looked down at the table. "I might . . . I might not have if I'd been here."

Silas wanted to say the opposite, but knew that wasn't true. His father had been so private, so insistent on dealing with *Mamm* his way. After Silas's fight with Faith, he understood. Yet that didn't mean they should have been fighting this alone. "I want to see her," he said.

"You will when she comes home. Right now they want her to rest. She hasn't slept well in *daags*. Neither have I." He got up and rolled his shoulders. "I feel like

I could sleep for a month, now that I know she's going to be all right."

Silas nodded. "I'll take care of the shop," he said.

Daed put his hand on Silas's shoulder. "I know you will. You've proven *yerself* through all this, Silas. I underestimated you."

"I needed to grow up."

"And you have. I'm looking forward to joining you back at work, as soon as *yer mamm* is settled at home."

"That sounds great. But right now, you need to get some sleep."

His father nodded and left. Silas sank down onto the chair, bent his head, and prayed, giving thanks that his mother would be all right. When he finished, he realized he was starving. He had just started to fix himself some eggs when there was a tap on the back door of the kitchen. He peered through the window and frowned. What was Faith doing here?

. . .

At first Faith didn't think Silas would open the door. Not that she blamed him. For the first time she realized how much she had hurt him, not just by accusing him of being irresponsible but also by ending their relationship. Through the kitchen window she could see how tired he was. Even at this distance the dark shadows were evident under his eyes. He stared at her for a moment through the glass. Maybe this was a bad idea. Maybe she should turn around and go to work. She was late as it was, but Grace said she would explain to Mr. Furlong why Faith was running late. Just as she was about to turn around, Silas moved and opened the door.

"Why are you here?" he asked in a flat tone.

"I wanted to know how *yer mamm* is doing . . . and how you're doing."

"She's fine." He leaned against the door, the tension in his face lessening a bit. "They had the wrong diagnosis. She's on new medication and after a couple of *daags* in the hospital she'll be able to come home. She should be back to normal soon enough."

"That's wonderful news." Faith smiled.

"It is." He glanced down at the floor, then back at her. "*Danki* for praying for her . . . for us."

"You're welcome." She threaded her fingers together. "Can I come in? We need to talk."

He nodded and opened the door wider. "I was just about to make breakfast. Do you want anything?"

"*Nee.*" She was about to sit down, then changed her mind. "Why don't I make you breakfast?"

Silas turned around, and she almost laughed at the shock on his face. "Seriously?"

"*Ya.* You look exhausted."

He nodded. "I am."

"Then let me fix you something to eat."

Without a moment's hesitation he nodded, then sat down at the kitchen table. She was able to find things in the tidy kitchen quickly, and soon she had coffee percolating and eggs and bacon frying on the stove. She poured a cup of coffee and added a little milk to it, remembering how Silas liked it. She turned to give

it to him and saw that his head was down on the table.
She set the mug down beside him, but he didn't stir.
Something inside her broke free, and the love she used
to feel for him surfaced. She touched his hair, brushing
a thick, curly brown strand from his forehead.

Instantly he sat up, then looked up at her. "Sorry.
Must have dozed off." Then he picked up the coffee mug
and took a sip.

"Does it need more milk?"

He shook his head. "It's perfect."

"The eggs and bacon will be done soon." She started
to walk away, then stopped when she felt his hand on
her arm.

"Why are you doing this?" he asked, his eyes filled
with confusion.

"Because I want to." She went back to the stove, surprised at how natural and easy things seemed between
them. As if making breakfast for him was something
she should have been doing all along. But when she slid
the eggs onto his plate and placed three pieces of thick,
crispy bacon beside them, a knot formed in her stomach. She'd come here with a purpose, and she couldn't
put that off any longer.

"Here," she said, setting the plate in front of him.
Then she sat down, not waiting for an invitation to join
him. She folded her hands, staying silent until he finished praying.

When he was done, he opened his eyes and picked
up his fork. "You're not eating?"

"I already had breakfast." Which was only half true.
She'd eaten part of a banana nut muffin, not having

much of an appetite. It was hard to admit she was wrong, that she was sorry. It was difficult to swallow her pride, but she had to do it, for both her and Silas's sakes. "I didn't just come here to check on *yer mamm*. I came here to apologize."

Silas stopped mid-chew. "Really," he said, then swallowed a mouthful of eggs. "Two apologies in a week? That's got to be a record." Quickly he raised his hand. "Now I'm sorry. I shouldn't have said that."

"It's okay." She looked down at the table. "One of the reasons I can't stand sarcasm is that it always holds a bit of truth. In this case, a lot of truth."

"Faith, it's okay." He put down his fork and looked at her. "I appreciate *yer* apology."

"You don't even know what I'm apologizing for."

"Doesn't matter. The fact that you're here and we're talking without fighting . . ." He smiled. "I'll take it."

His smile reached all the way to her toes. He was so handsome. Charming, sweet, and creative. Now she knew he was loyal, and had been so devoted to his family that he hadn't betrayed their trust. Perhaps he always had been loyal and she'd been too self-absorbed to see it. "I shouldn't have broken up with you the way I did."

"Are you talking about the one-sentence letter you sent me?"

"Um, *ya*. That. And refusing to see you after. That was selfish of me."

He picked up a piece of bacon and took a bite. "*Geh* on," he said around the food.

"You're not going to make this easy on me, are you?"

"Should I?" His voice was soft. "You tore out *mei* heart, Faith. I wanted to marry you. To spend the rest of *mei* life with you. I deserved more than a letter and the silent treatment."

"I know." She started to tug on the string of her *kapp*. "I handled it wrong. I should have explained why I couldn't marry you. When *Grossdaadi* died, I was devastated. I also felt guilty."

"His death wasn't *yer* fault, Faith."

"But I could have helped him. If I'd been paying attention instead of being so focused on working in the woodshop, I would have heard him collapse." Tears stung her eyes as she looked at Silas. "He died right outside the door."

He took her hand and held it tight. "Faith, the aneurysm took him instantly. Even if you had heard him right away, there was *nix* you could have done."

Tears ran down her cheeks. "That doesn't make me feel any better. I miss him so much, Silas."

Silas turned his chair so he could face her. Then he took her other hand. "I know that now. And I wasn't there for you like I should have been. I was late for the funeral. Then I didn't come by *yer haus* until hours after."

"I needed you to be by *mei* side," she said, sniffling.

"And I should have been." He let go of her hands. "I don't have a *gut* excuse, other than I didn't take *yer* pain seriously. I was also a coward."

She looked at him. "What?"

"I've had a pretty easy life, one I've taken for granted. *Daed*'s business has always been *gut*, so we never wanted for anything. *Mamm* was always there for me.

She and *Daed* had never been sick, and I never knew *mei* grandparents. They all died before I was born. I'd never lost anyone I loved. Until you left me. And even then, I didn't really understand how deep grief is . . . until I thought I would lose *Mamm*." He reached for her hand again. "So if anyone needs to apologize, it's me. What kind of husband would I have been if I couldn't be there for you when you needed me most?"

"Silas, I . . ." She didn't know how to respond. He'd said the perfect thing. The mature thing. "We both made mistakes," she finally admitted. "You're not the only one who had some growing up to do. So I wanted you to know—I'm not going to build the cabinets for Martha."

Silas frowned. "Why not?"

"Because I don't know what I'm doing. I have to be honest about that. I would slow down the process, and I know how much you need the money and the work. It's better that another carpenter work with you, one who is more experienced."

He shook his head. "We can work together. And you're not giving *yerself* enough credit."

"*Nee*, I've given myself too much. I've been prideful, Silas. I'm glad Martha has faith in me, but—"

"She's not the only one," he said, his eyes holding hers. "I know you have talent. The only thing you lack is experience."

His words gave her a warm feeling. "Which is why this isn't the right time for me to gain that experience. So I'm going to tell Martha today to find another carpenter."

"Are you sure?"

"I'm sure. I can make something else for Martha and Melvin." She chuckled. "Maybe a bread box."

"Faith," Silas said, moving closer to her. *"Danki."*

She couldn't stop looking into his eyes, and she saw something familiar in them. Love. But a different kind of love this time. One that was deeper. More mature. One that she strongly felt in return. When he leaned forward and kissed her, she didn't resist. Everything felt right—kissing him, giving up what she thought was her chance to prove herself, laying down her pride.

He pulled away from her and smiled again. "Wasn't sure you would let me do that."

"I'm glad you did."

"Tell you what. How about you help me with *mei* part of the kitchen job? I could use *yer* design and help with measuring, and you can keep me on schedule."

Excitement grew within her. She would be a part of the project after all. "I think I can do that."

"Gut. Because there's an added bonus in it for me."

"What's that?"

"We'll be together."

She put her arms around his neck and whispered in his ear, "That's a bonus for me too."

CHAPTER 9

"O kay, both of you close *yer* eyes." Faith tried to stem her excitement as she led Martha into the finished kitchen, Melvin at her heels. When they were all in the middle of the room, she said, "Now you can open them."

"Oh, Faith." Martha looked around the kitchen, tears in her eyes. "This is perfect."

Melvin walked over to Silas, who was standing next to the gas stove on the opposite side of the room. He shook Silas's hand. "*Gut* job," he said, grinning.

"She seems to like it." Silas tilted his head toward Martha, who was turning around in the middle of the room.

"Here," Faith said. "Let me show you around." The kitchen was simple and utilitarian, like she initially designed. But Silas had added his artistic touch, not only using the oak wood from her grandfather's shop but also mixing different types of wood—cherry, maple, and some birch—to give the cabinets a unique look. The pantry was deep and had a sliding door instead of one that opened out. The stain was light oak, but the knots and character of the wood shone through. While Silas and another carpenter, Levi Beachy, had done most of the building, Faith had done a lot of the finishing work, mostly sanding and staining.

"Faith, I love it." Martha hugged her cousin. "Now that the rest of the *haus* is nearly finished, I can't wait to move in after the wedding."

Silas appeared at Faith's side. He looked down at her as Martha and Melvin continued to take in the kitchen, remarking on the flooring, which Silas had put in himself. Now that his father was able to work in the shop because his mother was better, Silas had had more time to devote to finishing the kitchen, which he completed as scheduled.

"We should probably *geh*," Silas said, leaning down and whispering in Faith's ear.

"*Ya*. I doubt they'll even know we're gone."

She and Silas told them good-bye. Martha and Melvin waved to them, and they left. A short while later while they were riding home, Faith expected Silas to take her to her house. Instead he took her to his home.

"Why are we here?" she asked.

"I want to show you something. *Geh* on in the *haus*. I'll be there in a minute."

While he put the buggy away, she walked inside. Over the past month she had spent a lot of time here, and she didn't feel the need to knock on the door. When she walked into the living room, she saw Emma sitting there, her knitting needles clacking with rapid speed. "Hi, Faith," she said, her smile sweet and calm.

She looked happy, and most of all, healthy. The thyroid medication had worked, and although she'd have to take it for the rest of her life, she would be okay. "Where's Silas?"

"Putting up the buggy." Faith sat down on the edge of the couch. "He said he had something to show me."

"Oh." Emma put down her knitting. "Can I get you something to drink?"

"*Nee*. I don't want to interrupt *yer* work."

"You're not. I was just sitting here . . . waiting."

But Faith didn't miss her small smile. "Do you know what Silas is going to show me?"

Emma picked up her knitting again. "You'll have to wait and see."

"Hmmph," Faith said.

After several minutes Silas came inside. He bent over and kissed his mother on the cheek. Faith smiled. Since her illness he hadn't been shy with showing his affection for her, even though it wasn't typically the Amish way.

Emma put her knitting in the basket beside her chair. "I'm heading for bed," she said. "*Yer* father is probably sound asleep by now. *Gute nacht.*" She touched Faith on the shoulder as she passed by the couch and left the room.

"I'm so glad she's feeling well," Faith said when Silas sat down next to her.

"Me too."

"Did you ever ask her who Tommy was?"

"*Ya.*" He sighed. "She has *nee* idea. She didn't know anyone named Tommy growing up. Her doctor said some hallucinations don't have an explanation." He angled his body toward Faith. "I don't want to talk about *Mamm* right now. I brought you here for another reason." He pulled a piece of paper out of his pocket and handed it to her.

She unfolded it. It was a sketch of a small house—a *dawdi* house, to be exact—attached to a larger house, which looked suspiciously like the Grabers' home. Faith looked at him. "Is this what I think it is?"

"*Ya*. I figure I'll need help building it. And I'd rather work with you than Levi anytime—not that he isn't a nice guy. He's just not as pretty as you are."

She blushed as she looked at the paper again. Unlike her neat drawings, this was a more abstract sketch than she was used to. "I don't understand, though. Why are you adding on a *dawdi haus* now?"

"Because where else will *Mamm* and *Daed* live after we're married?"

Faith's eyes widened. "Married?"

He moved from the couch to kneel in front of her. "*Ya*. Married. I want to marry you, Faith. I don't think I ever stopped wanting to be *yer* husband." He grew serious. "But don't answer right away. I want you to be sure. And if you say yes, I want you to mean it."

She glanced at the paper again. "Do you have a pencil?"

He frowned and stood up. "*Ya*." He went to the side table near his mother's rocking chair and pulled out the small drawer. He took out a pencil and handed it to her.

She took it from him and started writing on the paper. Silas sat down next to her, and when he tried to see what she was doing, she angled her body away from him. When she finished, she handed him the paper.

He looked down at what she'd written.

Yes, I will marry you. And yes, I mean it.

He let out a whoop, stood, and scooped her up in his arms, whirling her around the room. "But there's one thing I want to change," she said, when he put her down. "If it's okay with you."

"Anything. I trust *yer* judgment."

She beamed as she took the paper from his hand. How long she'd waited for someone other than her grandfather to have confidence in her abilities. Now the most important person in her life had given her his approval, even though she now realized she'd had it all along. "The bathroom needs to be over here." She drew an arrow from one side of the house to the other. "Oh, and I think *yer* parents need more than one window in the living room. If we lengthen this wall—"

He silenced her with a kiss, and she forgot all about the *dawdi haus* and carpentry. All she could think about was how much she loved him, and about the future they would build together.

DISCUSSION QUESTIONS

A RECIPE FOR HOPE

1. Eve and Rosemary have spent much of their lives judging each other even though their actions adversely affected their relationship over the years. What are some examples of each woman judging the other?

2. Elias and Amos both fall for the same girl. Elizabeth believes that she can have her choice of either twin. Do you agree with Amos's decision not to court Elizabeth in favor of brotherly love? Was Elizabeth really "right" for either of the boys?

3. Rosemary was so afraid of becoming like her own mother that she denied Eve both discipline and affection when Eve was growing up—which left Eve feeling unloved much of the time. But both women feel closest to each other when they are cooking together. Why do you think that is?

4. This story is largely about the mother-daughter relationship. What is your relationship like with your mother or daughter? Do you see areas that need work? Have you ever been guilty of judgment, either as a mother or daughter? What do you hold most dear about your relationship with your mother?

5. In many Amish settlements, folks are embracing more and more of our *Englisch* ways. Cell phones are widely accepted, propane lighting is found in most homes, and many of the homes are decorated much like our own. Do you agree with the changes taking place, like Eve does? Or do you think things should remain simplistic, like Rosemary prefers? Can the Amish have it both ways?

LOVE IN STORE

1. At the beginning of this story, Stella is a bitter person with a sharp tongue. As the story progresses, we learn more of her past and perhaps we understand how she came to be this way. Have you ever felt yourself fall prey to bitterness? If so, what things helped you to change back to the person God calls you to be?

2. At first the problems at the market are inconvenient, but not actually harmful. Soon they become more serious. We have things in our lives like that—habits and sins that seem to hurt no one, but soon become destructive. What does the Bible say about becoming a new creature?

3. David is willing to move to live with his daughter, to help her through a difficult time. He wants to care for her and support her as well as the grandchildren. In what ways can you support someone in your life?

4. The letter David receives refers to Leviticus 25:10.

"Consecrate the fiftieth year and proclaim liberty throughout the land to all its inhabitants. It shall be a jubilee for you; each of you is to return to your family property and to your own clan." Obviously the writer of the letter in this story has misconstrued its meaning. What could this verse possibly mean to us today?

5. David and Stella find that God has brought them together, though the path they've lived has curved and dipped and sometimes even reversed itself—in the end the path God laid out for them brought them to one another. Psalm 119:105 reminds us that "Your word is a lamp for my feet, a light on my path." Share three Bible verses that have helped you to follow God's path.

BUILDING FAITH

1. Since the death of her grandfather, Faith has retreated into herself as a way to deal with her grief. How have you helped a loved one deal with grief?

2. Silas had a lot of growing up to do, and it took his mother's illness in order for him to mature. In what other ways does God use events to help us grow in our faith?

3. While Silas's issue was immaturity, Faith's was pride. Why is it so difficult to recognize pride in ourselves?

4. Faith has an unusual hobby for an Amish woman—carpentry. Do you have an unusual hobby/interest? What drew you to that particular hobby/interest?

5. What character qualities did you admire in Faith and Silas? Why?

ACKNOWLEDGMENTS

A RECIPE FOR HOPE

Much thanks to my friends and family for your encouragement and support, and especially to my husband, Patrick, who puts up with my tight deadlines and related mood swings. Love you, dear. ☺

To Janet Murphy, the best assistant on the planet—it's an honor to dedicate my novella to you. Thank you for all your help getting folks to test the recipes. You are a gem. Irreplaceable.

Thanks to my agent, Mary Sue Seymour. I hope another trip to New York City is in our future. What great memories!

To my editor, Natalie Hanemann—the journey continues, and I'm so incredibly blessed to have you in my life.

Barbie Beiler, thank you for making our "girls weekend" in Lancaster County so much fun. You are the best. Miss you!

And to Kelly Long and Amy Clipston—it was so great working with both of you.

And last, but certainly not least—thanks be to God for all He is in my life.

LOVE IN STORE

This book is dedicated to my associate editor at HarperCollins Christian Publishers/Thomas Nelson, Jodi Hughes. Jodi is a real pleasure to work with. She answers my emails in a timely fashion, gives me good feedback, and maybe most importantly—laughs at my jokes. We also share a love of all things Miranda Lambert. Hugs to you, Jodi, and thank you for all you do to bring my fiction to readers.

Thanks also to my pre-readers: Kristy and Janet. You ladies were able to do this on a quick turnaround, and I appreciate that. I'd also like to thank my agent Steve Laube who guided me through the contractual aspects of this story and always provides judicious advice when I need it. A special thank you to the folks at Amish Acres who gave my husband and me our first real glimpse into Amish life. If you happen to be passing through northern Indiana, I encourage you to take a few hours to visit the Amish Acres facility in Nappanee.

And finally . . . *always giving thanks to God the Father for everything, in the name of our Lord Jesus Christ* (Ephesians 5:20).

Blessings,
Vannetta

BUILDING FAITH

A huge thank you to Becky Monds and Jean Bloom, for being the fabulous editors you are. As always, thank you, dear reader. It's a joy and a privilege to go on this writing journey with you.

RECIPE FROM VANNETTA CHAPMAN'S *LOVE IN STORE*

OATMEAL CHOCOLATE CHIP COOKIES

1 1/2 cups chocolate chips
6 cups all-purpose flour
3 teaspoons baking powder
1 teaspoon salt
1 teaspoon ground nutmeg
1 teaspoon ground cinnamon
1 1/2 cups shortening
3 cups white sugar
2 cups quick cooking oats
3 teaspoons baking soda
1 cup buttermilk
1/2 cup dark molasses
4 eggs

Sift flour, baking powder, salt, nutmeg, and cinnamon into a very large bowl. Cut in shortening using a pastry blender until mixture forms fine crumbs.

Add ground chocolate chips, sugar, and oats. Mix well. Dissolve baking soda in buttermilk in small bowl. Add molasses and 3 of the eggs, and beat with rotary beater until blended. Add to flour mixture, and mix well with spoon.

Drop by heaping tablespoons about 3 inches apart on greased baking sheets. Flatten each with floured bottom of a drinking glass. Beat 1 egg in a bowl until blended. Brush tops of cookies with egg. Bake at 375 degrees F (190 degrees C) for 8 to 10 minutes or until golden brown.

RECIPES FROM KATHLEEN FULLER'S *BUILDING FAITH*

MUD HEN BARS

1/2 cup solid shortening
1 cup white sugar
1 whole egg
2 egg yolks
1 tsp. baking powder
1 1/2 cups all-purpose flour
1/4 tsp. salt
1 cup nuts
1/2 cup chocolate morsels
1 cup mini marshmallows
2 egg whites
1 cup brown sugar

Preheat oven to 350 degrees. Mix first seven ingredients and press into 13x9-inch pan. Sprinkle with nuts, chocolate morsels, and marshmallows. Beat egg whites until stiff; fold in brown sugar. Spread on top. Bake 30–40 minutes.

Makes 18 bars.

OVERNIGHT AMISH POTATO SALAD

12 cups shredded potatoes
12 hard-cooked eggs
3 T. prepared mustard
4 tsp. salt
1 1/2 cups chopped onions
2 cups white sugar
1 1/2 cups chopped celery
1/2 cup milk
1 cup sour cream

3 cups Miracle Whip *or* 3 cups mayonnaise and 3 T. vinegar

Cook and shred potatoes and eggs. Place in large bowl. Mix remaining ingredients and pour over salad. Refrigerate overnight. Makes 20 servings.

ABOUT THE AUTHORS

BETH WISEMAN

Beth Wiseman is the award-winning and bestselling author of the Daughters of the Promise, Land of Canaan, and Amish Secrets series. While she is best known for her Amish novels, Beth has also written contemporary novels including *Need You Now*, *The House that Love Built*, and *The Promise*.

You can read the first chapter of all of Beth's books at: www.bethwiseman.com

VANNETTA CHAPMAN

Vannetta Chapman is author of the bestselling novel *A Simple Amish Christmas*. She has published over one hundred articles in Christian family magazines, receiving over two dozen awards from Romance Writers of America chapter groups. In 2012 she was awarded a Carol Award for *Falling to Pieces*. She discovered her love for the Amish while researching her grandfather's birthplace of Albion, Pennsylvania.

* * *

Visit Vannetta's website: www.vannettachapman.com
Twitter: @VannettaChapman
Facebook: VannettaChapmanBooks

KATHLEEN FULLER

Kathleen Fuller is the author of several bestselling novels, including the Hearts of Middlefield novels, the Middlefield Family novels, the Amish of Birch Creek series, and the Amish Letters series as well as a middle-grade Amish series, the Mysteries of Middlefield. Visit her online at KathleenFuller.com, Twitter: @TheKatJam, Facebook: Kathleen Fuller.